Renew online at
www.librarieswest.org.uk
or by phoning any Bristol library
Bristol Libraries

PLEASE RETURN BOOK BY LAST DATE STAMPED

D0363013

Also by Alan Gibbons

Hell's underground 3

RENEGADE

ALAN GIBBONS

Orion
Children's Books

First published in Great Britain in 2009
by Orion Children's Books
This paperback edition first published in Great Britain in 2010
by Orion Children's Books
a division of the Orion Publishing Group Ltd
Orion House
5 Upper St Martin's Lane
London WC2H 9EA
An Hachette UK Company

3 5 7 9 10 8 6 4

A catalogue record for this book is available from the British Library

ISBN 978 1 4440 0079 5

Typeset at The Spartan Press Ltd,
Lymington, Hants

Printed and bound in Great Britain by Clays Ltd,
St Ives plc

The Orion Publishing Group's policy is to use papers that
are natural, renewable and recyclable products and
made from wood grown in sustainable forests. The logging
and manufacturing processes are expected to conform to
the environmental regulations of the country of origin.

www.orionbooks.co.uk

One

Chaim Wetzel learned at an early age that the streets of London were as likely to be paved with horror as with gold. On more than one occasion he'd seen the skeletal, wasted remains of some poor wretch being dragged away, unloved and unremembered, to a pauper's grave. He'd become accustomed to the many random acts of violence and cruelty that went unpunished in the mean neighbourhood where he lived. He'd heard it said that everybody gets what they deserve. He didn't believe it any more. Who deserves to be born into a hell on earth?

He also knew that somewhere, just a few miles away from Spitalfields, there was another London. Here there was wealth and grandeur, concerts and feasts. Great gentlemen and ladies attended lavish balls and stepped straight from sumptuous red carpets into their fine carriages.

Chaim was standing on the corner of Bell Lane and

1

Wentworth Street on the February day in 1839 it all began. He was looking for a boy by the name of Israel Lazarus. Israel was thirteen, Chaim two years older. Israel was a distant cousin as well as a neighbour and, like Chaim, attended the Jews' Free School. At least, he used to.

Chaim couldn't shift the great plug of unease that had been lodged in his throat ever since Israel disappeared. With two other children to raise and a husband in the burial ground on North Street, Israel's mother was in no position to search for her son, though she was sick with worry. It had fallen on Chaim to look for young Israel.

The trouble was, it was two days since Chaim had sighted Israel being swallowed up in the thronged streets. They'd had a furious quarrel in the moments before Israel went off with another boy, refusing to even listen to Chaim's pleas to him to come home.

There was sleet in the air that afternoon. It stung Chaim's eyes and made him squeeze the collar of his thin jacket tight shut against the whipping wind. To his great disappointment, the first familiar voice he heard wasn't Israel's. It belonged to Moses Cohen, a pupil monitor at the Jews' Free School. The job of the monitors was to teach the younger children reading, writing and mathematics under the supervision of the schoolmaster. But Moses thought he was a real *k'nocker*, a bigshot who didn't have anything to do with the younger boys.

'Are you still looking for Israel?' Moses asked.

'You know I am.'

Moses gave an exaggerated sigh. 'You might as well look for stars in a puddle,' he observed. 'He's moved on to pastures new, you mark my words. The little *putz* has done a runner.'

'You're wrong,' Chaim told him. 'He wouldn't do that. Israel's a good boy.'

'That's not what I've heard,' Moses said. 'Fighting and stealing's his game lately, ain't it?'

'Where did you hear that?' Chaim asked. He felt humiliated that Israel's shameful behaviour had become public knowledge.

'It hardly matters,' Moses said. 'The point is, I know. You're not denying it, are you?'

'Do you want to hear me admit it?' Chaim said. 'There, it's done. You're right. Israel's been getting into a lot of trouble recently. But why would he just walk out of school without a word? He wouldn't worry his mother like this. He's devoted to her.'

'What do you know?' Moses scoffed. 'You only see what you want to see. Take my advice. The little *shtoonk* has found himself work and a bed somewhere. You won't see him again.'

'What's the matter with you, Moses?' Chaim snapped. 'Why do you always have to think the worst of people?'

By way of an answer, Moses pointed wearily towards the end of the road. 'That's why.'

Chaim knew very well what he was pointing at. Spitalfields, so close to the City of London, was a maze of dank, narrow courts. Many of the houses in the labyrinthine slum were mouldering with age, their time-grimed walls teetering on lakes of filth, endlessly fed by ditches, open sewers and cesspits. The backwash of humanity ended up here. Even at this hour, on the steps of Christ Church there were half a dozen

3

starving children. Not one of them had a home to go to so they huddled together in their pitiful rags and shivered. Chaim looked at their wasted, shrunken faces and he couldn't help wonder if that was what lay in store for poor, wayward Israel.

'If you don't know by now why I always think the worst,' Moses said, 'then I feel sorry for you.' He pinched Chaim's cheeks. 'Face facts, my friend, these streets are full of human wolves ready to gobble up the first little lamb to wander by. Forget about Israel and look out for yourself. It's the only way to get on in this world.'

With that, he went on his way, shoving through crowds of ragged people. Chaim watched him go, seething with shame and embarrassment. Moses was right, of course. But no matter what misfortune had befallen Israel, if he was able to put one foot in front of the other, he would find his way home to his mother.

Chaim waited another half hour, hopping from one foot to the other. The soles of his boots were so thin that the cold of the pavement struck right through into his feet. It was a bad day to be standing on a street corner looking for a lost child. He was about to go when he saw a pinched, familiar face among the strangers.

Chaim's heart leaped. His patience had been rewarded. It was Israel.

Chaim was just going to call his name when he saw that Israel wasn't alone. Two boys were walking one either side of him. Each had hold of one of Israel's arms. They reminded Chaim of a pair of gaolers accompanying a prisoner. One was red-haired, about

4

thirteen. Chaim recognized him as the boy Israel had gone off with two days earlier. The other was older with lank, dark hair that fell onto his collar. He was maybe seventeen or eighteen. Though his clothes had seen better days, they were flamboyant enough to make a statement. He was a big man in the neighbourhood. The older boy was wearing a brown velveteen coat, breeches, lace-up half boots and white cotton stockings. He had a dark blue belcher handkerchief around his neck and a battered stovepipe hat jammed on his skull. The brim of the hat was drawn low over his eyes and the belcher was partly pulled up over his mouth to offer some protection against the biting cold.

Chaim continued his vigil for a minute or so. He decided against announcing himself. He would have little chance if Israel's companions were to turn on him. It wouldn't help Israel much either, if it alerted his captors to the fact that somebody was looking for him. He would probably vanish for good.

Falling in behind the trio, Chaim tailed them as far as Flower and Dean Street. He drew a deep breath. It was a notorious neighbourhood, even for the East End. It had a deserved reputation as a den of thieves. Here, at the top end, the street was fifteen or sixteen feet wide. At the far end it narrowed to no more than ten. From the upper windows, the residents could almost shake hands across the street.

Chaim allowed Israel and his guardians thirty seconds, then followed them into the heart of the Flowery, as the neighbourhood was known. Most of the houses were three stories of smoke-blackened brick and timber. Around them clustered shanties of timber frames and courts that were little more than shambles of brickwork, filthy water and dirt. The street was full of common doss houses where you could get a night's lodging for as little as two or three pence, though you might have to share the room with lice and bedbugs. If you ever sank low enough you had to sleep sitting up, leaning against a rope tied across the room.

Chaim pursued his quarry as far as a narrow, gloomy alley. It led to a makeshift wooden bridge that spanned an open sewer. The planks were slippery with green slime. Taking care not to give himself away, Chaim crept after them. Eventually, they entered a large, crumbling tenement, propped up by a wooden beam. Chaim stood outside.

He'd told his mother he wouldn't be late but it was going dark already and the gas lights were stuttering to life all around him. Even so, he would never forgive himself if he abandoned Israel now. After some hesitation, Chaim tried the door. It opened to admit him into a gloomy hallway. Hearing the tread of the three boys on the stairs, Chaim started up after them. He'd got as far as the second floor when he heard people talking on the landing above. If he took another step, he'd be bound to be spotted. Heart pounding, he shrank back, looking round desperately for somewhere to hide. He felt a door-knob at his back. Twisting it hurriedly, he let himself into the room.

'Oi,' a female voice protested behind him, 'what's your game?'

Chaim spun round to see a shabbily-dressed young woman, no older than he was, sitting in a worn arm-chair. Her toes were poking through her boots.

'You gave me a right turn,' she said. 'I thought it might be . . . . well, no matter.'

6

'I need to stay out of sight for a while,' Chaim said.

'It sounds like we both had the same idea,' the girl said. 'I come down here from time to time to be on my own. Lord knows, I don't get much in the way of privacy.' She stirred herself. 'Look, you'd better leave. I ain't sharing my little refuge with nobody.'

'Shush, will you?' Chaim said, gesturing desperately to get her to pipe down. 'You're going to give me away with your yap. I'd pay you to keep *shtum*.'

At the mention of money, a light came into her eyes. 'How much?'

Chaim winced. He only had two penny pieces to his name and he was loath to give them up. 'I'll give you a penny,' he hissed. 'Just be quiet.'

'Make it two,' the girl replied, 'and you're on.' She pinched finger and thumb together. 'Show me the colour of your money. Betsy Alder don't trust nobody.'

Chaim wondered how Betsy could have guessed how much he had on him. Aware that he was in a weak bargaining position, he tossed a penny on the bed. Betsy snatched it up and it vanished into the folds of her faded green dress.

'You can have that now,' he said. 'The other will follow when I know you're not going to give me away. I don't trust nobody neither.'

He listened at a door for a few minutes then eased it open a crack. As he prepared to leave, he felt Betsy's bony fingers dig into the flesh of his upper arms.

'Oh no you don't,' she said. 'Another penny, if you please.'

Chaim handed it over. He'd been hoping to get away before she could call him back. 'Now you keep your side of the bargain,' he said. 'I'm going to have a look upstairs.'

At that, Betsy's face drained of colour. 'Upstairs? What do you want to go there for?'

Chaim whispered his reply. 'They've got my friend.'

'This friend,' Betsy asked, 'he don't go by the name of Izzy, do he?'

She had Chaim's attention. 'That's right, his name's Israel Lazarus.'

'So who's looking for him?' Betsy asked guardedly. 'Got a name, have you?'

'It's Chaim. Chaim Wetzel.'

'You don't want to follow him in there,' she whispered. 'That's the Rat Boys' lair, that is. You've heard about Samuel Rector and his devil children, ain't you? It's my home too and I wish to God it wasn't. It ain't no place for decent folks, if you get my meaning. The day Izzy threw his lot in with Samuel, he put himself beyond salvation, just like me. If he's in there, you've already lost him. God washes his hands of any poor wretch that winds up here.'

'Don't talk like that,' Chaim retorted. 'I'm here to take him home.'

Chaim had heard the stories about Rector and his infamous lair. The word on the street made him out to be half-giant, half-demon from Hell.

'Not while Samuel Rector lives and breathes, you ain't,' Betsy said. 'You don't want to go tangling with the guv'nor. He's a bad 'un and no mistake.' She darted panicky looks around the room, as if Samuel might step out of the shadows at any moment. Her voice was breaking. 'Why, if Samuel knew I'd helped somebody track down one of his Rat Boys, he'd slit my gizzard for me.'

'You keep quiet about me,' Chaim said, unsettled by the terror in her eyes, 'and I'll keep quiet about you.' He'd heard the name Samuel Rector but he still wondered why the man terrified poor Betsy so. 'Agreed?'

Betsy nodded. Together, they stood at the door, listening. After a couple of minutes, Chaim heard at least half a dozen people going downstairs, their boots scraping on the floorboards out on the landing.

'That sounds like the entire gang,' Betsy said, 'right down to your friend, the new boy.'

'Then I'll be on my way,' Chaim murmured. 'Thanks, Betsy.' He paused at the door. 'You're very pretty, you know. Did anybody ever tell you that?'

'Men say it all the time,' Betsy answered. 'They only start their flattery because they want something from me.'

Chaim shrugged. 'Well, it's true and I mean it sincerely.' He held her gaze. 'Don't worry, I don't want anything from you.'

Once the Rat Boys' footsteps reached the front door, Chaim ventured out onto the landing and peered down over the banister. Israel was now part of a substantial group. There were eight or nine boys, ranging from thirteen to eighteen years of age and an older individual, a great bear of a man. This had to be the one Betsy was afraid of, the notorious thief-trainer.

Chaim waited until the gang had set off down the street, then followed them onto Rose Lane, across Wentworth Street and into an alley lit by a single lamp. At the end of that dismal, dark street there was an old-style gin palace, the kind that was everywhere in the days of the old King, before strong ale became the tipple of choice. Chaim gazed apprehensively into the smoke-filled taproom and wondered if he dared go in. The atmosphere inside was hot and humid in sharp contrast to the winter chill outside. Gaslights flickered in the gathering gloom. He looked at the drinkers dressed in their fustian or cheap cotton, swallowing down tumblers of gin punch. Chaim drew the attention of a man with muttonchop whiskers and retreated into the alley to ponder his next move.

He was still wondering what to do when a woman with gin-ravaged features pushed past, and vanished into the shadows. For a moment he thought she must be a ghost but there was a simpler explanation. He'd failed to notice the disguised alley over to his left. He pursued her through pitch darkness to the far end and saw her slip through a rotting doorway. On the other side of the door he could hear the sound of raised voices and barking dogs. There was another sound, the unmistakeable squeal of rodents. It was a ratting contest. Chaim knew he was bound to be challenged the moment he tried to enter so he searched the walls for an open window. He was in luck. A hurried scramble up the flaking brickwork and he was inside.

He dropped lightly to the floor and looked around. He was standing in a disused gallery overlooking the ground floor. Below him the ratting was underway. The hubbub was deafening. The crowd, mostly men, were clutching betting slips and pots of ale. They were shouting and cursing at the tops of their voices as a mastiff tore a stream of attacking rats to shreds. In addition to the yelling of the men, the barking of the dogs and the scream of the rats, there was much clanking of dog chains as terriers and bulldogs strained to break free of their leashes and join in the fight.

Chaim had heard about these gatherings though he'd never seen one. Around the walls were tubs and barrels, railed boxes and kennels. The rat pit was in the middle, surrounded by boards about four feet high. On a shelf that ran round the full perimeter of the rat pit were many iron-wire cages of squealing rats, scratching to be free. On either side of the rat pit there was a blazing brazier. For a moment Chaim stared at the bulging-eyed audience and wondered at mankind's cruelty. Then his attention strayed back to the mastiff in the pit which was finishing off a pair of sewer rats the size of cats. The mastiff's owner staggered forward, clutching a pewter tankard and his winnings.

'See that,' he roared drunkenly, 'my Caesar could clear the whole of London of its rats. Just look at him. He's killed twenty of the blighters and he hasn't even got started.'

Some of the audience who'd bet on the dog killing fewer started booing and whistling. A moment later, they fell silent. Samuel Rector had made his appearance, followed by his Rat Boys. Some of the onlookers fell back. They whispered in awe of Rector and his entourage. Some said Rector was just a vicious thug. Others hinted that he was so much more. The fearsome mastiff Caesar registered their approach in his own way, whimpering and retreating into a corner of the pen with his tail between his legs. There he cowered, the whites of his eyes showing.

'Devil children,' hissed one man.

11

'And the Satan of Spitalfields himself,' murmured another.

The Rat Boys fanned out across the floor, taking command of the room. Chaim leaned forward. His heart was pounding. *Please God, don't let them see me.* He clung to the shadows and watched the group's progress. Rector stood with his legs akimbo, dominating the scene. So this was the man who'd ordered Israel's abduction.

'Don't go quiet on account of me,' Samuel told the crowd. 'Let nobody say Samuel Rector ever spoiled another man's pleasure.' He ran his gaze over the assembly. 'Who wants to see my party piece?'

'Go on, Sammy,' one man shouted. 'I'll bet a shiny shilling that you lift seven of the blighters tonight.'

Immediately, the rest of the crowd started shouting their bets. Chaim wondered what they were betting on. He soon found out when two of Samuel's lieutenants, including the dark-haired boy in the top hat, lifted a barrel into the rat pit. The betting rose to fever pitch. Chaim leaned forward.

Samuel shrugged off his woollen great coat and his dark blue frock coat, then handed his billycock hat to one of his boys. Next, he peeled off his shirt to reveal a greyish vest underneath. His thick, muscular arms were bare and criss-crossed with scars. He stood there for a moment or two, most probably for effect, Chaim thought, then nodded to the two boys. They removed the lid from the barrel and Samuel shoved his arm inside. Instantly, there came from the barrel a deafening chorus of rodent squeals and shrieks. Now Chaim understood. The vermin had been starved to the point of madness. Samuel glanced across the room at a man with a fob watch. The man counted to thirty. Not once did Samuel flinch or give any indication that he might be in pain. No wonder the people of the abyss thought him more than human. For a moment Chaim felt sour bile rise in his throat. He thought he was going to be sick.

'Time's up!' the time-keeper shouted.

Samuel removed his arm from the barrel and the two boys secured the lid. At least ten rats were clinging to Samuel's arm, biting and tearing for all they were worth. It was a stomach-turning spectacle. But it was about to get worse. Without so much as flinching, Samuel marched over to one of the braziers and plunged his arm into the red hot coals. Chaim stared hard at Samuel's flesh. Why didn't it blister? Is this how he earned the name Satan of Spitalfields? The rats were less well-protected than the man on whom they were feasting. The dying creatures' squeals were like fingernails on slate.

'Eleven rats,' the time-keeper shouted. 'Let's see any winning bets.'

There were none.

Samuel's dark eyes feasted on the rats as they burned. Once his appetite for dead rodents was satisfied, he turned towards Israel who'd been looking on in horror.

'See this young gent?' Samuel shouted to the throng. 'He wants to join my Rat Boys. Ain't that right, Israel?'

'Taking up with the Hebrews now, are you, Sammy?' a man from the crowd shouted. There was sarcasm in the question.

In response, Samuel stiffened and swept the crowd with his eyes, searching for the speaker. 'Is that a

13

problem?' His dark eyes seemed to spear the man. 'Oh, it's you O'Shaughnessy. Still a warehouseman at the London Dock?'

'Y-es,' O'Shaughnessy said warily.

O'Shaughnessy was in the company of a woman in her late twenties or early thirties. He was reluctant to lose face in front of her but retreat was called for.

'But that's not your major source of income, is it? Who's that, with you? It wouldn't be the lovely Kitty Flaherty, would it?'

'You know exactly who I am, Samuel,' Mrs Flaherty retorted.

'I see you're as fiery as ever, Kit. I do miss our little skirmishes.'

Samuel made his way towards her and patted her cheek. She recoiled and flashed him a look of pure hatred. That only made him laugh.

Mrs Flaherty slapped his hand away. 'Get away from me, Samuel Rector.'

O'Shaughnessy looked put out by the exchange but he wasn't fool enough to pick a fight with Samuel.

'What's your latest sideline, O'Shaughnessy?' Samuel asked, shifting his gaze from Mrs Flaherty to her companion. 'Is it housebreaking, street robbery, or have you found something more lucrative?'

O'Shaughnessy blanched.

Samuel held his gaze. 'That's right, I know my territory inside out. You think you've got my measure? Well, I'm the one with the all-seeing eye.' He let the words sink in and pressed forward through the crowd towards O'Shaughnessy. 'Now, I just asked you if you had anything against my young Hebrew friend. What's your answer?'

14

'No,' O'Shaughnessy answered hurriedly, 'nothing at all. You know me, Sammy, when I've had a tankard or two of porter I do let my mouth run away with me.'

'Here's a piece of advice,' Samuel said, 'one that may save your life, O'Shaughnessy. Watch who you're taking a pop at in future. You might just pick the wrong man.' He glanced at Mrs Flaherty. 'I thought you'd have given your flunkey better advice, Kit. He's going to get himself killed, the way he's behaving.'

Mrs Flaherty remained cool. O'Shaughnessy, on the other hand, was trying to babble an apology but Samuel was having none of it.

'One more thing,' he said, 'the next time you address yours truly, don't call me Sammy. I don't appreciate it. It's got to be Samuel or Mr Rector or guv'nor. Is that understood?'

'Sure, Sa— I mean, Mr Rector.'

Some of the men around O'Shaughnessy shook their heads at him. Samuel had made him lose face in front of the entire criminal fraternity.

Samuel turned his attention back to Israel. 'Did my boys tell you there was an initiation ritual?'

Israel, quite terrified, shook his head.

'It's like this, see,' Samuel said. 'A Rat Boy ain't a Rat Boy until he's eaten a rat.' He enjoyed the look of disgust on Israel's face, then plucked a charred rodent corpse from the coals. 'Don't you worry, though. It don't have to be a raw one.' He dangled the roasted vermin. 'They take a bit too much chewing. Here's one that's well cooked. That's right, he's toasted through to his wicked, little heart.' He handed it to Israel by the tail. 'Eat up. Six bites should do it.'

Israel took the rat and stared at it. Mrs Flaherty tried to intercede.

'Don't make him do this, Samuel,' she protested. 'He's just a child.'

'Keep out of my business, Kit,' Samuel warned.

Then, grimacing, Israel raised it to his lips and prepared to take a bite. Chaim could see the tears welling up in his eyes. He wanted to stop him, but he didn't dare reveal himself. Before Israel could tear off a single morsel Samuel clapped him on the back and tossed the rat back in the brazier.

'That'll do,' he said, glancing at Mrs Flaherty. 'I only wanted to see if you'd obey me.' He put his arm round Israel's shoulder. 'Good lad. You're Sammy's boy now. You're in.' He raised the boy's arm. 'Ladies and gentlemen, a toast. To our latest Rat Boy.'

Israel was treated to loud acclamation, though Chaim noticed that, here and there, some of those present looked sullen and resentful, none more so than O'Shaughnessy who was slinking from the room. Mrs Flaherty stayed for a moment, staring at Samuel with barely-disguised hatred, then followed O'Shaughnessy outside.

'Was it something I said?' Samuel quipped.

Two thirds of the room laughed. The rest looked away. Even now, Chaim noticed that one woman was kissing a small crucifix on a chain before tucking it into the bodice of her dress. The Rat Boys were feared and loathed in equal measure. Once the betting on the rat fights had resumed, Samuel took Israel to one side. Chaim, listening from above in the balcony, managed to follow some of the conversation. The rest he guessed.

16

'You're one of us now, Izzy,' Samuel said. 'I've got a very important job for you.'

'What is it?' Israel asked.

'Not yet, young Sir, not yet,' Samuel said. 'You've got an apprenticeship to serve first. The boys will show you the ropes and introduce you to our company's general business.'

Chaim had been craning forward to hear every syllable. To his horror, he leaned just that bit too far and his cap fell from his head. He watched it fall and land with a loud slap on the floor by Samuel's right boot. Chaim threw himself back from the balustrade but not before Samuel had spotted the sudden movement on the balcony.

'Who's there?' he demanded.

Chaim flattened himself against the wall.

'We've got a spy up there,' Samuel roared. 'A guinea for the man or boy who catches the white-livered cur.'

There wasn't even time to check for passers-by on the street outside. Chaim closed his eyes and forced himself to jump out of the window through which he'd gained entry. He fell heavily, the jarring impact shuddering through his spine and exploding in his skull. Scrambling groggily to his feet, he pounded down the alley and ran in the direction of Brick Lane. The gin palace spewed his pursuers into the night, cursing and shouting. Chaim didn't break his stride. His hair was damp with sweat in spite of the cold. At the corner of one alley, a strong arm grabbed him and a hand covered his mouth.

'Down that way,' the man hissed. 'I'll send them the wrong way.' He shoved Chaim on his way. 'I owe the guv'nor for what he did to me tonight.'

17

It was O'Shaughnessy. Mrs Flaherty was standing next to him.

'Thank you,' Chaim said, glancing back gratefully.

'Forget it,' Mrs Flaherty replied, 'we're not doing it for you. We owe Mr Rector one. Now get on your toes boy, and good luck.'

On and on Chaim ran, but he wasn't safe yet. He was keenly aware of the thudding beat of his boots on the cobbles. Every time a pedestrian turned a corner his heart pattered. The city was alive with horrors, but where were the Rat Boys? Suddenly, he heard an ominous scuttering sound behind him. It was them. His pursuers were swarming through the narrow streets, light, agile and remorseless. Some closed on him from behind, others tried to outflank him, forcing him to backtrack. He skidded to a halt, darting glances. He soon saw a blur go past on the opposite side of the road. Then he realized who it was.

Top Hat.

Chaim turned to escape down the alley to his right but the red-haired boy had also appeared, blocking his way.

'We've got him cornered, Noah,' he shouted at Top Hat.

Chaim retreated a few steps, his heart pounding.

'Good work, Malachy,' Noah said.

Chaim knew he had only seconds to make his getaway before the rest of the crowd arrived.

'Come on then,' Noah sneered, reading his intentions, 'try it. See if you can get past me.'

Chaim chose what he thought was the easier option and lunged at the smaller, slighter Malachy. Still sore from the fall, he was no match for the agile Malachy. The

18

Rat Boy skipped across and lashed out with his right leg, catching Chaim's ankle and sending him crashing to the ground. Chaim jarred his elbow but there was no time to nurse the injury. He rolled over on his back and saw both Noah and Malachy looking down at him.

'Get up,' Noah ordered, dragging Chaim to his feet. 'Oh, Samuel's going to enjoy meeting you. He don't like spies.'

'No,' Malachy confirmed, 'he don't like them one bit. He scalped a man once for sticking his nose in. He'll rip your heart out, and eat it with boiled potatoes and cabbage.'

Noah and Malachy were grinning fit to burst, obviously anticipating a rich reward for delivering Chaim to the guv'nor. The smiles lasted only a few seconds. Suddenly, Malachy screamed. Out of nowhere, there had come a sudden rush of scalding heat. His clothes were on fire.

'What the devil?' he cried.

He tore off his jacket and set about beating out the flames. Simultaneously, Noah spun round to see what had caused Malachy's clothing to catch light so inexplicably.

'Who the 'ell are you?' he demanded, seeing a shadowy figure approaching.

The stranger simply stretched out his arms. Instantly, a second searing jet of flame cleaved open the gloom and temporarily illuminated the newcomer's face. It seemed to have boiled up from within him and sprung from his fingertips. Impossible, Chaim thought, just impossible.

'Run!' the stranger told Chaim, taking advantage of Noah and Malachy's surprise.

Chaim didn't need further encouragement. He spun round and fled, still wondering how the stranger had harnessed those intense jets of flame. He raced through the streets as if all the legions of Hell were on his heels. He lost his saviour along the way but he hardly cared. Soon he was climbing the stairs to the three rooms he shared with his mother, father and sister Rebekah. That night, as he lay awake in bed, he had two questions for the night. What had Israel got himself into and who was the mysterious stranger who had probably saved his life?

Two

*From the diary of Arthur Strachan, deputy chief
engineer, London Commercial Railway
Monday, 4 February, 1839*

*I*t has been a most perplexing week. Work on the new
line from Minories to Blackwall, hitherto progressing
at a most satisfactory rate, has been halted by unforeseen
circumstances. Last Wednesday, a gang of tunnellers
uncovered part of a wall, concealed beneath layers of
clay and shale. It appears ancient, possibly even Roman.
It is of a remarkable sturdiness and solidity. Is it any
wonder the modern age has such an admiration for the
works of antiquity? But there is something more note-
worthy than the quality of the construction. It is the
curious effect the discovery has had on the labourers.

   On Wednesday, two men were taken ill with an ague
whose onset was as sudden as it was extreme. That
was only the beginning. By close of work on Thursday,
the number suffering from curious and unexplained

maladies had grown to nine. Every one of them complains of hearing strange noises, though I am unable to confirm any such thing from my own observations. They speak of a hideous screeching, as if all the dark angels of the night had been let loose in their brains. Though I am sceptical about the wilder tales the men are telling, there is no doubting their fear is genuine.

Something is affecting them very badly indeed. I have witnessed them being physically sick until they were bringing up blood. Strong men have been reduced to mewling kittens within hours of excavating a stretch of the wall.

I have investigated what the men have been eating and drinking, hoping to find some rational explanation for the outbreak of insanity. For a while, I even feared it was cholera. I thought that there might be something in their victuals that would account for this sudden onset of sickness. My enquiries have come to naught. There is no common thread which might explain the outbreak. I confess that I am quite confounded.

Friday saw the strangest incident yet. Two of my most trustworthy employees, men with whom I have worked on the construction of two bridges, and who have always been the greatest of friends, were discovered trying to beat one another to a pulp. Even I, the most rational of men, am unable to comprehend one detail of the incident. At one point they started speaking in tongues. It sounded uncannily like Gaelic. Naturally, I had them removed from the site. Oddest of all, when I interviewed them not half an hour later, neither of them could explain what had provoked the barrage of fisticuffs. Nor could they reproduce a single word of the strange dialect in which they had been speaking. They seemed to have no recollection whatsoever of their behaviour. I have suspended them for five days.

This episode is most regrettable. Only a week ago the Chief Engineer on the line, Mr Robert Stephenson, stressed to me that the project must be completed by the summer of next year. I will speak to him urgently on this matter. Robert is a north Briton like myself and a most doughty and reasonable man. I am sure that together we will find a solution.

Three

The morning after his dramatic flight from the gin palace, Chaim ate a breakfast of oatmeal porridge and tea, then got ready for school. His *mamme* wanted to know if he had any news about Israel. Mrs Lazarus had been asking. Chaim decided that the events at the ratting contest would do nothing to put Mrs Lazarus's mind at ease.

'No,' Chaim said, 'but I'll keep looking. He'll turn up. I'm sure he hasn't gone far.'

'What makes you say that?' *Mamme* asked.

Chaim shrugged. 'I've been talking to people. They say he's still about.'

'I just hope you're right,' *Mamme* said. 'You hear such stories.'

Chaim made his way to Bell Lane, picking his way through the crowds of muffin men, costermongers and baked potato vendors. He peered into the coffee houses and penny pie-shops along the route, just in case Israel was hanging around one of them. He wasn't. All

Chaim saw was working men and women downing their bread-and-butter breakfasts. Part of what he'd told *Mamme* was true, of course: Israel hadn't gone far.

Soon after Chaim arrived at school, he heard the clanging bell announce the start of the day. The school consisted of two large, barn-like rooms, one for boys and one for girls. Chaim was both pupil and teacher, taking lessons from the schoolmasters and teaching some of the younger boys by rote under a lantern roof supported by cross beams. Hundreds of pupils were packed into the teaching space so the roof was paved with sacks to deaden the sound. The walls were constructed out of unplastered, whitewashed bricks. Draughts cut across the stone floor, discomforting everyone. To make things worse, the only heating was provided by a single stove that did little to off-set the bitter cold.

Chaim was lucky. He taught a group of middling ability boys. Some of the other monitors had more unruly pupils and struggled to maintain control. Moses was the strictest of them, thinking nothing of cuffing his charges round the ear for the slightest misdemeanour. A tap's no use, he would say, it just shows them you're soft. They need a thrashing to keep them in order. Once or twice he'd been as good as his word, even catching up with boys after school to give them a sound beating. Chaim disliked Moses intensely. He was cold, brutish and selfish and many thought he preferred beating his young charges to instructing them. There was no doubt that one day there would be a settling of accounts between them. But this morning, Chaim was too busy trying to control a particularly fractious boy by the name of Solly Jacobs to worry about Moses.

'Do try to concentrate, Solly,' Chaim urged him.

'What for?' Solly demanded. 'My old lady might fancy me as a rabbi or a surgeon, but it ain't going to happen, is it? At best, I'm going to be a *schneider* like *Tatte*.'

'In school,' Chaim told him, 'you'll say tailor not *schneider* and Dad not *Tatte*. Mr Henry wants his boys to grow up to be English gentlemen.'

'Gentlemen!' Solly guffawed. 'There ain't many gentlemen in the East End, excepting your good self, of course, you being a cut above the rest of us.' He winked to his classmates.

'Cut it out, Solly,' Chaim warned him.

But Solly was in flow. He adopted a mock-posh accent. 'Your Majesty, may I h-introduce His Lordship, Mr Chaim Lardy-dah Wetzel.'

The other boys laughed. Chaim knew that this was a major challenge to his authority. Either he dealt with it, or every successive day the task of controlling the boys was going to get harder.

'You'll apply yourself to your English grammar this moment, Solly,' Chaim warned, 'or I'll know the reason why.'

'Here's the reason, if you're so bloomin' interested,' Solly retorted. 'I don't want to. So there!'

Chaim could see some of the other boys being emboldened enough to copy Solly. A few 'lardy-dahs' were starting to float around the group. It was time to act. Grabbing Solly by the scruff of the neck, Chaim boxed his ears firmly.

'Now,' he said firmly, 'pick up your slate and write down what I tell you.'

Solly still looked grudging so Chaim shoved a clenched fist under his nose.

'Do it!' he ordered.

Solly's resistance broke and he started to scrape pronouns onto his slate. He paused for a moment, but it was only to brush away a tear. He still looked resentful but he didn't raise another objection. Chaim caught the eye of the other boys who might be tempted to follow Solly's example. 'You lot, too,' he said.

His boys were twelve or thirteen. Some of them would be leaving Bell Lane soon. He was supervising his pupils' work when he caught Moses' eye. Moses grinned. He'd seen the confrontation. Chaim argued that resorting to corporal punishment was a sure sign you'd lost control and that physical chastisement should be avoided where possible. How he hated the superior expression on Moses' face.

After his victory over Solly Jacobs, Chaim lunched with the other monitors. He took advantage of a lull in the conversation to ask if his companions knew anything about the Rat Boys.

'What makes you ask about those low-life scoundrels?' David Marks asked.

'Simple,' Moses said, interrupting, 'Chaim thinks young Israel Lazarus has got in with bad company.' He winked. 'I'm right, ain't I?'

Chaim hesitated. 'It's a possibility.'

'Didn't I tell you?' Moses said. 'I always knew he was born to swing from the gallows. Yes, any day now he's going to learn to do the Newgate jig.'

'That's a wicked thing to say,' Chaim protested. 'Well, do any of you know anything?'

'I might,' David said. 'My *zaydeh* has a shop in

Hanbury Street.' David's grandfather sold hosiery. 'He gets to hear things.'

'What kind of things?' Chaim asked.

David started to explain what his grandfather had told him. 'Samuel Rector's the one behind the Rat Boys. A right villain, he is. They say he's got a few murders to his name. Some even say he dabbles in the Dark Arts, stewing his victims in a cauldron so he can cast spells.'

'Just the facts please, David,' Chaim said.

David revealed what he knew. 'He's got two boys under him who he's training to take over from him some day.'

'Does one of them wear a top hat and a blue belcher?' Chaim asked, reliving the confrontation in the alley. He gave David a description of the boy he'd seen with Israel.

'That sounds like Noah Pyke,' David said. 'The other one's called Jacob Quiggins. You want to stay out of their way, if you know what's good for you. They're as vicious a pair of cut-throats as you'll encounter anywhere.'

'What about the others?'

David thought for a moment. 'My *zaydeh's* told me all their names. He says I'm to steer clear of the lot of them.' He named the rest of Samuel's gang. There were Ezra Flitch and Ethan Lockett, Jasper Logan, Malachy Doran and Enoch Wild. He didn't mention Israel. 'You'd be wise to keep your distance too, Chaim. There ain't a worse bunch of miscreants in the whole of London. If the Rat Boys have got their hooks into Israel, you may as well forget you ever knew him.'

'That's exactly what I told you,' Moses said, very superior. 'But you wouldn't listen to me, would you?'

Chaim did his best to ignore the interruption. 'There's a girl too, isn't there?' he asked.

'Oh, there are always girls,' David said. 'Samuel's got a string of them working for him. He plucks them out of the gutter then bends them to his will. They might be grateful in the beginning because he's put a roof over their heads and food in their bellies but a life on the streets is no life at all. They come to rue the day they ever set eyes on him.'

'Do you know any of their names?' Chaim asked.

'Let me think,' David said. His face cleared as he remembered. 'One's called Molly Vale. She's got a mean streak. The other goes by the name of Betsy something, Betsy . . . Yes, Betsy Alder, that's it. The poor wretches go in my *zaydeh's* doorway to shelter from the rain but they're bad for business. I think my *zaydeh* feels a bit sorry for them. It ain't their fault circumstances have brought them to such a condition.'

Moses snorted. 'I've little sympathy. Nobody makes them walk the streets.'

'No,' Chaim retorted, 'and nobody helps them get away, neither!'

'It ain't help they need,' Moses said, 'it's a spell in the workhouse.'

'And what good would that do them?' Chaim hissed, struggling to control his temper.

'Oy, let's not quarrel,' David said.

He didn't have much more to tell, only that the Rat Boys provided most of the stolen handkerchiefs and wallets sold along Petticoat Lane and most of the broken noses and bruised eyes handed out around

29

Fashion Street. Chaim digested the information then returned to his post for the afternoon session. He doubted whether he would have any more luck drilling his pupils in arithmetic than he had had explaining the principles of grammar and spelling. For all that, he never doubted the importance of what he was doing. Chaim had an ambition. One day he was going to be the Master of a great school.

It was growing dark by the time he left. He stood at the bottom of the steps to Christ Church for a while gazing up at the white spire. There was smoke and fog on the east wind. He shuddered and regretted the loss of his cap. He took in the neighbouring houses with their blackened chimneys and gable ends, their mouldering shutters and their broken windows stuffed with paper to keep out the cold. The mud was thick on the stones. He made the short walk to Flower and Dean Street and stood at the corner. He pictured the rat-infested passageway leading to the dark, tumbledown house where Israel now lodged with the Rat Boys.

I'm going to get you out Israel, Chaim thought. I just don't know how yet.

He was still imagining the dark staircase and the room where he'd met Betsy when he saw something move in a doorway. He peered through the gloom. He wasn't mistaken. Halfway down the Flowery, there was a shadowy figure. Chaim's first instinct was to turn and run, but there was something familiar about the stranger. Then he realized why. It was the boy who'd come to his rescue the previous evening. Chaim hurried forward, keen to thank his saviour, but by the time he reached the spot where he'd been standing nobody was there.

Four

At the top of the darkened staircase that still haunted Chaim's imagination, beyond a heavy, oaken door that was bolted and locked, Israel was trying to get used to his new life with the Rat Boys. As he lay on a straw mattress on the floor in the corner of the largest room, watching the others, he couldn't help but relive the circumstances that had brought him to this awful place. Until his thirteenth birthday, he'd been a happy, ordinary boy, intelligent, even gifted. He'd rarely given his mother a moment's worry. He'd always been studious, thoughtful and quiet and everybody had great hopes for him. But that was before he met the terror man. That's what he called the apparition that started to haunt his dreams.

Israel had known for a while that something was happening to him. When he asked his friends about it, they would start talking about forthcoming Bar Mitzvahs and the changes you went through in early adolescence. But Israel knew it was more than that:

the strange, dark pounding in his head, the fire that raced in his blood, the desire to smash and destroy and hurt. He had a devil inside him. One evening, back in November, Israel had been alone in the pair of rooms he shared with *Mamme*. She was talking to Mrs Wetzel on the next floor.

He sensed the danger even before he felt the blast of hot, sulphurous air. At the first rush of wind every hair on the back of his neck had stirred. Soon, a flurry of dust brushed his face. Turning, Israel had seen the floor seeming to dissolve, replaced by a dark, swirling vortex. He'd continued to stare in awe even when every instinct was screaming at him to flee. But he didn't flee. It wasn't just terror he felt. There was something else, a deep fascination with the apparition that was taking form in front of him. It was as if he'd imagined this scene before in his dreams. For several weeks the same unsettling thoughts had been gathering at the furthest margins of his mind. Now they rushed forward, clinging to the monstrous figure that was rising from the pit. Israel had watched the terror man floating before him and a name had come to his lips.

'Lud.'

'Yes,' the phantom answered, 'you know me, don't you, boy? I am your future. I am Lud.'

Every night, macabre dreams would invade Israel's brain. There was one that visited him over and over again. He would see himself in a misty burial ground, a sleepwalker among the dead. Beneath a full moon he would brush the soil aside from a coffin and lift the lid. His breath would mist then envelop the mask-like face of the corpse. Then the coffin's occupant would stir. Its eyelids flickered and its mouth yawned, spilling writhing maggots down its chest. Finally, with a momentary shudder, the creature climbed out of its grave. It stretched and groaned mournfully before starting to walk. Each new dawn Israel would wake clutching his head, wondering if he was going mad.

If Israel's nights were disturbed, his days became riots of mischief. He was no longer content to sit at home studying. The words on the page blurred and danced until he could make no sense of them at all. His old self crumbled like rotten plaster from a wall. He was restless. Sit for more than a few moments and it was as if his blood had caught fire. Soon he was running wild in the streets near his home, driven by the drumbeat of urges he didn't understand and couldn't control. Nothing he did made sense. It wasn't as if he made any profit from his thieving. He would steal from the hawkers just for the devil of it, raising a hullabaloo in the dense, crowded streets. If he robbed cakes he would eat one then throw the others away, inviting the street urchins to fight over them like squabbling pigeons. The more they scratched and gouged and bit to get one of the precious cakes, the more he enjoyed it. He didn't steal to eat like some of the wretches who shivered in rags on every street corner. He stole for the pure devilment of it.

He started to pick fights too. He remembered the first one. He challenged a boy two years older than him and they found a quiet alley where they could settle accounts. He had no right to win. The boy was much stronger, almost a man, sturdy and well-muscled. But Israel fought like a wild beast. He gouged and scratched, clawed and bit until his opponent was glad to give in. There was one reason for this fever of rebellion and one reason only. Its name was King Lud.

In the weeks that followed, Israel often asked himself who or what he was, this King Lud, this dark ghost that had risen and taken root in his soul, but Lud never explained himself. He just floated at the far fringes of Israel's mind. Once in a while, he thought about trying to summon Lud, but he never dared. So he waited. The waiting ended when Malachy and Noah came for him. Curiously, he didn't once try to resist them. Their coming was pre-ordained, so was his surrender. Now he was lying on a filthy mattress in a squalid room, missing home desperately and wishing he could escape. He heard Ezra Flitch talking.

'What's up with his nibs? Don't he talk?'

He means me, Israel thought. He pressed his nose to the wall and tried to blot out their conversation.

'He's a close 'un,' Jasper Logan said, 'he don't give nuffin' away.'

'Do you think he's deaf?' Ezra asked.

'No, he can hear,' Jasper said. 'He just doesn't want to talk to the likes of us. We ain't high-falutin' enough for His ruddy Lordship.'

Realizing that they weren't going to let him be, Israel glanced at them. 'What do you want me to say?'

'Oh, so you do speak then?' Ezra said. 'You don't look happy.'

'Happy?' Israel repeated. 'Why would I be happy when I've been snatched from my home?'

'What do you mean snatched?' Jasper said. 'You didn't put up much of a fight.'

'Hey, don't you like it here?' another boy demanded.

34

He grinned. 'Ain't you dazzled by the palatial surroundings of His Majesty Samuel Rector?'

This was Enoch Wild, by all accounts the best pickpocket in Spitalfields.

'I hate this place,' Israel said. 'Why can't I go home?'

'Home?' Enoch said. 'Why, this is your home now, Israel. You won't have no other.'

'That's right,' Jasper said. 'I had a mother once, before Samuel came to take me away, but she don't hardly figure no more. The Rat Boys are your mother and your father now.' He pronounced the words *mavver* and *fawver*. 'We're all the family you need.'

'But I don't belong here!' Israel cried. 'I've a home to go to. *Mamme* will be wondering where I am. I hate to think of her sitting at her window wondering what's happened to me.'

'It'll pass, little 'un,' Enoch told him.

'But I don't want it to pass!' Israel objected. 'I want to go home.'

His companions darted nervous glances, first at each other, then at the door to Samuel Rector's room.

'Don't go creating a fuss, Israel,' Ezra hissed. 'You don't want to go upsetting the guv'nor. He's a tolerable enough cove when you get used to him, but he won't have anybody carrying on. When you come to live at the Rats' Nest, you play by his rules. You give up all attachments to the world outside.'

'You said you wanted to be a Rat Boy,' Enoch said. 'I heard you with my own ears.'

'That wasn't me speaking!' Israel cried. 'That was him, Lud. Every time I open my mouth, it's his desires that come out.' He tried to bury his fingers in his temples. 'Lud's the one who's making me do these things. I wish I could reach inside my head and pull him out. I wish I could hurl him in the nearest fire.'

'Israel, Israel,' Jasper said in a calming voice, 'don't take on so. All of us were a little bit homesick at first. You'll get used to it.'

But all Israel saw was filth and cobwebs and rat droppings, and behind the whole squalid mess the ever-present shadow of Lud.

'It will never be home,' he protested. 'It's a prison, that's what it is.' To prove his point, he rose from his mattress and tugged at the door handle. 'See, it's locked. I might as well be in Newgate.'

By now, the three boys couldn't take their eyes off Samuel's door.

'You'll rouse Samuel the way you're carrying on and you don't want to do that,' Jasper told him. 'He's a terror and no mistake. He gets into such foul rages when people disturb him.'

But the damage was done. A moment later, the door burst open and Samuel appeared in corduroy trousers and the same greying vest he had worn when he climbed into the rat pit. He treated everyone in the room to a lowering glare.

'What's all the racket in here?' he demanded. 'I can't get a decent kip for your belly-aching.'

'It's the new boy,' Ezra stammered. 'He's upset – he don't like it here.'

Samuel turned his stony gaze on Israel. 'Is this true?' He folded his arms over his barrel chest. His tone of voice surprised Jasper and the others. It was calm, even understanding. 'Are you disappointed in our hospitality, Izzy?'

Israel nodded. 'I'd like to go home, please.'

36

The plaintive tone sounded out of place in the Rats' Nest. Enoch giggled but Samuel cut him dead with a stare. Israel saw Samuel's cold, unblinking eyes and the skin on his neck stiffened. What was the monster going to do to him? Israel was aware of Ezra, Enoch and Jasper backing away. They'd seen the look before and they were anticipating violence.

'Noah, Jacob,' Samuel shouted, 'where are you, you good-for-nothing rogues?'

The older boys came running, eyes wide with panic.

'What's the matter, guv'nor?' Noah bleated.

He and Jacob were Samuel's lieutenants and often the first port of call for his fiery wrath.

'Israel here's unhappy,' Samuel told them.

Noah and Jacob looked horrified.

'I'm shocked,' Samuel continued, 'shocked, I tell you.' His voice fell to a deep growl. 'Why ain't you entertaining our guest?'

Noah and Jacob swapped glances.

'We didn't know he was miserable, Samuel,' Noah said. 'Honest we didn't. He never said nuffin'.'

'He shouldn't have to say anything,' Samuel murmured. 'If you're to be my right-hand man, Noah, I expect you to anticipate his needs.'

Samuel let his gaze smoulder at Noah for a few moments.

'Well, make sure you do something to make our latest acquisition feel more at home,' he said. 'Here's a simple fact I want you to get through your thick skulls: Israel matters more than all the rest of you good-for-nothings put together.'

Israel heard but he didn't understand. Why did he

matter so much? What had he done to earn this monstrous brute's protection?

Samuel gave a wintry smile. 'So we're all going to help Israel settle in, aren't we?'

When nobody answered, he slammed his fist into the wall, sending dust and plaster spraying across the room. Israel found himself staring at the brawny arms and the huge knuckles, wondering how the burns from his performance at the ratting contest could have healed so quickly.

'So think of something,' Samuel thundered. 'I want Israel to feel at home and I mean now.'

There were hasty nods all round. Rector dropped into an armchair by the fire and put his feet on the fender. 'Come on, look lively. You know what they say. There's no time like the present.'

A murmur went round the room. What were they meant to do? Noah was the first to come up with an idea.

'Do you know what we haven't done, boys?' he said. 'We haven't properly introduced ourselves.' He waved Israel over to him. 'Did you ever wonder why they called us the Rat Boys?'

Israel offered the first answer that came into his head. 'You eat rats.'

That set off a chorus of laughter.

'Oh, that's us,' Jacob said. 'Toasted rat for breakfast, rat stew for dinner and skewered rat for supper.'

'And all lightly dusted with ground rat,' Jasper said, joining in.

'Quite right,' Ezra said, 'and the whole kit and caboodle followed up by a tasty rat pudding and a chilled rats' blood cordial to wash it all down.'

'It's a good guess, Izzy boy,' Noah said, 'but it ain't strictly correct. Watch.'

He snapped his fingers and Ezra, Enoch and Jasper came running. Immediately, they launched into the most astonishing display of acrobatics, leaping high into the air in a complex set of aerial manoeuvres. Not once did they collide.

'There you go. Some people think Rat Boys is just the name of yet another street gang. Now you know different. We're special.'

Noah snapped his fingers again. Ezra, Enoch and Jasper dropped to their knees. Malachy Doran and Ethan Lockett sprang onto their shoulders.

'Come on, Israel,' Ethan shouted. 'Complete the pyramid.'

Israel scrambled to the top and balanced on Malachy and Ethan's shoulders. To his delight, the whole pyramid started to move round the room as if it were one living organism.

'Right,' Malachy said, 'down you get, Israel.'

Israel did as he was told and the pyramid broke up.

'Go to it, boys,' Noah shouted, 'show Israel what you can do.'

At his signal, the five younger boys started to caper and somersault around the room, scurrying up the walls and leaping over the furniture. Israel watched the acrobatics and smiled despite himself. Enoch put on a performance, picking the pockets of everyone present. Ezra took half a dozen knives from a drawer and juggled them effortlessly. Israel clapped until his hands were sore. But it was King Lud who was enjoying the spectacle, experiencing it through Israel's eyes.

'There you go,' Noah said, 'you're feeling better already.'

Not to be outdone, Jacob Quiggins joined in the performance.

'Jasper,' he said, 'Israel will be impressed by your special trick.'

'Happy to oblige,' Jasper said.

He untied his cravat and let it hang loose. Jasper breathed deeply and stared hard at Jacob. In the hush that followed, Israel saw the ends slide across Jacob's chest and slowly, very deliberately, knot themselves as if manipulated by human fingers. But there was nothing moving the cravat. It seemed to have a mind of its own.

'That's astonishing,' Israel said. 'Can anyone else do a trick?'

'Of course we can,' Jacob said. 'Malachy, come here, you red-haired devil.'

Malachy waited patiently for his instructions.

'Show Israel why they call you Play Dead,' Jacob said.

Malachy started to race round the room. Suddenly, he stiffened as if shot in the back and crashed to the floor. His face turned pale. His lips were blue.

'Examine him,' Jacob said. 'Go on, look for signs of life. You won't find none.'

Israel bent over the fallen Malachy. There was no pulse. He didn't appear to be breathing either. What's more, he was stone cold.

'Here,' Jacob said, 'use this mirror.'

Israel held it to Malachy's lips. It didn't cloud the glass.

'Is he dead?' he asked in an awed whisper.

Jacob shook his head. 'Nah, he's only bluffing.'

'But how's that possible?' Israel asked.

'Every one of us here has a number of talents,' Jacob said. 'Some of us have extra abilities. Malachy's is to play dead. He could convince them down at the morgue.' He glanced at Samuel. 'That's why the guv'nor chose us.' He bent over Malachy. 'Hey, Play Dead,' he said, 'rise and shine, you idle wretch!'

Instantly, Malachy sprang to his feet. Gone was the deathly pallor.

'That's amazing,' Israel said. Then he frowned, remembering his dreams of the risen dead.

'What's wrong?' Noah asked, worried that he might still get a beating from Samuel.

'Oh, nothing,' Israel replied. 'But what about me? You could be the greatest mountebanks and performers in the whole of Europe. But what talent do I have? I'm here on false pretences.'

'Nonsense,' Samuel said. 'As it happens, you're greater than any of us. You've got the most miraculous power of all.'

Israel felt the oddest mix of emotions. He was horrified yet flattered at the same time.

'I have?' he asked.

'That's right, young Israel. You just don't know how to use it yet.'

'Will you show me?' Israel asked.

'Oh, I'll show you all right,' Samuel said, 'in good time.'

'But why not now?' Israel asked.

'Patience, my boy,' Samuel said. 'Patience.'

He laughed and the Rat Boys joined in. Even Israel laughed, though quite why he couldn't say. But he did

41

feel better. The moment his companions started to display their abilities, it had made him feel at home. Loathe the Rats' Nest though he did, somehow it was his destiny to be here. He was about to return to his mattress when he heard the rustle of skirts on the landing outside.

'That'll be Molly,' Samuel said. 'Let her in, Ezra.'

Ezra rushed to the door and slid back the bolts. A young woman of seventeen or eighteen appeared. She was wearing a burgundy dress and bonnet and her face was heavily made up. She made straight for the fire and rubbed her hands over the flames.

'I'm going to die of exposure one of these nights,' she complained. 'You shouldn't send me out when it's this cold, Samuel. It ain't right.'

But the show of temper was a ruse. She flounced away towards the small kitchen but Samuel had seen through her play-acting.

'Not so fast, Moll,' he said. 'Haven't you forgotten something? There's an entrance fee to the Rats' Nest, a token in respect of my hospitality.' He rubbed thumb and forefinger together. 'Where's the money, lady? You have got it, haven't you?' His eyes hardened. 'Because if you haven't . . .'

He didn't have to finish the sentence. Molly hastily dropped a drawstring purse into his hand. It jangled with coins.

'This feels a bit light,' Samuel said, weighing it in his hand. 'You wouldn't be holding anything back from me, would you?' He stroked Molly's cheek with the fingernail of his right forefinger. 'You know how I hate it when my girls try to cut into my profits. How's a businessman to make ends meet if his employees have their hands in the cash box?'

Molly stood stock still while he traced a line across her lips with his finger.

'You're right,' she said, pulling away. 'There's more.'

She didn't offer an excuse. Instead, she held out four shiny silver crowns.

'Four dollars,' Samuel said, adding the coins to the purse. 'Now what made you forget about them, Moll? Was you cogitating on the meaning of life?' He rubbed his fleshy nose. 'Or was you perhaps composing a great symphony?'

Israel's throat was dry. Samuel took Molly's jaw in a vice-like grip. The girl held herself rigid, barely daring to breathe. All the while, Samuel searched her face. Israel had never seen such menace as there was in Samuel's features at that moment.

'What's the cause of this absent-mindedness?' he asked.

'I don't know, Samuel,' Molly said, her voice little more than a frightened whisper. 'It won't happen again.'

'I know it won't,' Samuel said, letting go. 'How could I stay angry when I see those baby blue eyes looking up at me, all tearful and afraid?' He tightened his grip until Molly winced. 'We'll forget about it this time.' He relaxed his hold. 'How's that, my sweet Moll?'

'Thank you, Samuel,' Molly said.

'Think nothing of it,' Samuel told her. 'There's some brandy over there to warm the cockles of your heart.'

Molly crossed the floor and poured herself a glass.

Israel could tell by the erratic cluck of the liquid that her hands were still shaking. After a while, Molly put down her glass and whispered something to Jacob and Noah.

'Something wrong?' Samuel asked.

'I ain't seen Betsy all night,' Molly said. 'I've been to all the usual places. I looked everywhere. I'm worried something might have happened to her.'

'Oh, don't you worry about Betsy,' Samuel said. 'I gave her the night off. She's been here with me all along.'

Molly looked in the direction of Samuel's room. Israel did likewise. He hadn't noticed the girl before. She was just visible through the half-open door. He'd spoken to her a couple of times in passing but he didn't know much about her. She was around Molly's age. Her copper-coloured hair fell in an untidy, tangled mane over her bare shoulders. She was hugging her nightdress close but the gesture failed to disguise what everyone had noticed. Betsy had a cut lip and her arms and neck were covered in bruises and ugly, red welts.

'Lord save us, Samuel,' Molly gasped, rushing towards her friend, 'what did you do to her?'

Before Molly could reach the door, Samuel seized her by the wrist and pulled her to him.

'Now now, my girl,' he said, 'I thought we'd just come to an agreement.'

Molly struggled fiercely.

'Why did you have to beat her like that?' she cried. 'She ain't a bad girl. Why do you have to hurt people, Samuel?'

'Are you shouting at me?' Samuel snarled.

Without any warning, he swung Molly brutally

44

against the wall. She cried out in anguish and slid down to the floor, hugging her ribs.

'You ever raise your voice like that again,' he growled, 'and I swear, I'll tear out your spine.'

'I hate you, Samuel Rector,' Molly croaked weakly, pain written into her features. 'I wish you were dead.'

'Oh, Molly, Molly, Molly,' Samuel said, kneeling beside her, 'what am I going to do with you? How long have you been with me?'

'Too bleedin' long,' Molly cried, trying to squirm away from him.

'All this while under my roof,' Samuel said, 'and still you don't know how to behave yourself. My young ladies are supposed to be refined and gentle. So why are you belly-aching like an old fish wife?'

She was still shoving against him, trying to push him away.

'Now, you just stop that,' Samuel said, raising his right hand while restraining her with his left. 'I hope you're not going to give me any more trouble.' He made a swipe at her but didn't make contact, stopping his hand just inches from her face. 'Who's the guv'nor here?'

Molly resisted his grip for a moment or two then she went limp against him.

'I'm calm now, Samuel,' she said, not daring to meet his stare. 'It was seeing Betsy like that. I lost my mind for a moment.' She looked up at him like a frightened rabbit. 'Don't hurt me.'

Samuel stroked her throat. She flinched visibly. He glanced at Betsy through the open door. 'It's all a misunderstanding anyway. Betsy stumbled and fell against the washstand. Ain't that right, Betsy girl?'

Betsy nodded. 'Yes, that's right, Samuel. Clumsy, that's Betsy Alder, always covering herself with bruises.'

'There,' Samuel said, 'didn't I tell you? You're always jumping to conclusions, Moll. You've got to learn to control that temper of yours before it gets you into trouble. Now what have you got to say to me?'

Molly forced out an apology. 'I'm sorry.'

'And why are you sorry?'

'I thought you'd hurt Betsy,' Molly said. It was obvious she had to force the words out through gritted teeth. 'I can see I was . . . mistaken.'

Samuel yawned and let Molly go, then returned to his room, closing the door. The Rat Boys slunk away to their beds leaving Molly standing in the middle of the room, staring at Samuel Rector's closed door. Now that Samuel was gone, she could allow her true feelings to creep back into her face. Her eyes were blazing with hatred. After a few moments she felt Israel's gaze.

'What are you looking at?' she demanded.

'Nothing,' Israel answered. 'I'm sure Betsy's going to be all right.'

'You know that, do you?' Molly asked. 'How do you know? You some sort of surgeon? Or are you one of them clairvoyants?'

Israel wished he hadn't spoken. He lowered his eyes. 'I didn't mean anything.'

Molly watched him for a moment or two then softened and came to sit next to him. 'What's your name again?'

'I'm Israel.'

'You're new, ain't you?' she asked.

Israel nodded. 'Yes, Noah and Malachy came for me.'

'So how did you come to pitch up here among all us dead souls?' she asked. 'Don't you have no home to go to?'

The Rat Boys' performance had cheered Israel for a moment but the effect was starting to wear off. It was that part of him that was owned by Lud that had revelled in the demonic mayhem. 'Of course I've got a home. *Mamme* and I live off Wentworth Street.'

'So what are you doing here in this hell hole?' Molly asked. She glanced at the others. 'You ain't a devil child? You ain't got the seed, have you?'

'I'm sorry, I don't understand. The seed?'

'Do you mean to say you're here under the master's roof and you ain't never heard of the demon seed?' Molly asked.

'No,' Israel replied, 'never.'

'Let's put it another way,' Molly said. 'Did you ever get a visit from a rotten, filthy creature that goes by the name of Lud?'

Israel stiffened. 'You know about Lud?'

Molly nodded. 'Everybody that sets foot in this house knows about Lud.' She lowered her voice. 'He's made us all his disciples. Samuel lords it over us but it's Lud that pulls his strings.'

'Yes,' Israel said, 'I do know Lud. He mostly comes in my dreams. I see him almost every night. Until I came here and met other boys like me, I thought he was my own private nightmare.'

In that instant, Molly's attitude to him changed.

'So I was right not to trust you,' Molly said. 'You're just like them, you sly little scoundrel. You've got the

47

demon seed. Well, if you're acquainted with Lud, then there's nothing more I can do for you.'

'But, Molly . . .'

She threw up her hands. 'Stay away from me. You're all damned, every last one of you.'

For a moment, tears glistened in her eyes, then she brushed them away with the back of her hand. She'd realized she'd said too much. Her tone changed from anger to distress.

'You won't tell, will you?' Her eyes were wild. 'Please don't you go running to Samuel over this,' she said, fear flooding her voice. 'Promise you won't go blabbing what I've just said. I'll do anything you want.'

'I never will,' Israel said, gentleness creeping into his voice. 'I promise.'

Molly stared at him. 'Now ain't you an oddity? Every one of those boys out there would have shopped me at the drop of a hat. You don't sound a bit like them.'

'Really?' Israel said. 'So what makes me so different?'

'I can't put my finger on it,' Molly said. 'You don't seem to have the same mischief in you at all. Are you sure there ain't something you haven't told me?'

'I don't feel sure of anything,' Israel admitted. 'Tell me about the demon seed.'

'It's what connects you to Lud,' Molly said. 'It's what makes your blood race and your mind fill with black thoughts.'

Molly seemed to be trying to make sense of the situation. Was this sensitive boy really another of the terror man's disciples?

'I wonder what Samuel wants with you,' she murmured.

Before she could say another thing, Noah and Jacob made their way over.

'What are you saying to Israel?' Noah asked.

'Nothing,' Molly answered.

'Don't give me that,' Noah said. 'I heard you muttering. Samuel won't like you spreading rumours about him, Moll. Don't you never learn your lesson?'

Molly went to protest but Jacob interrupted.

'You're going to get yourself killed one of these days,' he added, 'and it will be your own stupid fault. You're too proud by half.'

'I didn't say a thing about the guv'nor,' Molly said. 'Cross my heart and hope to die. You can tell 'em, can't you, Izzy?'

'We were just talking,' Israel said.

'What about?' Jacob asked.

'How I got here, that's all.'

'There,' Molly said, 'didn't I tell you?'

'Well, that's enough talk for one night,' Noah told her. 'You run off to bed, Moll.'

Jacob tugged at her blond hair. 'Yes, that's right, you run off to bed like a good girl.' He made a grab for her. 'But before you go, give me a kiss.'

Molly pulled away. 'I'd rather kiss the Devil himself.'

Jacob sighed. 'You disappoint me, Molly. Ah well, maybe you'll have sweet dreams about me.'

For a moment it looked as though Molly was going to come up with a smart riposte, then she thought better of it.

'Quite right,' she said, almost jauntily, 'it's time I

turned in. A girl needs her beauty sleep. Goodnight, *gentlemen.*'

'Goodnight, Moll,' Noah said. 'Don't have nightmares.'

Israel watched her go then he curled up on his straw mattress. Images of Samuel, the Rat Boys, Betsy and Molly revolved in his mind. But, by the time Samuel re-emerged from his room to check on the boy, he was fast asleep. Jacob and Noah joined the thief-trainer by Israel's bed.

'What's so special about this one?' Jacob asked. 'I mean, what's his trick? Why's he so important?'

'Do you really want to know?' Samuel asked.

'If you don't mind, guv'nor,' Noah said.

'See these?' Samuel said, enclosing the sleeping boy's hands in his massive grip. 'They're going to raise an army. They're going to make me the most powerful man in London.'

Five

From the diary of Arthur Strachan
Tuesday, 5 February, 1839

*T*he tunnellers exposed more of the wall today. My
suspicions were correct. The construction definitely
belongs to antiquity. I have just spent several hours
exploring it with my own eyes. Did I say it might be
Roman? I doubt whether that's true. The reliefs are
pagan but they bear no resemblance to any classical
deity with which I am familiar. What I saw in these
carvings wasn't Jupiter or Mars, Venus or Pluto. I have
scoured my library for some clue as to the age and nature
of this edifice but I am mystified. If it isn't Roman, then
what in the Lord's name is it? The Saxons, Vikings and
Celts aren't known for building such great and intricate
structures of brick and stone.

I will record in these pages one of the reliefs. It depicts
a creature, more devil than man, a kind of primitive
Satan that has been cornered by four priests in flowing

robes. Each of these four hooded figures bears a trident. With their weapons, they are pinning the creature to the earth. Around this scene there is a great wall. At each corner of the four-sided enclosure there rises a fortified gate. Four gates, four priests, one imprisoned demon. I returned to my studies and discovered that there were once seven gates to the city. So why were there four depicted in the relief? The numbers did not match. What was I to make of the mystery?

At first I was stumped, so I consulted an old friend, Professor Melling of the London Museum. He explained that some of the seven gates were built fairly late in the history of the city. The most ancient of the gates, the ones which had their origin in the Roman city Londinium, were four in number as shown in the relief. There was Aldersgate to the North, Aldgate to the East, Ludgate to the West and the Bridge Gate to the South. Professor Melling gave me a mischievous grin and told me that the four gates marked the boundary of the dark city. They were the chambers of London's savage heart. I laughed off his tales as mere superstition.

'Arthur,' he said, 'what is superstition but that part of reality we fail to understand?'

Regardless of the historical significance of the wall, I have one more question. What property does this assemblage of stone possess that reduces grown men to sobbing children? I experienced it myself this afternoon. I had been there some two and a half hours when I felt the most morbid thoughts blooming in my mind. It was as if a host of unseen creatures was tearing my flesh and clawing my spirit. After a while I barely knew who I was or why I was in that odious place. Had one of my

52

foremen not dragged me physically from the spot, who knows what might have befallen me?

Perhaps it would be best if we re-routed the line and left the wall to Professor Melling and the other gentlemen of the British Museum. Why, if I'm not mistaken, it could be a treasure as great as the Elgin Marbles themselves and it is a treasure forged within these islands, not in antique Hellas. I have invited Robert and his wife to dinner tomorrow night. I will raise the matter with him then.

Six

The following evening two workmen were drinking at the Frying Pan pub in Brick Lane. The interior was lit by oil-lamps, turned down low so that the drinkers sat in shadow. The tap room was packed with flower girls, labourers and tradesmen. Some worked in the slaughterhouses and wore aprons spattered with dried blood. Thick tobacco smoke swirled around them, impregnating everything with its acrid reek. The first of the workmen, Tobias Gumm, drained his glass and rested his forehead on his palm.

'Are you all right?' his drinking partner, Albert Murray, said.

Tobias sighed. 'I'll be better when we've laid this line. There's something not right with the place. I tell you, Bertie, it gives me the collywobbles.'

Albert chuckled. 'Put it out of your mind, you muddle-head. It ain't nuffin' a pint of stout won't clear away.' He laid a handful of pennies on the bar and caught the eye of the barmaid. 'Two jars of stout, my darling, and your best smile for two working men.'

The barmaid shook her head. 'You can have your beer, you old charmer, but smiles are extra.'

Albert laughed and collected the drinks. 'There you go, Toby,' he said, 'let good lady ale ease your troubles away.'

'Don't you feel it though, Bertie?' Tobias asked. 'It's the ground. It's haunted. I swear, it's sewn with dragons' teeth, it is. I read about such a place once. I can't sleep nights for thinking about it.'

'There's a bit of an atmosphere down at the workings, I'll give you that,' Albert conceded, 'but nuffin' you don't get in a churchyard.' He grinned. 'Did I tell you about the time I got rotten drunk and took a short cut through the cemetery?'

'I can't say I recall.'

'Well, that's exactly what I did. There was a fair old pea souper and I got myself lost among the graves. You know what, I only went and fell asleep on one of them there tombs.'

Tobias's eyes were as round as saucers. 'What happened?'

Wrinkles appeared at the corners of Albert's eyes. 'You really want to know, Tobe my old mate?'

Tobias nodded, his eyes fixed on his drinking partner.

'Well,' Albert continued, 'I woke up in the middle of the night with this winged creature leaning over me. It had its arms outstretched like so.' He demonstrated. 'I tell you, Tobe, I nearly jumped out of my ruddy skin.'

Tobias was listening with rapt attention. 'What was it, Bertie?' he asked.

Albert let out a loud belly laugh. 'What do you think it was, you great donkey? It was one of them stone angels.' He shook his head. 'Don't you know when somebody's pulling your leg? No wonder you've got yourself believing them workings are spooked.'

'I know you think I'm stupid,' Tobias said, grumpily sipping at his stout. 'This is different. I've never been one to believe in ghosts and ghouls.' He took a deep swallow. 'But this has got me mightily spooked. Bertie, I've been thinking of walking off the job altogether.'

'You can't do that!' Albert said. 'How will you pay your lodgings? Good God, Tobe, do you want to end up sleeping on the street like some penniless vagabond?'

Tobias refused to be mollified. 'I'm starting to think I'd rather sleep rough than go back to that place.'

Albert was about to impart another piece of advice when he heard the scrape of a stool being drawn up. He half turned to see a burly, heavily-browed man in a woollen greatcoat. The smell of sweat and tobacco hung around him.

'If you don't mind,' Albert said, 'this is a private conversation.'

Tobias turned too. The newcomer seemed strangely familiar.

'I couldn't help but overhear you, gentlemen,' the intruder said. 'You work for the Commercial Railway, don't you?'

Albert was cautious. 'That's right. What's it to you?'

'The name's Samuel Rector,' the stranger said. 'I've got an interest in the new line.'

The moment Samuel introduced himself, Albert

glanced at Tobias. The exchange demonstrated that they'd both heard of him.

'Rector?' Tobias said. 'I thought I recognized you. Would you be the bare-knuckle fighter?'

'You mean we're sitting next to the man who beat Phineas Shrike over twenty-five rounds a few years back?' Albert gasped.

'The very same, Sir,' Samuel said. 'I fought old Phineas twice, in fact. The contests were some months apart. He gave me a run for my money the first time.' He rubbed his knuckles against the stubble on his chin. 'The second contest was a somewhat shorter affair, mind. I broke his jaw in the first round. That jab quite ruined his smile. I'm told he's a pot man in Bethnal Green these days. Seems he lost his appetite for the fight game after he came up against me.'

'So what made the difference between the two fights?' Tobias asked. 'Why did he last so long the first time?'

'Did it take you a bit to get used to his style?' Albert asked. 'Was you working out your tactics?'

'You're barking up the wrong tree, my friends,' Samuel told him. 'It had nothing to do with Phineas. It was me. I wanted the bout to last a while.'

Two pairs of eyes fixed him.

'I was toying with the cove, see,' Samuel explained. 'I let him pummel me for the first fifteen rounds.'

'I don't get it,' Tobias said. 'Why let him pound you like that if you had the beating of him? It don't make sense.'

'It's simple enough,' Samuel said, 'I was putting myself to the test. I wanted to know how much punishment I could take.'

'Are you serious?'

Samuel's eyes narrowed. 'Do I look like a man who tells jokes at his own expense?'

'So what's the answer?' Albert asked, wishing he'd never spoken. 'How much can you take?'

Samuel winked. 'A lot. I'm a quick healer. One time, this cove shoved a blade in my back down to the hilt. The blow would have killed any ordinary man. All I've got to show for it is a half-inch scar that itches when it rains. I've got a hide like an ox, see, and muscle to match.'

Albert ventured another question. 'Rumour has it you once killed a man in the ring.'

'You're well informed,' Samuel said. 'He went by the name of Danny Flaherty.' He yawned. 'I hit him so hard, something snapped in his brain.' He shook his head. 'It was such a pity. He fought bravely. Still, that's the fight game for you. There can only be one winner.'

'And the law didn't take no action against you?' Tobias asked.

Samuel shook his head. 'There were a few Bobbies watching that night. They would have liked to slap me in irons for what I did.'

'Why didn't they?'

'They'd been attending an illegal contest.' Samuel chuckled. 'They'd been laying a few bets too. So there was nothing they could do.' The smile faded from his face. 'Flaherty was unlucky, that's all.'

'Yes,' Albert said, 'unlucky he came up against the Satan of Spitalfields.'

Samuel laughed. He was enjoying the attention. While Albert and Tobias were probing him with questions, he spied a street urchin peering through the door.

'Hey you,' he said, 'yes, *you*, boy, I could do with your help. Do you want to earn yourself a florin?'

The boy's eyes widened, then distrust crept in. 'What do you want me to do for it?'

'It's simple enough,' Samuel said. 'I want to prove my strength to these fine gentlemen.' The boy glanced at Albert and Tobias. 'All you have to do is sit on this chair while I lift you.'

'And that's it?' the boy asked. 'You'll pay me a whole florin for that?'

'That's about the size of it,' Samuel confirmed. 'Generous to a fault, that's me.'

He was showing off his wealth and power. The two workmen wondered why.

'Get to it,' Samuel said. 'Hop on the chair.'

The boy did as instructed. The demonstration had attracted the interest of most of the tap room. Samuel winked at his new friends and gripped a chair leg. Then, in one steady movement, he lifted chair and boy higher and higher. His arm didn't even tremble. He continued to lift until the lad tapped the ceiling with his fingers. The whole room immediately rocked with applause and Samuel rewarded the boy with his florin.

'That's some right arm you've got, friend,' Albert said.

'There's nobody stronger in the whole of London,' Samuel told him.

He snapped his fingers at the barmaid and she hurried over with a round of drinks. Soon, Samuel had lubricated Tobias's and Albert's tongues sufficiently to put his questions about the progress of the new Minories station. 'I hear it's jinxed.'

'Cursed is more like it,' Tobias slurred.

'Cursed?'

'It's this wall we found,' Tobias explained. 'You've never come across anything like it. There are pictures carved all over it.'

'What sort of pictures?' the Satan of Spitalfields asked.

'Devils,' Tobias told him. 'It's like Dante's Inferno. Yes, there's all manner of horrors down there. It makes my blood run cold to think of it.'

'So what does the engineer say about it all?' Samuel asked.

'Mr Stephenson?' Albert said. 'He hasn't seen it yet. It's his deputy, Mr Strachan, who's been in charge of things lately. There's a rumour he wants to re-route the whole line.'

Samuel leaned forward. His eyes blazed with keen interest. 'What happens to the wall if he does that?' he asked.

'Who knows?' Albert said. 'We might cover it up again or hand it over to these Harky-hologists.'

'Archaeologists,' Samuel said, correcting him.

'That's what I said, ain't it?' Albert grumbled.

'Some of the men say we ought to just smash it to pieces and sow the ground with salt,' Tobias said. 'I'm with them on that. If a thing's evil, you need to crush it into dust before it does the same to you.'

Samuel gave him a bleak stare before asking his next question. 'What's he like, this Mr Strachan?'

'He's a Scotsman,' Albert said. 'He's a bit humourless but he's always been fair to his men.'

'What's his full name?'

'Arthur,' Albert replied, 'Mr Arthur Strachan.'

'Does he have any family?'

'He's a widower,' Albert replied. 'He's got a daughter, though. Victoria's her name.' He paused. 'Here, what are all these questions in aid of?'

'Can't a man show some interest in his locality?' Samuel asked.

Albert and Tobias had been emboldened by the drink they had consumed. They didn't like the direction Samuel's enquiries were turning.

'Interest is one thing,' Albert said, 'but you're crossing the line, my old cove. You ain't a gang master, are you?'

Tobias picked up the thread. 'Oh, so that's your game. You're waiting for us to walk off the job so you can put your own men in.' By then, the drink wasn't so much talking, as screaming. 'You're right, Bertie. Why, I bet it ain't the wall that's been making us feel bad after all. This cove's probably been poisoning our food the whole time.'

Samuel held up his hands. 'Now now, boys, don't go jumping to conclusions.'

'Oh, giving orders now, are you?' Tobias slurred.

Samuel scowled. 'Stop right there, my friend.'

'There he goes again,' Tobias roared, 'giving orders.'

He tried to stand but Samuel slapped a meaty fist on his forearm. That just made Tobias even angrier. He tore Samuel's arm away and rose unsteadily to his feet. Some of the other customers turned to watch. The barmaid gave the landlord the nod that trouble was brewing.

'Calm down, gentlemen, please,' he said from the bar.

'It's him you should be talking to,' Tobias complained. He took a swing at Samuel's head. He was soon made to pay for his mistake. The ex-boxer allowed the punch to sail past his right ear and simultaneously seized Tobias's fist in a vice-like grip. Tobias cried out as the powerful fingers crushed his knuckles. A split second later his face drained of blood and his knees buckled.

'Now now,' the landlord called, still not budging from the safety of the bar. 'I'll have no fisticuffs in here.'

But he made no move to separate the two men. He knew better than to interrupt the Satan of Spitalfields when he was chastising somebody. Samuel leaned in close, relaxing his grip only slightly. He whispered some advice to Tobias. 'I'll let you go on one condition. You don't take another swing at me. Agreed?'

Tobias looked at Samuel's huge fists with their big, bony knuckles and croaked his agreement. 'Just let go of my hand.' He could feel his bones grinding against one another. The pain was excruciating. 'Hell's bells, you've got a grip like a bleedin' ape, you have.'

The Frying Pan's other customers continued to stare at the commotion but nobody tried to intervene. One of the onlookers, watching from a booth, was Kitty Flaherty, the woman Samuel had approached at the ratting contest.

'The show's over,' Samuel announced. He waited until the drinkers had resumed their conversations and hissed a question at Albert and Tobias. 'Are you two ready to listen to me?'

Both men nodded.

'Good,' Samuel said. 'Look here, my lively lads, I don't want your jobs. That ain't it at all. You see, I've a bit of an interest in the railway industry myself.' He lowered his voice. 'I mean a financial interest. It's like this, I mean to be a man of property one day. I've had enough of bare-knuckle boxing and unofficial trading.'

Albert glanced at Tobias. That was a euphemism for receiving stolen goods.

Samuel continued. 'Let's say there's money to be made buying and selling the land around the line when it's finished, and that means I need to know where it's going. That way, I can buy the right plots at the right time.'

'But I thought the railway company owned the whole area,' Tobias said.

'Oh no,' Samuel said, 'there's plenty of room for the small investor.'

Tobias and Albert started to relax again.

'So this is the deal,' Samuel continued. 'I meet you in here now and then and you keep me abreast of developments on the site.'

Tobias was still flexing his sore hand, wondering how any human being could exert such vice-like pressure.

'What's in it for us?' he asked.

'A crown each to start with,' Samuel said, handing over the money. 'There'll be more if the information is good. Well, are you in?'

Albert gave a greedy smile. 'Oh, we're in all right. We're only earning a pound and ten shillings a week on the railway. A little bonus would be most welcome.'

Samuel grinned. 'I thought the money might come in

handy. Let's say I like to give an honest working man a leg up in life.'

Tobias chuckled appreciatively. 'You're a regular charitable institution, that's what you are.'

'Exactly,' Samuel said. 'Now, there's one last thing before I go. It's worth another George each.'

'Half a crown!' Albert said. 'What do you want to know?'

'Just this,' Samuel said. 'I'm thinking foundations. I need to know what's under there. How far down do these workings go?'

'Well, we did sink a couple of deep shafts,' Albert said. He wracked his brains for some information that might prise the half crowns from Samuel's fist. He turned to Tobias. 'Didn't you say you'd seen a gatehouse or something like?'

Samuel was hanging on every word. 'A gatehouse, you say?'

'That's what it looked like to me,' Tobias said. 'I only had a lantern and it was a ruddy big hole but I could have sworn I saw a door down there.'

'Go on,' Samuel said, 'tell me everything. What kind of door?'

'That's just it,' Tobias said, 'it wasn't like anything I've ever seen before. It was pure white, like marble. From time to time it seemed to glow faintly.' He shuddered. 'It don't bear thinking about.'

'But I want you to think,' Samuel said. 'When it glowed, did you see a handle?'

Tobias frowned then his brow cleared. 'Why, no I didn't! Well, what do you make of that, Bertie? It never occurred to me until now. A door without a handle, ain't that an oddity?'

Samuel thought for a moment, then spoke. 'Do me a favour, gentlemen, if anybody comes sniffing round the site, leave me a message here.'

'You want to know about competitors,' Tobias said. 'That's it, ain't it?'

Samuel smiled. 'Got it in one.' He handed the men their coins. 'Tobias, Albert,' he said, 'it's been a pleasure. I must take my leave now. I look forward to doing business with you again.'

Tobias smiled and jingled the money in his pocket. 'Not half as much as we're looking forward to seeing your good self, Mr Rector.'

With that, Samuel stepped into the foggy evening, leaving his two companions quite mystified. Kitty Flaherty let him go then made her way over to the pair. She wanted to know what Rector was up to. Mrs Flaherty had little difficulty persuading Albert and Tobias to talk. They were only too happy to serve two paymasters.

Seven

Israel woke to see the grey light of a winter morning struggling through the dusty, tattered curtains. In the unforgiving glow of the sun it was impossible to disguise how far he'd fallen by throwing in his lot with the Rat Boys. He'd dreamed of the graveyard again and the walking dead that rose from the earth. He forced the nightmare to the back of his mind and sat up. The other boys were strewn around the room, sleeping where they'd lain down the night before.

Israel grimaced at his surroundings. The ceiling and walls were black with dirt and age. Soon, he made out the sound of splashing from the small scullery where Samuel brewed his coffee in a saucepan. He padded across the floorboards and peered through the half-open door. There he saw Molly and Betsy, 'Samuel's girls', sitting together at the wooden table that dominated the room. Molly was treating her friend's cuts and bruises with a cloth dipped in warm water.

'Somebody ought to do for the blighter,' she said.

'He's got no right to hurt you. You ain't done nuffin' wrong.'

Betsy winced.

'Did that sting?' Molly asked. 'I can't help it. Like my old mum used to say, God rest her soul, a hurt's got to get worse before it gets better.' She paused to inspect her handiwork. 'That's the best I can do, Bets. Put on a bit of rouge and you'll cover up the worst of it.'

'Thanks, Molly,' Betsy said, 'you're a treasure.'

'Ain't that the truth?' Molly said. 'I'm a real lady. It's a pity some City gent don't see me and set me up in a fine house with a little dog to stroke. That's all I want, Bets, a bit of comfort and consideration. I've been poor all my life. Don't I deserve a change of fortune?'

Betsy patted Molly's hand. 'That's all any of us want, Moll, the chance of a bit of love and affection.'

Molly cut two slices of bread and buttered them. She handed one to Betsy and kept one for herself. 'Not while Samuel's beating you like this,' she said. 'Why does he do it, Bets?'

Betsy shrugged. 'He has a taste for it, simple as that.'

'Some day, I'll find a way to get even,' Molly said.

Betsy shushed her with a finger. 'You've got to stop taking such risks. One of these days Samuel's going to catch you cursing him. You shouldn't yell at him the way you do.'

'Why ever not?' Molly demanded. 'I mean what I say. Somebody ought to do for the swine.' She placed her fingertips under Betsy's chin and turned her friend's face so that she could examine the bruises in the sunlight that was streaming in from the open window. 'What kind of man does that to a girl?'

Instinctively, Molly glanced at the door. She made

out a shadow and paled. Seeing her friend's reaction, Betsy spun round.

'Who's there?' she asked.

Betsy shrunk back, terrified that it was Noah or Jacob. But it was Israel who stepped into the scullery.

Molly gave a sigh of relief. 'Oh, it's you, Israel. You gave me such a turn.'

Betsy still looked scared out of her wits.

'Don't you worry about Israel. He's a good boy, ain't you, Izzy?'

'Good boy?' Betsy snorted. 'Are you mad, Moll? You can't trust a Rat Boy. He might seem all right at the moment but don't forget that he belongs to Samuel and the pair of them belong to Lud. You can't trust a word he says.'

Israel hung his head.

'Look at that,' Molly said, teasing Israel in spite of everything Betsy had said. 'You've gone and hurt his feelings.'

Betsy finished her buttered slice. 'I don't give a fig for his feelings. A Rat Boy might be nice enough to begin with but you know how they all turn out. Don't you remember what Malachy was like when he first came?'

'I remember,' Molly said, 'you was like a mother to him back then, cradling him until he slipped off to sleep.'

'That's right,' Betsy said. 'Look at him now, Moll. He's one of the worst of them.'

'I'm sorry,' Israel said, forcing himself to interrupt, 'but I don't know what you're talking about. What happens to the boys?'

68

'Are you pulling my leg?' Betsy demanded. 'You must know.'

Israel turned his gaze towards her. 'I know I'm meant to do something . . . special.'

'Has nobody explained it?' Molly asked. 'Don't you understand what's happening to you?'

Israel shook his head. 'I knew I had to go with Noah and Malachy. I know I can't go home. There's something in my head telling me so.'

'You ain't spinning us a line, are you?' Betsy asked doubtfully.

'I'm telling the truth,' Israel said. 'I really don't understand why I'm here or what's to become of me. You've got to help me.'

'Well, it goes like this,' Molly said. 'If you've got the demon seed in you, you're normal enough until you turn thirteen. The moment you start developing into a man, you change.'

'How?'

'Surely you've noticed,' Betsy said. 'Didn't you start to feel different?'

'I've been getting into fights,' Israel told her, 'stealing, that kind of thing.'

'And was that your nature before you came into adolescence?'

'No,' Israel answered, 'not at all. I've always been quiet.'

'There you go,' Betsy said. 'You're becoming one of them.'

Israel glanced over his shoulder at the sleeping Rat Boys. 'And what are they?'

'Monsters, hell-fiends, *demons*, that's what they are,'

Molly told him. 'You've seen them, the way they ain't quite human.'

'And you think I'll go the same way?'

Molly snorted. 'We know so!'

Betsy stroked his cheek. 'Moll's right. You'll go the same way, my lamb, I can guarantee it.'

'There's no hope for you here, Izzy,' Molly told him. 'I've seen boys try to fight it, but they all surrender in the end. There ain't one of those boys out there that won't kill for Samuel if he's asked.'

In the main room somebody stirred.

'No more talk,' Betsy said anxiously. 'Samuel gave me a bad enough beating last night. I wouldn't survive another one.'

'Why does he hurt you?' Israel asked.

'Why?' Betsy said in a kind of despairing sigh. 'There ain't no why in the Flowery, Izzy boy. Samuel hurts people because he likes it, and that's all there is to it.'

Ezra appeared at the door, cutting the conversation short. 'You got any more of that bread and butter, Bets?'

Betsy cut him a slice and passed it to him. Ezra munched it hungrily. At that point, Noah strolled in and asked, 'You ready for your first day's work, Izzy?'

'I suppose so,' Israel answered. 'What do I have to do?'

'We're going to show you the tricks of the trade,' Ezra said, mumbling through a mouthful of bread and butter.

'I hope you learn quickly,' Noah added. 'I don't want you slowing us down.'

'You don't have to worry about me,' Israel said.

'Glad to hear it,' Noah said. 'Ezra, go rouse the others.'

Ezra woke Jacob first. While the boys rose one by one from where they'd been sleeping Israel watched Noah. He seemed very interested in Betsy. Noah caught him staring.

'What are you looking at, Izzy?' the older boy snapped. 'You wait over there while I have a chat with Betsy here.'

Ezra dug his elbow into Israel's ribs. 'Noah's sweet on our Bets. The guv'nor would beat his brains out if he knew.'

Soon the Rat Boys were ready to go. Jacob tapped on Samuel's door and told him they were off. There was a grunted reply. Outside in the street, Israel put a hand to his mouth and nose. A sickening smell of sewage and animal dung escaped into the houses and yards. Here and there, he had to step over dead rats. They made their way through pot-holed streets and broke up into groups to hang around the pie-shops and coffee houses. By midday they'd filched half a dozen hand-kerchiefs, two wallets and a fob watch.

'Hey, Licker,' Noah said, handing the stolen goods to Ethan. 'Run these back to the Rats' Nest.'

Ethan took the haul back to Samuel while the rest of the gang carried on working.

'Why do you call him Licker?' Israel asked.

'It's his name,' Noah said, 'Licker Lockett. You'll find out why we call him Licker soon enough. We'll be needing his talents one of these days.'

Israel didn't have a chance to puzzle over it for long. Jacob wanted to continue his training.

'Follow me, young Izzy,' he said. 'We're going to try something a bit more ambitious.

Malachy fell in step beside them and they cut through Brushfield Street towards the city. They slunk along, trying not to be noticed. Soon Jacob spotted a suitable victim: a middle-aged city gent.

'Show Izzy what to do,' Jacob said. 'I'll follow you.'

Jacob explained the situation. Armed with his instructions, Israel walked past the gent and down the narrow alley behind him. There he waited. Once he was in position, Malachy snatched the man's handkerchief and set off down the alley towards Israel. The gent gave chase. Malachy led the prospective victim to the far end of the alley, past Israel then turned round. Though their victim didn't realize it, he had placed himself in the jaws of their trap.

'Give me my handkerchief,' the gent said, 'or I'll call the police. Hand it over and I'll forget all about it.'

Malachy made a show of handing over the handkerchief. The moment the gent reached out, Israel scrambled up his back and yanked his top hat down over his eyes. Clinging to the brim, he held on for dear life while the man struggled. Meanwhile, Malachy deftly stripped him of wallet, watch and cravat.

'Let's go,' Malachy said.

But Israel let go a little too quickly and the gent managed to pull his hat from his eyes. He made a grab for Israel. It was a bad mistake. Already, Jacob was striding towards him, his eyes dark with rage.

'I think not,' the gent said. 'I'm going to hand him over to the Bobbies.'

72

'No,' Jacob said, 'you ain't. Get your hands off him. Let him go and you can still walk away.'

'What impudence!' the gent bellowed. 'I'll do nothing of the sort. The boy's a thief. Get out of my way, you young scoundrel.'

'Is that your final answer?' Jacob asked.

'It is.' With that, the gent started to call for the police. 'Police! Police! I've apprehended a thief.'

Jacob sighed. 'I warned you.' He grabbed the gent by the collar and fixed him with a stare. Instantly, the man's face changed.

Israel glanced at Malachy, wondering what was happening.

'Just watch,' Malachy told him.

The gent's face was ablaze with terror. 'No!' He started to scream. 'No, dear God, no!' He fell back against the wall, foam forming on his lips.

Israel was bewildered. Jacob didn't seem to be doing anything but gazing into the man's eyes.

'That'll do,' Malachy said. 'You don't want to kill him, Jacob.'

Jacob nodded and the three of them walked away, leaving the man crouching on all fours in the alley, sobbing like a smacked child.

'What did you do to him?' Israel asked, glancing back.

'You've got a lot to learn,' Malachy said. 'You've just witnessed one of the marks of the Rat Boys. Every one of us has the ability. I made him live through his worst nightmares. We can scare a man to death with a look.'

'Does that mean I can do it?' Israel asked.

'All demons can. I'll show you how when we get

73

back to the Flowery.' Malachy tugged Jacob's sleeve. 'How much is in the wallet?'

'Thirty shillings.'

'Thirty!' Malachy cried. 'Fancy carrying such an amount about your person. The cove's got more money than sense.'

'Let's get a bite to eat,' Jacob said. 'Samuel can have twenty. We'll split the rest.' He glanced at Israel. 'Keep quiet about it, young 'un. No blabbing to the guv'nor about this. We have to skim some of the money off the top or we'd starve. Samuel never gives us enough to eat.'

Twenty minutes later they were sitting in a booth in a coffee house. They each ate a bowl of oatmeal porridge and a plate of poached eggs. Around them the air was rich with pipe-smoke and damp air but Israel felt happy. He kept reliving the moment he sprang onto the gent's back and pulled the top hat down over his head. There were two voices in his head. One told him it was wrong. The other said it was fun.

'Did you see how Izzy did for a first-timer?' Malachy chuckled. 'He gave his man a right bonneting.'

'Yes,' Jacob said, 'you're a natural, young Izzy. You've just got to be a touch quicker on the getaway. You'll learn.' He slurped his tea. 'Mind you, none of us are going to be filching for long.'

'You mean Samuel's ready to hatch his plan?' Malachy asked.

'Almost,' Jacob answered. 'Samuel's got great expectations of us, boys, great expectations indeed.' He leaned forward conspiratorially. 'If all goes well, our thieving days will soon be over. We're going to change the whole bleedin' world, you mark my words.'

Sitting there, listening to his companions, Israel felt a rush of excitement and just the slightest tingle of dread too.

Eight

From the diary of Arthur Strachan
Wednesday, 6 February, 1839

Mrs Weaver did us proud this evening. Informed of the fact that Mr Robert Stephenson is a most important and prominent man, she laid on a feast fit for a King. There was turtle soup, turbot, several meat dishes, a lobster vol-au-vent, and, for dessert, a fine tart made from apple preserves. I swear, Her Majesty the Queen will not have dined better this year.

Over cognac I broached the question of the wall. I listed the curious events that have bedevilled the project and suggested that we might re-route the line altogether. It seemed a not unreasonable request but Robert would have none of it. He explained the budgetary constraints imposed upon us by the investors, which excluded the possibility of even the most minor changes. Reluctantly, I had to agree to continue on our present course, however challenging that might prove. Robert was equally

76

opposed to any delay while an archaeological survey was carried out. In his own words: 'If we must build over it or through it, Sir, that is what we must do. The line and the station must be delivered on time.'

There we have it. Work will continue as before. If we have to demolish a work of antiquity, then so be it. Such is progress.

Nine

Chaim was tired. He had taken a great risk spying on the house in Flower and Dean Street. So far, he didn't think he'd been spotted. *Mamme* was often curious about how he was spending his time, but never once did she try to stop him looking for Israel. He had come to the conclusion that there was only one real-istic chance of springing Israel from the clutches of Samuel Rector, and that was to rouse him from his bed before the others had woken. To achieve his aim, he would need an accomplice, somebody who would aid him on the inside. The very person was over there, shuddering on the corner of Dorset Street.

'Betsy,' Chaim said. 'Can we talk?'

Betsy stopped and stared. She recognized the boy who'd burst in on her the other evening. Molly Vale ran suspicious eyes over him. Evidently, Betsy hadn't mentioned him.

'What do you want to talk to me for?' Betsy asked.

Caution crept into her voice. 'Why did you come back?'

'Yes, what's your game?' Molly demanded, stepping protectively in front of Betsy. 'Hook it.'

'There's no need for that,' Betsy said. 'He don't mean me no harm.'

Molly didn't look happy but she drifted away, leaving Chaim and Betsy to it. Their breath misted as they spoke and every sound seemed magnified in the cold East London air.

'I'll only keep you a few minutes,' Chaim told her.

Molly looked on from the street corner. There was no disguising the expression on her face. She was ready to defend Betsy any way she could from the attentions of this stranger. Molly had a small but lethal knife hidden in the folds of her dress. Spend a few days frequenting the beer halls of the East End and you'd be sure to come across somebody who was sporting the marks of Molly's handiwork. She wasn't afraid to use her trusty blade in self-defence.

'It's all right, Moll,' Betsy said, regretting her own over-reaction. 'He means well. He just don't know what he's getting himself into.'

She laid her hand on Molly's and the knife remained in its hiding place.

'I do know I've got to get Israel out of that place,' Chaim said stubbornly.

'You know Izzy?' Molly asked.

'Chaim's his pal,' Betsy explained. 'This ain't the first time I've come across him.'

'I worked that much out,' Molly said. 'You was as thick as thieves just then. So where do you know him from?'

'He came to the Rats' Nest,' Betsy said. 'He came looking for Israel.'

'Israel and I live in the same building,' Chaim explained. 'Well, we did. I'm meant to take care of him.' He grimaced. 'I haven't done a very good job of it.'

Betsy glanced at Molly. 'We like Izzy. We know he's bound to turn sooner or later but he's putting up a real fight. If I didn't know better, I'd say he could beat it.'

Chaim frowned. 'I don't understand. What do you mean *turn*?'

'Don't you know what's happening to him?' Molly asked. 'Izzy was in the dark too. You're in for a shock, you are.'

'There's something inside these boys,' Betsy explained, 'it makes them turn bad.' Her voice trailed off. 'I can't say no more.'

'I'll keep a look out,' Molly said. 'For God's sake make it quick.'

'Can we trust her?' Chaim asked Betsy as Molly made her way to the corner.

Betsy was offended by the question. 'I'd trust Moll with anything,' she told him. 'We're more like sisters than friends. She'd lay her life down for me and I'd do the same for her.'

Chaim accepted her word. 'It's like this,' he said. 'I've been watching the house whenever I get the chance. There's only one time of day I can get Israel out of there and that's early morning when they're still asleep.'

'It won't work,' Betsy said. 'Nobody leaves the Rats' Nest without Samuel's say so.'

'I know,' Chaim said. 'That's why I need you.'

Betsy looked at him for a moment then it dawned on her what he was asking her to do. 'Oh no,' she said. 'You want me to go against Samuel? You've got to be soft in the head.' She shook her head fiercely. 'If I get caught going behind the guv'nor's back, they're going to have to fish me out of the Thames the next morning.'

Chaim wasn't about to give up yet. 'I only want you to unlock the door and draw back the bolts. Samuel won't blame it on you. He'll think Israel did it. You said he was trying to fight back.'

'What if the guv'nor finds out?' Betsy said. 'He damned near killed me the last time he lost his temper.'

She showed Chaim the marks on her face and drew back the collar of her dress to show him the welts and bruises on her shoulders.

'Do you want to be responsible for more of this?' Betsy demanded.

Chaim winced at the injuries. 'He did that to you?'

'That and a lot more,' Betsy said. 'He turns on all of us from time to time; me, Moll and the boys. I want to help you, truly I do. But I can't risk another beating like this.'

'Please Betsy,' Chaim said, 'you're my only hope. You know what's going to happen to Israel if he stays there. You said it yourself, he's going to turn into a demon like them. You don't want that to happen, do you?

'It's not that I don't want to help you,' Betsy said. 'I can't. I ain't a bad girl, Chaim. I'm weak, that's all. Molly's always had to take care of me.' She thought of the knife.

Molly appeared at that very moment. 'We've got to

go, Bets. I just saw Jacob and Noah outside the Ten Bells. What if they're checking up on us?'

'I'm sorry, Chaim,' Betsy said, 'I truly am, but there ain't no way I can help you.'

Molly was suddenly curious.

'Why,' she asked, 'what's he asking you to do?'

Betsy was darting worried looks in the direction of the Ten Bells. 'Chaim, I know you mean well, but we can't be seen talking to you.'

'I'm not going to give up,' Chaim said. 'You must know that.'

Betsy was trembling. 'You're going to be the death of me, truly you are.'

'I'll only ask you one more time,' Molly said, annoyed that they were ignoring her, 'what are you after? What's it going to take to get you off our backs?'

Chaim explained that he wanted somebody to unlock the door to the Rats' Nest and slip the bolts. A change came over Molly.

'And that's it?'

'Yes,' Chaim said, 'that's it.'

Molly's eyes lit with defiance. 'Well, why didn't you say so!'

Betsy stared at her. 'You're never going to do it.'

'I ruddy well am,' Molly said. 'It's time our high and mighty guv'nor got his come-uppance. Old Sammy Rector's got high hopes for his little Izzy. Israel's the apple of his eye. He's part of some big plan.'

'Do you know what it is?' Chaim asked.

'No,' Molly said, 'but that don't really matter. I just want to see the guv'nor's face when you steal him away from under his nose.' Her eyes sparkled. 'I'll help you.'

Betsy was wearing a mask of terror. 'No, Moll, he'll do for you.'

'He's got to catch me first,' Molly said. 'I've lived in fear too long, Bets. I just want to look myself in the mirror and know I tried to do the right thing for once.'

Betsy hissed a warning. 'There's Jacob. He's looking for us, all right.'

Molly drew Chaim over to her. 'You ain't going to back out, are you? You're going to help Israel, no matter what happens?'

'Yes,' Chaim answered, 'I give you my word.'

Molly continued to press him. 'You change your mind and I'll come after you. I'll kill you with my own bare hands.'

'I told you I'd go through with it.'

'No matter what?'

'No matter what.'

Molly seemed almost convinced. If she was going to risk her life, she had to know Chaim was genuine. 'And there's nothing that'll stop you? You'll do all you can to take him away from Samuel?'

'Yes.'

Betsy's eyes were hard with fear. 'Molly, you can't be serious! This is Samuel Rector you're going to double-cross.'

'Oh, I'm serious,' Molly said. 'I'm sick of being in that monster's pocket. Look at the pair of us, Bets. Yes, it'll be worth it just to spite Samuel.' She leaned forward and kissed Chaim on the cheek, making him blush. 'God bless you.'

'What did I do?'

'You reminded me what life's about.'

Without another word, Molly took Betsy by the hand and led her across the road towards Jacob and Noah. Chaim waited for a few minutes then slipped away among the crowds. Nobody had noticed the keen observer, watching the entire scene from a nearby pie-shop. It was Mrs Flaherty.

Ten

From the diary of Arthur Strachan
Thursday, 7 February, 1839

I have had a visit from a most disreputable character,
a man of obviously low morals and brutish tastes. He
announced himself to me as one Samuel Rector. I had
never heard his name until this day. On making enquiries among my staff, I have discovered that he is a rogue of
some notoriety in the East End. He seems to be surpris-
ingly well-versed in the history of the Minories to Blackwall line. It's as if he's privy to the engineer's plans. He's
got to have inside information. Tomorrow, I shall press
upon the men the necessity of not discussing details of
construction with strangers.

The rogue had the impertinence to make demands. He
expects me to re-route the line and sanction unauthorized
excavation of the wall, all on his say-so! He wants me to
cordon off the wall and give him exclusive access. He even
offered me payment for my services, as if I were some

dishonest clerk taking a bribe. Needless to say, I dispatched the blackguard with a firm refusal. Even then, he wanted to have the last word.

'You'll soon change your tune,' he retorted.

When I insisted that I would buck the trend, he simply smirked.

'I have an interest in seeing the area excavated,' he told me. 'I usually get my way in the end.'

'Well, you will not get your way this time,' I answered.

I told him that I hadn't studied engineering for four years at Edinburgh University and spent twenty years building a reputation in the industry to throw it all away.

'Be gone, Sir,' I said. 'Be gone before I call the Metropolitan Police.'

Even then the villain continued to act in the most carefree and arrogant manner.

'Is that your last word?' he asked.

I told him that it was. Then he gave his last word.

'It seems I'll have to find a way to persuade you,' he said. 'It shouldn't be difficult. I'm used to twisting arms. There isn't a man alive that don't have an Achilles' heel.'

I confess, for a moment I had a most uncomfortable feeling. But what could such a low individual do to harm a respectable gentlemen such as I? I have no secrets, no skeletons in the cupboard. I am as upstanding a citizen as ever was. Armed with faith, sobriety and the support of the law, I will withstand whatever assault he mounts against me. Do your worst, Sir, I say. Do your worst!

Eleven

That Friday morning, Molly woke early. She'd bedded down along the scullery wall to get some privacy. Samuel had announced that Betsy was his girl now. She wouldn't have to work the streets again. Molly only feared for her friend all the more. The guv'nor's rages were occurring more often lately and Betsy would be first in the firing line. Molly lay awake for several moments, wondering if she really dared go ahead with Chaim's plan. It was madness. But it was her chance to strike back at Samuel, no matter what it cost.

Padding across the floor in the threadbare nightdress she'd filched from the stash of stolen clothes, she looked down at the sleeping boys. As she watched, Malachy stirred. Molly held her breath for a moment, then, seeing he had slipped back into a deep sleep, she continued over to the door. Willing the key not to scrape in the lock, she turned it slowly to the left. The heavy, rusted tumblers groaned but nobody woke.

Now for the hard bit, Molly girl, she told herself. Bracing herself for the scrape of metal, she eased back the top bolt. So far, so good. She had the bottom bolt halfway across when something brushed her ankle. She stiffened and a shudder ran up her backbone.

Sweet Lord, what's that?

She stood there paralysed for a good minute, the cold draught seeping under the door and biting her toes. The object brushed her again and a cold tingle ran over her skin. What could she do? Here she was crouching low, holding the bolt, and something or somebody was stroking her ankle. She imagined Jacob or Noah behind her ready to grab her leg and drag her screaming to Samuel.

Please God, not that!

But she couldn't simply crouch there waiting to be called to account. She had to discover what kind of danger she was in. After an age she twisted round to see what was touching her. She gave a long, shuddering sigh of relief. It was only Jasper. He'd rolled over in his sleep and the back of his hand had come to rest against her leg. Easing away from him, she finished drawing back the second bolt. That done, she scampered over to the window and gazed down into the street. Chaim was waiting in the opposite doorway just as he said he would be. Molly stood for a second at the garret window and waved. Chaim nodded. Molly was trembling from a mixture of the cold and the clammy creep of fear.

Reassured that nobody had seen her, she returned to her bed and squeezed her eyes shut. It was one thing to be brave in advance. It was quite another to maintain

88

your courage when push came to shove. But you did it, Molly girl, she told herself.

Unfortunately for Molly, she didn't notice a drowsy Noah Pyke watching her from under his heavy eyelids.

Out in Flower and Dean Street, Chaim made his move. Molly had promised to unlock the front door before she retired for the night. Chaim twisted the handle and it opened.

You're a gem, he thought. He looked up the staircase and ran his hand over his face. There were two options. He could either creep up the stairs to cut down the noise, but run a greater risk of being caught on his way up, or he could stride boldly and snatch Israel in one quick raid. In the end, he did neither. Terror had its way of dictating the way he moved. He climbed the stairs two at a time, allowing his shoulder to slide along the candle-blackened walls. Eventually, he reached the top landing and paused. Every hair on his body was standing on end. He caught the glint of light under the door and hesitated. Then he remembered. Molly had told him there was always a candle lit in case there was a raid by the Peelers.

He turned the handle and entered. There was only the faintest squeal from the hinges. His eyes darted around the room. He was in luck. Israel was close, sleeping against the wall just beyond a skinny, red-haired boy. He was tossing and turning, as if in the throes of a nightmare. Chaim reached across Malachy Doran and put a hand over Israel's mouth. Israel woke with a start. His eyes widened to see Chaim but he didn't shout out. Molly had been right. They'd discussed whether to tell Israel in advance, but they'd decided against it. He had the demon contagion in his veins. What if he betrayed them? No, in his present state of mind, he could no longer be trusted. Better just to turn up and beg him to come. Chaim pointed at the door. To his relief, Israel nodded and followed. Half-way down, Israel froze.

'What is it?' Chaim asked.

'I thought I heard movement.' He turned. 'It came from upstairs.'

Chaim listened. 'I don't hear anything.'

They waited another few seconds then continued down the stairs to the front door. Chaim was amazed how easy it had been. His spirits were starting to lift. But, as soon, as he stepped onto the street, Israel drew back.

'What's wrong?'

Israel's gaze travelled up the crumbling walls. The Rat Boys had appeared. Defying gravity, they clung to the wall, heads pointed downward. 'Hook it!' Chaim yelled, tugging at Israel's hand.

But Israel stayed glued to the ground. All those pairs of black eyes had reduced him to a state of paralysis.

'Israel!' Chaim cried. 'You have to run.'

The Rat Boys were closing in. Israel watched them uncertainly, then he clasped his hands to his head.

'What's wrong?' Chaim asked.

In his imagination, Israel could see a dark mist slowly forming into Lud's face. The insane black eyes blazed. The booming voice ordered him to stop. None of it was seen or heard by his dismayed rescuer.

'It's him, Lud,' Israel cried, trying to shut out the snarling voice. 'He's inside my head.'

He couldn't shift the vision of the demon master's face either.

'Get away!' Israel sobbed, beating at a face he only saw in his mind's eye. 'Leave me alone!'

Chaim stared helplessly. He couldn't see the pitiless, demonic eyes that were burning through Israel's consciousness. He couldn't hear the irresistible commands that were echoing in his head.

'Run,' Israel groaned. 'Save yourself.' Turning his face away, he retreated from Chaim. 'I'm sorry but I can't come with you. You should never have tried to help me. My place is here. The Master said so.'

'Master!' Chaim cried. 'You have no master but God. Come with me, Israel. I'm begging you.'

Before he could say another word, Jacob dropped into the street, crouching low.

'You heard him,' he hissed. 'He's staying here with us, ain't you, Izzy?'

Israel nodded miserably. Meekly bowing his head, he trudged over to Jacob. He moved like a sleepwalker. There was a deep sadness in the way he surrendered to Jacob, as if he knew he was condemning himself by his actions. Chaim made a grab for Israel's hand but the Rat Boys gathered round their captive. Chaim's eyes swung back to the Rat Boys clinging to the walls overhead. For a brief moment, he looked at them then he ran.

The Rat Boys came leaping after him. Suddenly, Ezra dropped down, clamping himself to Chaim's back and scratching his face with razor-sharp fingernails. He drew blood. Instinctively, Chaim threw himself back against the wall. The impact made Ezra relax his grip. Chaim shrugged him off and ran, escaping out onto Rose Lane. To his horror, Jasper and Enoch were blocking his escape. In desperation, Chaim spun round and fled in the direction of Fashion Street. He ran on, sprinting down Red Lion Street. The Rat Boys were gaining on him. Chaim stumbled suddenly. He stared down in disbelief and saw that his bootlaces had untied themselves then knotted themselves together.

'That's impossible,' he gasped.

'Not when my friend Jasper's around,' Enoch said.

While Chaim desperately tugged at his laces, he ventured a backward glance. Why had the pair stopped when they had him at their mercy? Then he saw the reason. Between him and the Rat Boys there stood the stranger, the one he had encountered twice before. Chaim could see him clearly for the first time. The newcomer was about his own age, but taller. What struck Chaim was how pitifully thin his rescuer was, his ragged clothing hanging off him like a black shroud. He was barefoot. He would have looked like one more beggar on the street but for one detail. His outstretched hands were glowing scarlet, tendrils of energy leaping from his fingertips.

'Go back,' the stranger told the Rat Boys.

His voice didn't match his appearance. There was none of the thin, reedy pleading most beggars adopted. He barked out the command with all the confidence of a sergeant major.

'You again!' Noah cried.

'Go back,' the stranger repeated. The words crackled through the chill air.

'Why should we?' Noah demanded. 'It ain't just the two of us this time. It's seven onto one.'

The stranger stood his ground.

'Step aside, friend,' Noah reiterated, 'this has nothing to do with you.'

'It's eight onto one if we're counting Izzy,' Malachy reminded him.

'That's right,' Noah said, 'eight. That ain't good odds, my friend. So what are you going to do?'

The stranger didn't say another word. Instead, he held out his palms. They blazed with liquid, rippling waves of fire. Without a moment's hesitation, he swept the street with a long, swinging movement of his right arm. Flames leapt from the road and acrid smoke filled the air.

'Blow me!' Ethan cried, 'it's true what Noah said. You're one of us. You belong to the demon brotherhood.' He turned to the other Rat Boys. 'Did you see what he did!'

Jacob was coughing and spluttering, trying to see through the flames and the smoke.

By the time the fire died down both Chaim and his mysterious rescuer had vanished.

'Well, I'll be jiggered!' Ezra exclaimed. 'Where did he come from? Samuel swore that there weren't any more like us. I thought Israel was supposed to be the last of our kind.'

'I don't know anything about the fellow and I don't care,' Jacob said, 'but I'll tell you this for free. I don't feel like going home to tell the guv'nor we lost the intruder. Samuel will take it out of our hides.' He gestured to the Rat Boys. 'Spread out. We've got to find them.'

They were too late. Their quarry had already doubled back to the rear of Spitalfields Market. Never breaking their stride, Chaim and the strange boy were soon within sight of Wentworth Street and home, Chaim leading the way.

'We'll lie low at my kip,' he said. 'I owe you a debt of gratitude. I'm Chaim Wetzel. What's your name?'

The stranger answered in a hollow voice. 'I'm Paul, Paul Rector.'

Chaim stiffened. 'Say that name again.'

For a moment, there was hesitation in the other boy's voice, then he gave his answer. 'You heard right. My name is Paul Rector.'

'Are you chaffing me?' Chaim asked, recovering from his surprise. 'Is this some kind of joke, because I'm not laughing.'

'I wish it was different,' Paul said. 'But it's true.'

'You share a surname with the devil that's holding Israel prisoner,' Chaim said. 'He's the most dangerous villain in the whole East End. Rector indeed!'

'Yes,' Paul said, 'I can imagine.'

'What are the chances?' Chaim said. 'You and that monster, both called Rector.'

'Chance has got nothing to do with it,' Paul said. 'Didn't you see the flames? How do you think I did that? Samuel Rector and I don't just share the same name. We are of the same bloodline. The demon seed runs in my veins too.'

Chaim looked suddenly wary. 'So what are you doing helping me?'

'You're not the only one who's been watching the Rats' Nest,' Paul said. 'Samuel's planning something. I've got to stop him.'

'But if he's family, as you say,' Chaim objected, 'why are you taking sides against your own blood? It don't make any sense.' He was wondering if he'd done the right thing, taking Paul to his home. 'Is this a trick?'

'It's not a trick,' Paul said. 'Honest it isn't. You could call it a family falling out.' Paul wished he could come up with a better explanation. 'Samuel and his devil children are on one side. I'm on the other. They hate me. They call me the renegade. I don't know what else I can tell you.'

Chaim still had a dozen questions, but there was no time to ask them. At that moment, his mother opened the door to their cramped living room. Her eyes alighted on Paul.

'Oy! Who's this bedraggled specimen you've brought home?'

'His name's Paul,' Chaim replied. 'I was being chased by a gang of cut-throats. He saved me from them.'

Mrs Wetzel treated Chaim's account with some scepticism. She looked Paul up and down, wrinkling her nose at the state of his clothes. 'He doesn't look as though he could save himself. He's so thin and hungry a strong breeze would blow him over.' That's when something occurred to her. 'What were you doing out so early? I thought you were still in bed. I was about to wake you.' She tutted. 'Here you are running round the streets at all hours and you're meant to be in school.'

'It's to do with Israel,' Chaim said.

'Ah,' his mother sighed, 'I thought it might be.'

Chaim glanced at the clock on the mantelpiece. 'I'll still be in time.'

'And what about him?' Mrs Wetzel demanded,

looking at the dishevelled figure standing in the doorway. 'What am I supposed to do with this stray of yours?'

'Feeding him might be an idea,' Chaim said, heading for the door. 'Just look at him, will you? He needs some nosh inside him.'

'Then what?'

'Let him stay here until I get home,' Chaim said. 'Trust me, *Mamme*, I'll sort it out then.'

The Rat Boys scoured Spitalfields for over an hour but there was no sign of the invader or his mysterious rescuer. It was with a heavy heart that they returned to the Rats' Nest.

'Where's the guv'nor?' Jacob asked fearfully.

'He paced the floor a while,' Molly said, 'then he went out after you.'

'I didn't see him,' Jacob said.

While Molly and Jacob talked, Noah sought Betsy out. 'I've got a proposition for you,' he said.

'What do you mean?' Betsy asked.

'You know I like you,' Noah explained. He breathed the scent of her hair. 'I want you to like me too.'

Betsy tried to interrupt, but Noah pressed a finger to her lips.

'No, hear me out,' Noah said. 'It might change your mind. I know something, see. I know who let Izzy out.'

Betsy's eyes flashed with fright.

'I'll protect Moll,' Noah said. 'But there's a price to be paid for my silence.'

He slipped his arm round Betsy's waist. Immediately, she slapped him away.

'You must be crazy!' she hissed. 'The guv'nor seems

set on making me his girl. If he thought I was taking up with you, he'd go wild.'

Noah grinned and made a grab for her. 'I'll take the risk.'

Betsy pushed him away. 'Well, I won't. He hurts me, Noah. He hurts me bad. I can't risk making things worse.'

Noah took his hands off her. 'You've made a mistake, Bets.'

That's when she realized the power of Noah's threat. She was about to call him back when Samuel returned. He could cause trouble for her . . . and Moll.

'Well, well,' Samuel said, 'if it ain't my loyal soldiers, my eyes and ears.' He glanced at Betsy and Molly. 'Remember I was just telling you how alert and devoted they are?' The two girls lowered their eyes. 'No? You don't remember me saying that?' Without any warning, he spun round and crashed his fist into Jacob's face. The boy fell to the floor, blood spilling from his broken nose. 'That's because it ain't true!' He took Noah by the throat and slammed him against the wall. 'These two wastrels call themselves my lieutenants. They swagger round the East End, telling everybody what big men they are. Big men, eh? So why did they let an intruder break in and try to abduct our little Izzy right from under our noses?'

Israel met Samuel's gaze for a moment then dropped his eyes to the floor. Samuel paced around the Rat Boys.

'Would anybody like to tell me why there was nobody awake when the Wetzel boy broke in?' Samuel yelled. 'Anyone?'

Noah was rubbing his shoulder. 'I was awake.'

97

'Oh, that's right,' Samuel said. 'You were awake, weren't you, Noah? A regular watch dog. The trouble is, you didn't think to rouse me, did you? You let the Wetzel boy get all the way down to the street before you raised the alarm.'

'Guv'nor,' Noah pleaded, 'let go and I'll tell you something you'll want to hear.'

Betsy's heart turned over. She gazed at Noah, willing him not to say another word. But it was too late to stop him.

'I heard Molly, see, but I didn't think anything of it at first. Then I went back to sleep. I only woke up properly when I heard footsteps on the stairs.'

A shadow passed across Samuel's face. 'You heard *who*?'

'Molly,' Noah said, 'I saw her too. She was up and about before anybody else.'

Betsy's hand flew to her face. What have I done? she thought. Why didn't I agree to Noah's bargain?

Samuel speared Molly with a look. 'And what was Molly doing up at such an unearthly hour?'

Molly tried to say something but Samuel silenced her with a shake of his head.

'I know exactly what she was doing, Samuel,' Noah said. 'She was pulling back the bolts.' He spun round, jabbing a finger at the girl. 'It was her! She's the one that let the intruder in.'

At that moment, Israel saw the look of horror on Betsy's pale features. He instantly realized the consequences for Molly. He stepped forward to speak in her defence.

'No, it wasn't Molly,' he cried, 'it was me.'

'It ain't true!' Noah cried. 'You weren't awake but she was.'

'Let Israel speak,' Samuel said, interested in what the boy had to say.

Israel rushed to get his story out. 'I wanted to escape. I got up and drew the bolts. I'm sorry, Samuel. When I saw Chaim standing there in the doorway, I wanted to go with him. It was a spur of the moment decision. But when I got outside I heard Lud's voice booming in my head. It was so loud, I couldn't think. I had no choice but to change my mind.'

Samuel paced up and down the floor, turning the explanation over in his head. 'Now let me get this right. You didn't make your mind up until you saw Chaim in the doorway? Did I hear you correctly?'

Israel nodded. He was so scared he would have said yes to anything.

'Odd that,' Samuel said. 'You see, you just told me you were the one that opened the door for him. You turned the lock. You drew back two bolts. Is that right?'

Israel nodded. 'That's right.'

'So now you're saying it was all planned in advance?'

Israel realized his mistake. The two stories contradicted each other. He met Molly's terrified stare.

'Which means,' Samuel said, 'you knew he was coming all the time. That doesn't sound like a spur of the moment decision to me. Does it to you, Noah?'

Noah shook his head. 'It surely don't, Samuel.'

'Does it to you, Jacob?'

'No.'

'Does it to you, *Molly*?'

99

Sick at the thought that she was partly responsible for the peril Molly was in, Betsy stepped in front of her. 'You've got it wrong, Samuel. Izzy's got himself all mixed up, that's all.'

'Oh, he's mixed up all right,' Samuel said. 'He's mixed up because he's just invented the whole story. It wasn't Israel that pulled back those bolts, was it? It was you, Molly.'

'And I'm a witness to that,' Noah declared. He flashed Betsy a gloating look. This was how he was paying her back for rejecting him.

'Step aside, Bets,' Samuel said.

Betsy stood her ground. 'Don't hurt her, Samuel. Please.'

'Please, is it?' Samuel growled. 'Why don't I hear a please from you, Molly?' He looked over Betsy's shoulder at Molly's horror-stricken face. 'Go on, plead, beg for your miserable life. I know it was you that opened the door. I should have seen it coming. You've always been a thorn in my side, stealing from me and talking behind my back.' He picked up a pewter plate and hurled it across the room. Everybody stiffened. 'Well, I don't hear no begging. Don't you care for your low, worthless life?'

Fighting back the paralysing terror she felt, Molly forced herself to scream her defiance. 'I ain't going to beg no more, Samuel. I ain't going to tremble and cower neither. I hate you, Samuel. I wish you were dead.' She pulled the knife from the folds of her dress. 'I'd happily go to the scaffold if I could rid the world of your filthy carcass.'

Betsy was beside herself. 'Don't listen to her, Samuel.' She turned and started clawing at Molly's sleeve.

'Good God Almighty, Moll, have you taken leave of your senses?'

'No,' Molly told her, 'I've just regained them. I won't be his slave no more, Bets.'

Glancing over her shoulder at Samuel, Betsy continued to plead her friend's case. 'She don't mean it. She's a good girl, Molly is. She made a mistake. Tell him, Moll.'

But Molly continued to flaunt her defiance.

In despair, Betsy renewed her pleas for mercy. 'Punish her if you have to, Samuel, just don't kill her. You can't take my only friend from me.'

Samuel laughed. 'Ain't I your friend, Bets?' He slipped his arm round her waist and drew her away from Molly. He rested his chin on her shoulder, rubbing his stubble along the fabric. 'I thought we were real good friends.'

Betsy gnawed at her bottom lip. 'You know what I mean, Samuel. I need someone my own age.'

'What about my fine boys?' Samuel asked. 'Noah and Jacob are about your age.'

'A girl,' Betsy murmured.

Samuel guided her out of the way. Noah restrained her while Samuel approached Molly.

'Hear that?' he said. 'Betsy wants a friend.' He walked around the room, with his hands on his hips, acting out an exaggerated female walk. 'She wants another girl so she can discuss fashion and flowers and . . . love.' He fluttered his eyelids for a moment then snarled his contempt. 'It's up to you, Molly Vale. I'm prepared to show mercy. All you need to do is put that knife down then get on your knees and beg for forgiveness. What about it, Moll?'

Betsy struggled to break free of Noah. She was pleading with Samuel not to hurt Molly. Israel held his breath. What was Molly going to do?

'You're lying, Samuel,' she said, 'just like you always do. You ain't going to let me live, not after what I've done. You'll humiliate me and shame me, then you'll do for me anyway.' She tossed her blond hair. 'Yes, I know you. You'll come over all friendly then you'll strangle me in my sleep.' Her eyes flashed. 'Well, I won't do it no more, Samuel. I'll take no more orders from you. I made my decision when I agreed to help Israel escape.' She looked at him. 'You're a stupid boy, Izzy. The moment you got out on that street you should have kept on running.'

Israel started sobbing. 'I'm sorry, Moll. I've got this voice in my head. It won't let me go.'

'That's all right,' Molly said, 'you've got to be stronger, that's all. You've got a voice in your head but you've got a conscience too. You don't have to give in to Lud.' She sighed. 'You'll do the right thing some day.' She glanced at Betsy for a moment then she turned a defiant face towards Samuel. 'I ain't had such a great life so I won't miss it much. Just get it over with.'

Samuel rushed at her. Betsy struggled and fought to break free of Noah's grasp but he held her tight. She could only look on while Molly slashed with the knife. The blade sank into Samuel's muscular forearm. To her horror, he simply smiled, even though the knife was buried in his flesh right down to the hilt.

'You forget who you're dealing with,' he said. He reached across and gripped the handle. 'I serve the demon master.' Very slowly, very deliberately, he withdrew the knife from his flesh and let it clatter to the floor. There was only a smear of blood. 'A man who can let a dozen rats feed on him then plunge his arm into hot coals isn't going to feel much when some little piece of dirt sinks a blade into him, now is he?'

Betsy finally clawed her nails down Noah's cheek and broke free. She threw herself at Samuel, tears streaming down her cheeks. 'Let her go, Samuel. Please. We'll do anything to make it better, won't we, Moll? We'll work until we drop.'

Molly shook her head sadly. 'There's no making this better, Bets. I'm done for. Just remember I did this for you, to show you that even a working girl's worth something.' She glanced at Israel. 'That goes for you too, Izzy. This won't be the last chance you get to escape the monster's clutches. Next time you've got to do whatever it takes. Just get away from this life, you hear? Don't let me die in vain.'

Samuel listened with his head to one side, then started to applaud. 'Oh, what a lovely little speech that was. You ought to be performing at some penny gaff. The audience would love you. I can just see the posters: Molly Vale, the little bird that pecks back.' He looked at his wounded arm. He raised it and licked away the blood. 'What a sharp beak you've got, Moll. It's just a pity you don't have wings to go with it.'

Without any warning, he seized Molly by the shoulders and hurled her through the nearest window. The glass shattered and she vanished from sight with a cry. Betsy ran to the window and screamed. Molly was lying spread-eagled in the yard below, her neck broken. Samuel joined Betsy at the window.

'The little bird that tried to fly then fell to earth.' He

stroked Betsy's cheek. 'Have you got anything you want to say to me, Bets?'

Betsy had to force her knuckles into her mouth to kill the cry of horror that was welling up inside her. Her eyes flashed briefly then the fire in them died. Hopelessness took over. 'No Samuel, I ain't got nothing to say.'

Feeling a cold tear running down her cheek, she wiped it away with her sleeve.

'Good girl,' Samuel said. 'You know which side your bread's buttered, don't you? I did the right thing making you my girl. You ain't kicked up a fuss about Molly. That means you're the one for me all right, Bets. You're my princess from now on.'

Betsy's flesh was crawling but she didn't dare say what was in her heart.

Oblivious to her true feelings, Samuel gave his orders. 'Run for the Peelers, Enoch, and be sure to tell them how Molly Vale pulled a knife on your guv'nor and how he had to throw her out of the window in self-defence. Have you got that?'

Enoch grinned. 'Got it.'

Samuel walked to the centre of the room. 'The Peelers are going to want to know what happened here. It was self-defence and you're all going to say so.' He examined every face around the room. 'Just remember this lesson. Nobody crosses Samuel Rector and lives to tell the tale.' He noticed Betsy watching him through her tears. 'What's this? After what I just said to you, I hope you're not going to start moaning and crying over Molly.'

Betsy seemed to manage to swallow down the hatred and despair she was feeling.

'Of course not, Sammy,' she said, gagging on every word that passed her lips. 'I just want to say goodbye before the Bluebottles arrive. That won't do no harm, will it?'

Samuel yawned. 'I suppose not. You've got five minutes then I'm sending one of my boys down to get you.'

'Oh, thank you, Sammy,' Betsy said, flying from the room.

She went to Molly and sank to her knees.

'Oh, Moll,' she sobbed softly, 'my poor Molly.' She glanced up at the window. 'You were proud and rash and you had a temper you could light a fire with, but you didn't deserve to die like this.' She tore at her face. 'And it's all my fault. If there's a heaven, and you're up there listening to this, you've got to help me.' She gazed at the sky, searching for the brightest star. 'You've got to do something to give me the strength.' She cut a lock of Molly's blond hair then she removed a locket from her neck. 'This trinket is all I've got to remember my mother by, Moll.' She placed the lock of hair inside the locket and snapped it shut. 'You're the only one who ever treated me decent since she passed away. Your hair is going inside. I won't ever forget you.' Then she walked back indoors, pausing only to say a last goodbye. 'Farewell, Molly darling. I just hope there's an angel waiting in Heaven for you. Nobody can hurt you anymore.'

Twelve

It was nine o'clock in the evening before Chaim returned to his lodgings. He'd had a late class studying the Torah but he'd hardly taken anything in. All he could think about was the stranger who'd saved his skin.

'Is Paul much recovered?' he asked the moment he walked through the door.

'He's been sleeping like a baby since this afternoon,' Mrs Wetzel said. 'He had a good old nosh up then he went fast asleep in your *Tatte's* chair.' She gave Chaim the longest look. 'Wherever did you find him?'

Chaim stumbled through an explanation. *Mamme* listened through hooded eyes then left him to talk to his guest.

Chaim woke Paul gently. 'How are you?'

'Better,' Paul said.

'You look more dead than alive,' Chaim said. 'How long has it been since you ate a decent meal?'

'Two weeks,' Paul said before revising his answer. 'Nearer three.'

His gorge rose as he remembered the rotten scraps he'd been eating to stay alive, the rainwater he'd gulped from leaking barrels. Day after day, he had wandered the streets, trying to make sense of the world into which he had stumbled. It had been easily the most wretched period in his life.

'Where've you been sleeping?'

'Anywhere I could find,' Paul told him in a hollow voice, 'doorways, back yards, alleyways.'

The cold, lonely nights came back to him. He shuddered at the thought of returning to the streets of London.

'Don't you have no home to go to?' Chaim asked.

Home, Paul thought. The word hardly meant anything anymore. Every day he tried to remember his mother, his girlfriend, his friends and every day their images became fainter and less familiar. He fought back the tears and shook his head. 'I'm a fugitive. I don't really know where I belong.'

'But where are you from?'

How could he tell Chaim he had already lived through the twenty-first century and the Blitz of 1941? And what if he mentioned the real reason for his quest?

'I'm a Londoner,' he said. 'Mile End.'

'The new town?'

Paul smiled. There was nothing new about it for him. 'Yes, the new town.'

'You don't sound quite like you come from the East End,' Chaim said. 'You're educated. I can hear it in your voice.'

'You're educated too, Chaim,' Paul said, glancing at the books on the table. 'I've heard how much you study.'

'*Mamme's* been talking to you, hasn't she?'

Paul nodded. 'She's very proud.'

Chaim nodded then changed the subject. 'Do you know what's happening to Israel? I keep hearing about something called the demon seed.'

'That's right,' Paul said. 'Look, all of this is going to sound completely weird . . .' He saw Chaim frown and realized his twenty-first century rhythms of speech must sound quite alien. 'The demon seed is a contagion, a madness that's as old as time. It's the demon seed that brought me here.'

'Do you think I can save him?' Chaim asked.

'I'm not going to lie to you,' Paul replied. 'It's in your friend Israel's blood.'

Chaim followed with the obvious question. 'Do you have it too?'

'Yes,' Paul answered. 'My blood is tainted, just as his is. Down the generations, many men from my family have succumbed to its dark power. I am determined to break the cycle.' *If I can.* He sensed the unsettling thoughts that were always at the fringes of his mind then changed the subject hurriedly. 'Will you answer some questions about Israel for me?'

'Ask away.'

'Does he ever complain about feeling sick? Does he suffer from faints?'

'Yes,' Chaim said, 'all the time. It started a few weeks ago. Some days he would just collapse and lie senseless on the floor for several minutes.'

Paul nodded. He recognized all the symptoms. He'd

108

experienced the same attacks for months as the demon side of his nature asserted itself.

'Have his hearing and eyesight become more acute?'

Chaim thought for a moment. 'He didn't mention anything like that.'

That could be something that only affects me, Paul thought. 'Maybe he's started doing things that were out of character,' he said. 'Has he taken up fighting or stealing? Does he fly into sudden rages?'

'Rages,' Chaim said eagerly, hoping against hope that Paul would have a proper explanation of what was happening to Israel, 'yes, I recognize all that and more.'

'Then there's no doubt about it,' Paul said. 'He's becoming part of the demon brotherhood.'

Chaim grimaced. That wasn't what he wanted to hear. He was upset by Paul's words but he could no longer deny the evidence of his own eyes.

'While I live and breathe,' he retorted, 'I will never let him go. Hang on a minute. You've got the demon seed, just as he has. And yet you're standing here talking to me, all rational and decent. You helped me get away from my pursuers. You didn't go over to evil, did you? Why should Israel?'

Paul relived his life as freeze-frame images: the child who should have died, the brother returned from Hell, the monstrous destiny.

'I'm different,' he said simply. 'I'm the one that got away, a renegade who broke with his destiny.'

Chaim sounded angry. 'Oh, you're different, are you? You think you're superior to the rest of us, is that it?'

'No,' Paul said, 'that isn't it at all. I'm not proud of what I am. I'm sorry, it came out all wrong.'

Paul wanted to explain, to tell his new friend how he had the same instincts pulsing in his blood, but how he was able to master them in a way none of his stricken ancestors had ever done. Chaim wasn't in any mood to be pacified.

'Well, listen to me,' he said. 'We're all different, every one of us. That's why there's still hope for Israel. There's something about you, Paul Rector, something I don't understand. You're from the East End but not *this* East End. I sense it. It's like you're here but you don't belong here. You're . . . a ghost.'

'I'm no ghost,' Paul said wearily. 'Here, you can pinch me if you like. I'm flesh and blood, just like you.'

'All the same,' Chaim said, 'I have to know *why* you're different.'

He was getting too close to the truth. 'That I can't tell you,' Paul said, 'not the whole story, not yet.'

'Then tell me this at least,' Chaim said, 'and I want a straight answer. How did you start that fire, the one that stopped the Rat Boys in their tracks?'

'All who carry the demon seed have unnatural abilities,' Paul explained. 'The Rat Boys have great agility, as you've seen. Israel has yet to discover his power. It was . . . is the same with me. I have two abilities that I know of, fire and fear. The first you have seen.'

'And the second?'

Paul relived the moment he had first used his ability to terrify another human being to the point of death.

110

'That,' he said, 'you don't want to see. But other things are happening to me. My hearing is sharper, my eyesight keener. My transformation has only just begun.'

'What will you become?'

Paul remembered the horrors that had made him embark on his journey through time, the demon Ripper who had stalked his East End. He shrugged. 'I only wish I knew.'

Chaim allowed his mood to lighten a little. 'So you're like a little green caterpillar that's started to turn into a butterfly?'

'Something like that,' Paul replied, irritated that Chaim could joke about it.

'Tell me then,' Chaim said. 'I've seen what you can do. If you possess such powers, why are you reduced to starving and living in rags?'

Paul considered the question for a moment. 'Just because I can control fire, it doesn't mean I can conjure up money or food or any of the other comforts of life. I can't create four walls to shelter me or put a roof over my head.'

'No,' Chaim whispered, 'but you've got the powers to take what you need, ain't you? There's got to be something you can do to improve your present condition.'

Paul recoiled. 'I'm not going to steal, if that's what you're getting at.'

'Listen to me,' Chaim said, 'we're poor people. I'll do my best to persuade *Mamme* and *Tatte* to let you stay, but it can't be for ever. Some time you'll have to learn to survive the worst London's got to offer.'

'So what are you saying?' Paul demanded. 'You

want me to forget everything I've ever believed about right and wrong? You want me to become a criminal?'

'Don't go twisting my words,' Chaim told him. 'My *Mamme* and *Tatte* brought me up to be as honest and law-abiding as the next fellow. But look at yourself. You're wasting away. This is survival. You've got to take a leaf out of old Robin Hood's book. Steal from the rich and give to the poor.'

Paul listened but he didn't come to any decision.

'I don't like stealing any more than you do,' Chaim said. 'But this is a matter of life and death. Think about it, Paul. Nobody can make your mind up for you.' He walked to the door. 'I'll see you in the morning.'

Paul was soon asleep. Sometime in the small hours, he woke. Instantly, he felt a prickling sensation spilling down his spine. Somebody had been watching him as he slept. Raising himself up on one elbow, he looked around. He slowly became aware of a presence, real yet ephemeral. Lud? But there was no searing heat, no acrid reek of brimstone, no palpable sense of evil. Gazing across the room, Paul saw another familiar figure, a thing of mist and light, much like Lud himself. But this spirit was Lud's opposite. His presence was reassuring rather than threatening. Their first meeting had taken place one hundred and seventy years in the future, on the day Paul began his descent into Hell's Underground, the pathway into London's dark past. Since that encounter the fire-priest had become his guide through the tunnels of time.

'Cormac,' Paul said, 'you came.'

There was no greeting from the fire priest. 'Have you found your enemy?' he demanded.

'I've found the demon master's disciple,' Paul said. 'My ancestor Samuel Rector is planning his Lord's liberation. He intends to attack Lud's tomb.'

'Can you provide evidence of your claim?' Cormac asked.

Paul was ready for the question. 'He's found the Aldgate entrance to the crypt. He's assembled all the members of the demon brotherhood in this time. He's preparing an assault on the first seal.'

Cormac smiled. 'You've learned your lessons well, Paul Rector.' Incidents recollected from many centuries swarmed in the ancient priest's memory. He remembered his part in making the four magic seals which bound Lud in his underground tomb. 'This is your greatest test yet,' he said. 'You have repelled Lud's attacks thus far.'

'At a cost,' Paul murmured, remembering Evelyn and Cotton, who had died in another time.

'There are always casualties in war,' Cormac said.

'How can you be so heartless?' Paul wondered out loud. 'The people who perished were my friends.'

'You're young,' Cormac said. 'Passion races through your veins. That's good. Without it, you would never endure. But I am too old and too weary to share your indignation at death. I do what must be done.' He stopped talking for a moment, inviting Paul to have his say. When Paul held his tongue, Cormac continued.

'You know the story. Many centuries ago, I and my brother priests bound the creature you know as King Lud in his crypt. We built four gates to keep him interred. We did our work well. All four seals must be broken for the creature to rise. That is a powerful protection, but the danger is growing nonetheless. The assault Samuel is about to mount may be the first step to Lud's freedom.' He clenched his fist. 'You must understand. The past is being rewritten as we speak. The demon lord can unravel time. Everything you know as fact will vanish into mist and be replaced by horrors you dare not imagine.'

Paul nodded grimly. 'I understand.'

'I wonder if you do,' Cormac said. 'Lud will escape his bonds. The white chapel's defences are weakening. There is nothing anyone can do to reverse the process. For two millennia he has fought to be free. The great walls we established against his power are old and crumbling. The seals are relaxing their grip on the gates.'

'I'm not stupid,' Paul said. 'I heard what you said. He can change the future. If he gets his way, the world I come from will never have existed.'

'Precisely,' Cormac said. 'The stakes could not be higher. By now you know the demon master's nature. You must never underestimate him. In the long years of his incarceration he has been gathering knowledge, developing his powers in preparation for his liberation. If Lud breaks free in this era, no power on Earth will stop him. He will triumph, just as you say.'

'So why am I here at all?' Paul cried. 'It sounds like a losing battle. What's the point? Why have I gone through so much pain?'

Cormac answered patiently. 'Lud is determined to change the future. You can stop him. You only have to believe in yourself. The *mature* Lud would destroy you. Were you to face him now, he would crush you. The world you see around you would become his

114

playground. But if you can keep him chained and bound; if you can roll back the years and delay his escape, his strength will diminish and yours will grow. Your power will one day equal his. Only then will you be able to vanquish him.' He met Paul's look directly. 'Do you have the will to go on?'

Paul closed his eyes for a moment. He thought again about those he had left behind in the London of the future: Mum, Netty, his friends, then he gave his answer. 'Yes.'

'Are you sure?'

Paul thought for a moment. 'So this is it, this is my destiny. I have to keep him imprisoned.' Now he understood the prophecies, the talk of him as the renegade. If he persevered, if he fought on, he could overcome the monster. He glanced at Cormac. 'I alone have the power to prevent him changing the future.'

Cormac seemed satisfied. 'What do you know of the creature's plans? You're my eyes and ears in this time.'

'Samuel is assembling his army,' Paul said.

'Describe the forces at his disposal.'

'He has eight members of the brotherhood under his control.'

Cormac looked puzzled. 'Eight, you say?'

Paul nodded. 'Why, what's wrong?'

Cormac pondered the information. 'This is no army. It is too weak a force. You must understand, Paul, the crypt is protected by sorcery of great power. Lud once ordered a hundred of his followers against the walls. I witnessed it with my own eyes. Some burned. Others went insane and took their own lives. Every one of them died and still they could not force the slightest breech. A mere eight demons would never be enough. You must find out how he intends to gather sufficient forces to break through.'

'I've got one lead,' Paul said. 'There's a man called Strachan. I have to find him.'

'Is he the one you told me about?'

'Yes, I discovered the diaries he left to his ancestors. That's what brought me to this time.'

'Then go to it, Paul Rector,' Cormac said. 'You're learning fast. I knew you were the one who could champion our cause against the demon master.'

'But is there nobody to help me?' Paul asked. He found himself appealing to Cormac's sense of pity. 'I'm hungry and exhausted. I'm isolated and alone. I don't know if I can go on.'

'Alone you were,' Cormac said, 'and alone you will be until this battle is won.'

'Surely somebody can help me!' Paul protested.

Cormac looked doubtful. 'I don't know. I may be able to convince the Courts of Destiny.'

Paul frowned. He'd heard the words before. Only now did he realize that Cormac wasn't speaking metaphorically. 'Courts of Destiny? What does that mean?'

'You must be patient,' Cormac said. 'I can tell you no more. Not yet.'

'So there's no advice you can give me?'

'You must understand,' Cormac said. 'I am not a free agent. I can tell you this. You will achieve nothing if you're starving. I overheard your conversation with the boy Chaim. You would do well to listen to him.'

'So you expect me to steal too?'

'I want you to triumph over Lud,' Cormac said.

'Everything is subordinated to that aim. You may have to break the rules you lived by in your own time. If you have to steal in order to survive, then do it. If you have to kill, then you must do that too. The rules of the game are being re-written as we speak. You must do whatever it takes to triumph over Lud.'

'But what if the fight against Lud corrupts me?' Paul cried. 'Every time I use my powers, I get such terrible thoughts. I know what the demon seed did to my brother. What if I become all monster?' He dropped his voice to a whisper. 'What if I lose my soul along the way?'

'That is a risk you took when you began this quest,' Cormac answered. 'You knew you would have to contend with your dual nature. What did you expect? That you could embark on this journey and face no resistance? No human struggle is guaranteed success in advance. You must find your own way to redemption.'

In desperation, Paul put his question again. 'And you can't help me?'

'My time is past,' Cormac said. 'My bleached bones lie beneath the ashen ruins of this city. I am but a shadow, a voice, a memory. What is left of my presence in this world is but a guttering candle. Nor am I a free agent. I have to plead to greater forces to be able to help you.'

'So who is the real power in the world?' Paul cried. 'What are the Courts of Destiny? You can't just keep me in the dark. If they can help me, I've got to speak to them.'

'That's impossible,' Cormac said. 'You are not ready. You would never be admitted.' Paul went to protest but Cormac silenced him with a raised hand. 'You

117

must accept what little guidance I am permitted to give you. From time to time, I can shed a little light in the darkness. I can do no more than that.' He glanced behind him. 'I must go now, Paul Rector. As you are aware, a great evil is rising. Your foe is ruthless. You must match him blow for blow.'

'But how can I do good if I break the law?' Paul wanted to know. 'Surely there must be rules.'

'That is the problem you must solve for yourself,' Cormac replied. 'In this quest, you are the law. The rules are yours to make.'

'But I'm fifteen,' Paul cried. 'I'm stranded in a different time. There's got to be something else you can tell me.'

'I'm sorry,' Cormac said again.

With that, he was gone. Paul was left with the night, and his thoughts. For a while he wondered how Mum was coping. But it was Netty Carney who filled his mind. He could still remember the thrill when he'd asked her out for the first time and she'd said yes.

'Netty,' he murmured, 'I wonder what you're doing right now.'

Thirteen

Netty Carney stares out at the early February drizzle. She has a crumpled photocopy in her hand. She doesn't look at it. She has examined it dozens of times. There is a knock on the door.

'Come in, Mum,' she says.

Mrs Carney peers round. 'Is everything all right?'

Netty hesitates and Mrs Carney's heart misses a beat 'Is this about Paul,' she asks. 'Do you know where he is now?'

Netty nods.

'Look, Netty,' Mum says, 'it's three months since he vanished. How can you know what's happened to him?'

Without a word, Netty passes the photocopied news item to Mrs Carney. She's had it in her possession for weeks but this is the first time she's shown it to anyone but her best friend Charlotte. She watches her mother's eyes widen.

119

'But this is impossible,' Mrs Carney said. 'The date on the photograph, it's 1941.'

'Look at him, Mum,' Netty says. 'Tell me that isn't Paul.'

Mrs Carney blurts out: 'It's his spitting image, an uncanny likeness.'

'It's *him*, Mum,' Netty says. 'Let's not lie to each other. Have you forgotten what happened here?'

Mrs Carney looks away.

'You can't shut it out, Mum,' Netty says. 'A killer came into our home, a killer with supernatural powers.'

'Netty, you're letting your imagination run wild.'

'Stop it, Mum,' Netty says. 'You know there's no other explanation.'

'Netty . . .' The protest died in her mother's throat.

'There's no point trying to deny it, Mum,' Netty says. 'Even that policewoman knows I'm telling the truth. DS Hussein saw things she couldn't explain.' She watched as her mother sat on the edge of the bed. 'At least here, in our own home, we can talk about it honestly, can't we?'

Finally, Mrs Carney nodded. 'I will never forget his eyes.' She shudders. Then she turns to look at Netty. 'It is over, isn't it?'

Netty glances at the photo of Paul striding through Trafalgar Square. 'I don't know, Mum. But how can I move on knowing Paul is down there, in Hell's Underground? Everybody knows something's wrong. Charlotte's been asking about it. So has Afshana. I don't know if I can go on pretending that Paul has just run away from home.'

'But what are you saying?'

Netty shakes her head. 'I only wish I knew. Mum, I need to see Mrs Rector. She's the only one who really understands. May I?'

Mrs Carney smiles thinly. 'Something tells me you're going to go, no matter what I say.'

'But do I have your permission?' Netty asks. 'It matters to me.'

Mrs Carney rises from the bed. As she reaches the door, she speaks without turning to look at Netty. 'Do what you have to.'

Fourteen

*F*ire and fear. Paul had been trying to come to terms with the changes to his mind and body for months now. He was growing stronger, but so was the darkness within him. So was the need to inflict pain. There were mornings when he woke drenched in sweat, his mind still blazing with the images of slaughter that had come to him in his sleep. Sometimes the monster he saw in his nightmares wasn't Lud. It was himself.

He considered his powers. Demon kind were hardwired to hurt and destroy, to revel in mischief and suffering. By some accident of fate, here he was with many of their abilities but some resistance to their primal cruelty. He had the mental strength to resist the extremes of his nature. But it was still there, deep inside.

Was he doomed to surrender to Lud eventually? All through the night he had pleaded with Cormac to come back, to give him some guidance. But Cormac had left him alone, with his isolation, with the horror. Paul was still turning over these questions in his mind when Chaim appeared. '*Mamme's* made you breakfast,' he said.

Paul ate with the family and thanked them for their hospitality. Chaim heard the note of finality in his voice.

'Does that mean you're going?' he asked.

Paul nodded. 'I've got to leave.' The thought filled him with dread but he had no choice. 'Samuel is bound to come looking for me. I can't stay here. If I do, I will only endanger you and your family.' He waited until they were alone then put a question to Chaim. 'Do you know any thieves?'

Chaim looked confused at first, then he understood what Paul was thinking. 'Does that mean you're going to take my advice?'

'It looks like I've got no choice,' Paul told him.

He didn't mention Cormac's visitation or the long hours tossing and turning.

'What changed your mind?'

'Let's say I slept on it,' he answered. 'Now, where do I find a thief?'

Chaim shook his head. 'You're asking the wrong person, I'm afraid.'

'But you suggested it!'

'I said it was the only way you were going to survive,' Chaim reminded him. 'That doesn't mean I rub shoulders with pick-pockets and house-breakers. Your relative and his associates are the only thieves I know and they're not going to help you, are they?'

Paul rose. 'So I'm on my own.'

He was about to go when Chaim remembered the confrontation at the ratting contest. 'Just a moment,'

123

he said, 'I think I do know somebody who moves in the right circles and he's got no love for Samuel.' He told Paul what he knew about O'Shaughnessy the house-breaker then handed him a pair of battered boots. 'They've got holes,' Chaim said. '*Mamme* was going to get them repaired. You need them more than I do.'

Thanking Chaim and Mrs Wetzel, Paul stepped onto the frozen streets. After some asking around, Paul found the warehouseman staggering out of a tavern on the Ratcliff Highway, worse the wear for drink.

'O'Shaughnessy?' he asked.

O'Shaughnessy stopped and stared at the ragged figure before him. 'Who's asking?' he slurred.

At first, Paul hesitated. Then, knowing he was going to starve if he didn't go through with his plan, he continued, 'You don't need to know. Here's the thing, I need money.'

O'Shaughnessy burst out laughing. 'Don't we all, boy? Don't we all?'

'You don't understand.'

O'Shaughnessy gave a low chuckle. 'I've spent forty-five years on these streets, cocker. I think I understand very well.'

Paul forced himself to persevere. 'I was told you might be the kind of man who could help me get some money.'

O'Shaughnessy laughed and lurched unsteadily against the door jamb. He shoved at the door and shouted into the beery warmth of the tavern.

'Are you ready, Kit?'

Mrs Flaherty appeared at the door and saw the ragged youth next to O'Shaughnessy. 'Would you like to introduce me to your friend?' she asked.

'He ain't no friend of mine,' O'Shaughnessy snarled. He poked his forehead. 'I think he's a bit soft in the head. He came tapping me for money.'

'You must be Mrs Flaherty,' Paul said. 'I hear the pair of you frequent the same haunts as Samuel Rector. You know a bit about thieving, don't you?'

O'Shaughnessy froze. After a couple of moments he turned and examined Paul more intently.

'Who are you?' he demanded. 'Who's been flapping their jaws?'

Paul ignored the question. 'People say you're a house-breaker.'

O'Shaughnessy made a grab for Paul. 'I want to know where you heard that.' He balled his fist. 'So you just start talking. Do you know anything about this gutter rat, Kit?'

Mrs Flaherty said nothing. She'd noticed the way the boy spoke. He was no gutter rat – that was for certain. She was intrigued.

'Tell me how you know so much about me?' O'Shaughnessy demanded. 'Who's set me up? Was it Rector?' When Paul stayed tight-lipped, O'Shaughnessy threw other names at him. 'Barton then, or Willis? It's got to be one of the rogues. Come on, cough.'

Paul allowed the man to tighten his grip on his tattered clothing and waited for the moment when he would catch the warehouseman's eye. The moment he did, O'Shaughnessy saw something in his gaze and tried to look away. But the dark worm of terror was already burrowing into his mind.

'Keep looking, O'Shaughnessy,' Paul said, seizing the warehouseman's jaw and brow and holding his

125

head rigid. Something blazed between them and O'Shaughnessy's throat tightened.

'What are you doing?' he gasped.

'What are you afraid of?' Paul asked. 'Could it be the hangman's noose?'

'You ain't right in the head,' O'Shaughnessy protested. 'Let me go. Kit, give me some help here.'

Mrs Flaherty looked on, curious about the outcome. Tightening his grip, Paul gazed deep into O'Shaughnessy's eyes. Immediately, the terrified housebreaker's mind was flooded with the images that haunted him every night of his life. He saw the beak donning a square of black cloth and the slow climb to the scaffold. He heard the crowd's mocking laughter. He felt the rope tighten round his neck and the trapdoor creaking beneath his feet.

'Stop,' he cried. 'Oh God, please Kit, get this lunatic off me.'

But Mrs Flaherty continued to look on, fascinated by the spectacle.

'Are you ready to help?' Paul asked.

O'Shaughnessy heard the trapdoor snap open. Suddenly, he was kicking at empty air, clawing at an invisible noose. In his imagination he was dangling at the end of the rope, eyes popping, throat burning. The nightmare was invading every corner of his consciousness. He was being scared to death. 'For the love of God, stop.'

Paul's voice broke through the haze of terror. 'Are you going to help me?' He felt the dark fingers of night entering his mind. 'I'd advise you to say yes.'

'We'll help you,' Mrs Flaherty said. She grasped Paul's arm. At first he ignored the pressure. He

126

watched the terror he had unleashed devouring O'Shaughnessy. He drank in every twitch of the man's tortured face.

'Please. I don't know what you've done to him but you've got to stop.'

Her voice swam at the edge of Paul's consciousness. His demon side had taken over. He was enjoying torturing O'Shaughnessy, luxuriating in the man's tormented stare.

'He's no use to you dead,' she pleaded. She dug her fingernails into Paul's flesh. 'Stop!'

Paul finally returned from the dark mist and relaxed his hold. 'You'll help me then?'

Mrs Flaherty nodded. She still had her hand on his arm. 'You're the strangest vagrant I've ever met.' She narrowed her eyes. 'And the most interesting. I'll warrant you've an engaging tale to tell.'

Paul ignored the comment and told her what he wanted. 'I need money.'

'That can be arranged,' Mrs Flaherty said, her eyes continuing to explore Paul's face as if her were some curious breed of wild animal. 'I could use somebody like you.'

'You won't use me,' Paul said. He had terrorized O'Shaughnessy and it felt good. The feeling of inflicting terror still roared through his blood. He had a new confidence. 'I'm not interested in scraping a living working for you. I'll only be here a matter of weeks.'

'So what do you want?' Mrs Flaherty asked.

'I want to live,' Paul declared. Then he stopped. 'No, I don't just want to survive.' His eyes blazed. 'Listen to me, Mrs Flaherty,' he said. 'I have lived in rags long enough. I've felt the cold strike through me. I'm sick of being wet and hungry.' The power of the demon was still throbbing through him. He could have what he wanted. He could sleep between clean sheets and be warm and dry. 'This is the way it is. In the time I am here I'm going to live in comfort. I don't want to have to answer to anybody. That means I'll need cash, plenty of it. You're going to tell me how to get it.'

'You're very sure of yourself,' Mrs Flaherty said.

Paul almost laughed out loud. He was still on a high after the terror he had inflicted on O'Shaughnessy.

'If you're as well informed as you say you are,' he replied, 'then you'll know why.'

'Don't say a word, Kit,' O'Shaughnessy panted, rubbing at the non-existent burn marks on his throat. He was a little recovered from his ordeal. 'You ain't going to let a stranger profit from all our hard work, are you?'

'Oh, do shut up, O'Shaughnessy,' Mrs Flaherty said. 'This could be the start of a promising business relationship.'

'How do you work that out?' O'Shaughnessy asked.

'I've been keeping abreast of developments in the Flowery,' Mrs Flaherty snapped. 'If you were sober for more than an hour at a time, you might know something of this young gentleman's reputation. My ears on the street overheard Samuel's boys quarrelling. For some reason, they're afraid of Paul. That's got to work in his favour.'

Paul was surprised to discover quite how much she did know.

'That's right,' Mrs Flaherty said, 'I know your name. In fact, I've heard a lot about you lately.'

O'Shaugnessy gave Paul a cautious glance. 'He don't look much.'

'Maybe not,' Mrs Flaherty said, giving O'Shaughnessy a scornful glance, 'but he had you screaming like a whipped child and no mistake. Come with us, Paul. We'll talk business.'

Half an hour later, the three of them were sitting in front of a roaring fire in Mrs Flaherty's parlour. She'd watched while Paul peeled off what remained of his shirt and scrubbed away some of the filth of the street. As he dried himself, she handed him a set of O'Shaughnessy's clothes. O'Shaughnessy seemed quite put out by the act of generosity.

'So you can help me get my hands on some money?' Paul asked, wearing warm, dry garments for the first time in many days.

'That's possible,' Mrs Flaherty said, removing her bonnet and shaking out a mane of black hair. 'I've had my mind set on a house in Bloomsbury. A merchant owns it.'

'Kitty!' O'Shaughnessy protested. 'I've had my eyes on that one for months. You can't just hand it over to some lousy vagrant.'

'I'll do as I fancy, O'Shaughnessy,' Mrs Flaherty snapped. 'I started this business, not you. Left to your own devices, you'd have boozed away all our profits.' O'Shaughnessy dropped his eyes. 'Don't you ever forget who gives the orders round here.' She glanced at Paul. 'And don't forget that I had to plead for your life or this so-called lousy vagrant would have done for you.'

O'Shaughnessy scowled.

'A merchant's house,' Paul said. 'That sounds about

129

right. I need to know how to break in, what to look for, where I can fence any items.'

'Give him all the help he needs, O'Shaughnessy,' Mrs Flaherty commanded.

'But Kit . . .'

'Just do it, damn you!' Mrs Flaherty snapped.

Grudgingly, O'Shaughnessy described the Bloomsbury house. Paul's target would be a comfortable middle class home with steps leading up to the front door and a Saturday girl to scrub them. The address was number nine, Harker Terrace. O'Shaughnessy described the occupants in detail. There were five members of the family. The master of the house was a man in his fifties. He oozed wealth and standing in society. His wife was slightly younger. They had three children, a boy about Paul's age and two girls about ten and twelve years old. Paul quizzed O'Shaughnessy about the adolescent boy. The set of clothes he was wearing would do nicely. It was bound to fit better than O'Shaughnessy's cast-offs and it would certainly be cleaner.

'So you're satisfied with our arrangement?' Mrs Flaherty asked, drawing her chair closer to Paul's.

'Thanks for the information,' Paul said. 'But what do you want in exchange?'

'You're right, of course,' Mrs Flaherty said. 'I ain't in this for charity. But we can discuss the price later.'

She glanced at O'Shaughnessy. 'It's late,' she told him. 'Shouldn't you be on your way?'

O'Shaughnessy stared. For a moment it looked as though he was going to protest, then his shoulders sagged and he made his way to the door. The moment it slammed, Mrs Flaherty leaned forward, taking Paul's hands in hers. The firelight illuminated her features and made her eyes sparkle with mischief.

'I'd like you to stay,' she said. 'You can burgle the Bloomsbury house tomorrow.'

Paul glanced at a worn couch in front of the fire. 'I'll sleep here.'

'I meant . . .'

Paul looked purposefully at the couch. 'I said, I'll bed down here.'

Mrs Flaherty threw back her head and laughed. 'Suit yourself.'

With that, she climbed the stairs to her room.

Fifteen

Paul didn't leave Mrs Flaherty's house until late the following afternoon. She was an attractive woman and fine company. More importantly, she kept a warm fire burning in the parlour, and he was dreading the next few hours.

'You hate Samuel, don't you?' he said as he finished the mutton she had ordered in for their lunch.

'Oh, I detest him most powerfully,' she replied. 'He almost destroyed me.'

He saw the dark shadow that came into her face. 'What did he do to you?' Paul asked.

'He beat me, just as he does everyone he invites into the Rats' Nest. He took me in, you see, just as he picked Molly Vale and Betsy Alder off the street.' She hesitated before offering the next bit of information. 'I lived with the scoundrel for six years as his common-law wife.'

This came as no surprise to Paul. Chaim's account of

their exchange at the ratting contest had hinted that they had history.

'Why did you leave?' he asked.

'Why do you think?' Mrs Flaherty retorted. 'I made the mistake of keeping some of my earnings for myself. I wanted to buy a pretty dress and make myself look like a real lady.'

'You are a lady,' Paul said.

Mrs Flaherty gave him a pitying look. 'Don't go sentimental on me, Paul.' Her dark eyes held his gaze. 'You'd be wrong to put your trust in me. Surviving in the Flowery turns you into something you don't want to be. I fence stolen goods. I run a gang of pickpockets. I won't trouble you with the other ways I earn a living. I ain't much different to Samuel. Truth is, I'm his main rival. I've a good reason to want him dead. Samuel gave me such a thrashing one night, he thought I was at death's door. So he took me down to the river and threw me in. By rights, I should have drowned that night. Lord knows, I was too weak to swim. Yes, I should have gone under. But for poor O'Shaughnessy, I would have.'

'You mean he saved your life?'

'He did that,' Mrs Flaherty answered. 'He was working on the dock and he heard the splash. Jumped in after me, he did. That's how I got to know him. He nursed me back to health.'

'No wonder he's so protective,' Paul said.

Mrs Flaherty laughed. 'He adores me, the poor brute, but I treat him badly. You'd think I owed him something for diving into the filthy Thames to pull me out, wouldn't you? And for all the weeks he fed me and looked after me.'

'So why do you treat him so badly?'

'That's easily explained,' Mrs Flaherty said. 'Revenge is what moves me, not affection. I looked at O'Shaughnessy, hoping he was the man who could stand up to Samuel. When I saw he wasn't up to the job, I went looking for somebody who was. Do you know what I did? I just up and married the first strong man I could find. I wanted revenge that badly. I broke O'Shaughnessy's heart.'

'But he hung around?'

'He did,' Mrs Flaherty said, 'even though I rubbed his face in the dirt. O'Shaughnessy's devoted to me but he's a poor, weak wretch as your friend Chaim must have told you. I married a big ox by the name of Daniel Flaherty. I wanted him to cook Samuel's goose. My actions only went and got Flaherty killed. You must think me a wicked woman, Paul.'

'Of course not,' Paul said. 'You're trying to survive, same as me.'

Mrs Flaherty laughed. 'Ain't that the truth?'

'So what happened to Flaherty?' Paul asked.

'He was a bare-knuckle fighter in his own right,' Mrs Flaherty told him. 'He was strong as a bleedin' bull. Great powerful arms he had. But he was no match for Samuel. That cove ain't human. The guv'nor toyed with Danny for fifteen rounds, beating him to a bloody pulp.' She sighed. 'Then he finished it. He dragged Danny right over to me so I could watch the killer blow close up. That's Samuel Rector. He thrives on brutality. He's a monster, Paul.'

Paul nodded. 'I know.'

Mrs Flaherty pursed her lips. 'Do you?'

'Yes,' Paul answered, 'I've met his kind before.'

He thought for a moment before he spoke again. 'You think you know everything about me, Kit. You're wrong.'

Mrs Flaherty raised an enquiring eyebrow.

'Samuel and I have one or two things in common.'

'Meaning?'

He explained the best way he could without talking about a journey through time and ancient horrors. 'What do you think of me now?'

Mrs Flaherty's answer surprised him. 'I think you're a breath of fresh air. Will you stay?'

Paul shook his head. 'I can't, Kitty. I'm not going to work for you. I'm going to Bloomsbury.'

'Suit yourself,' Mrs Flaherty said, a teasing smile playing on her lips. 'You know where I am if you change your mind.'

Paul hurried out onto the street, crossing to the other side as a hansom cab clattered by. By the time twilight had begun to gather, he had put all his doubts about housebreaking to one side. It would be dangerous to throw his lot in with Mrs Flaherty. It was unlikely he could trust her. The two of them only had one thing in common, their need to destroy Samuel Rector.

The owner of number nine, Harker Terrace had money. That would mean independence from Mrs Flaherty. The family could afford to spare some of their wealth and he needed it more than they did. God knows, in his own time he had never had money. His computer was second-hand. Even some of his clothes had been hand-me-downs. He heard the noise of brass rings on rods as the servants drew the curtains for the night. He smelled their evening meal.

So it isn't just my sight and hearing that are becoming more acute. It's all my senses.

The family dined on sirloin of beef, roasted potatoes and broccoli. They followed the main course with a slice of damson pie. How he longed to be like them, part of a loving family seated around the table to discuss the day's events. But he would never be like them. He would never belong.

Just after eleven o'clock the servants extinguished the last gaslight in the house and retired to their quarters. Paul waited another half hour then slipped round the back of the house. He found a sash window and tried to open it. It wouldn't budge. Somehow he would have to reach the catch. Hitherto, his power to control fire had been chaotic and instinctive. If he was to do this, he must learn to bend it to his will. As he focused his concentration on the task in hand, the familiar dark floaters revolved around the edge of his vision. Soon, his right index forefinger started to glow. Though it took far longer than he had anticipated, he finally succeeded in directing a single, needle-thin beam of light on the window pane. It slowly burned a hole just beneath the catch. The circle of glass tinkled to the floor and shattered. Paul tensed and listened for footsteps. But the household slept on.

With a smile, he slid the catch back and lifted the sash window. He straddled the window sill and lowered himself to the floor of the servants' scullery. He was beginning to enjoy his night-time adventure. The meal he had eaten at Mrs Flaherty's seemed a long time ago. He raided the larder for some cold meat and potatoes, ate hungrily, then searched for some of that damson pie. He devoured three slices, then chased it down with a jug of milk.

Now that he had a full stomach, he set about finding the family's valuables. As he moved through the darkened house, he realized that he had no trouble seeing. The physical changes that he had been experiencing were accelerating. He discovered the study and explored the various drawers, finding a cheque book but no cash. It wasn't long before he discovered the reason. Hidden behind a wall painting there was a safe. Paul almost laughed. So there was a time they actually did things like this, just like in the movies. He read the manufacturer's name and the date of casting: Chubb of Wolverhampton, 1837. He grimaced. This wasn't going to be as easy as opening a sash window.

In the event, it took just over an hour to burn through the locks, but eventually the door swung open. Paul rummaged through the various deeds, certificates and bonds before coming across a wad of notes. He carried them over to the window to examine them in the moonlight. There was two hundred pounds. He tried to remember his history lessons. One pound in Victorian times was worth a lot more than in the twenty-first century. This bundle of paper had to be worth a small fortune. O'Shaughnessy had chosen well. Paul thumbed the wads of money and smiled. This would make him more than comfortable. He shoved the lot into his pocket. But he hesitated at the door.

No, taking such a large amount might ruin them.

After a few minutes he decided to return a portion of the money to the safe. It would still leave him with more than enough on which to live. There was one final thing to do. He was fed, he had money. All he needed now was a roof over his head and that posed a problem. He didn't want to go back to Mrs Flaherty's. That meant he had to find a hotel. He looked down at the ill-fitting, threadbare outfit he had inherited from O'Shaughnessy. If he went anywhere but the most disreputable lodging houses, he would be told to leave. He remembered the family's fine clothes, especially those of the teenage boy.

Soon, he discovered a laundry room in the cellar next to the scullery. The set of clothes he'd been looking for was folded neatly and hung over a maiden ready for washing. He cast off the ill-fitting workmen's outfit Mrs Flaherty had given him and dressed quickly.

He emerged from the room in a brown velvet waistcoat, brown trousers and a matching frock coat. He had the almost universal tall hat under his arm. He was missing only one item, a pair of shoes. What chance would he have of renting decent lodgings if he turned up barefoot? He found a sturdy pair of shoes in a cupboard on the landing. So, fed, dressed and with money in his pocket, Paul climbed back out of the window and went in search of a roof over his head. He soon found a hansom cab and quizzed the driver about accommodation in the centre of London.

'You've left it a bit late,' the driver said.

'Oh, I see,' Paul murmured, resigned to another night shuddering in a back alley.

The driver took pity on him. 'Tell you what, I do know the night porter at Hummums. Slip him a consideration and he'll see you right.'

Paul seized on the offer. 'How much?' he asked eagerly.

The driver suggested an amount. It seemed reasonable. Paul was in no position to haggle anyway. 'Hummums,' he asked, 'where's that?'

'Covent Garden,' the hansom driver told him. 'Will that suit your purposes, young sir?'

Paul put the key question. 'Is it . . . respectable?'

'Oh, I should say so.'

'Then I'm in your debt,' Paul said, starting to enjoy playing the part of the Victorian gentleman about town. He'd tried living honestly but wretchedly on the street. Dishonestly and comfortably was more like it.

The hansom duly delivered him to Hummums. Twenty minutes after crossing the night porter's palm with silver, Paul was lying between fresh, clean sheets. Yes, this was much more like it! For a while Mrs Flaherty's face floated through his mind, followed by Netty's. The succession of images troubled him but soon he was fast asleep.

Sixteen

Earlier that same evening, Samuel Rector had assembled his Rat Boys. Betsy made up the company. They sported all manner of cuts, welts and bruises. The guv'nor's fury spared nobody.

'It's like this,' Samuel said, addressing them, 'I've got great plans but there's somebody in the way.'

'We know where he lives, Samuel,' Noah said hurriedly. 'I've been asking around. His name's Chaim Wetzel. He's a senior boy at the Jews' Free School. We'll do for him, if that's what you're thinking.'

'I know all about the Wetzel boy,' Samuel said with a scowl. 'He ain't the real danger. You all know who I mean. I'm talking about the renegade, the one that got the better of you.'

'He got lucky,' Malachy said.

'It wasn't luck,' Samuel observed sourly.

'There ain't supposed to be any members of the demon brotherhood but us,' Malachy protested. 'He took us all by surprise.'

'There's always an excuse, ain't there?' Samuel snarled.

'But we don't know nuffin' about him,' Jacob protested.

A voice filled the room. 'I do.'

A hot wind roared. With it came a blast of brimstone. A dark vortex had opened behind them. At its centre there was a pulsating white light. The speaker was silhouetted against the glow. Lud had appeared. Samuel bowed his head and his Rat Boys followed suit. Only Betsy held her head up. She owed Molly this at least, a single moment's defiance.

'The renegade is special. He was still-born. But the Courts of Destiny had to meddle. The fools revived him. They'd been listening to the priests of Beltane. Because of this accident of birth he has the demon's powers but no obedience to his ancestral Lord. He doesn't share our taste for mischief. For this reason, he poses a real threat to our survival. He must be destroyed.'

'But where's he from, Master?' Noah asked. 'I've never heard any talk of another like us anywhere in London town.'

'That's because there are none,' Lud told him. 'The renegade has the help of the fire priests, the gaolers of my physical form. He comes from a world almost two hundred years in the future.' He saw the look of surprise on the faces of his audience. 'That's right, I am no longer alone in being able to open doors through time. Until he appeared, only my disciples could skip the centuries.'

The Rat Boys swapped glances.

'The renegade has an advantage over me,' Lud said. 'He can assume corporeal form.'

'What's he mean?' Enoch asked in a whisper.

'I hear you, boy,' Lud said. 'The renegade is flesh and blood like any of you, while I can only roam as a phantom spirit until the day of my liberation from this tomb. This invader alone can thwart my plans.'

'We'll find him for you, Master,' Jacob interrupted, not to be outdone by Noah. 'We'll turn over every house in London looking for him, won't we, boys?'

The Rat Boys agreed.

'You will do all that and more,' Lud said, 'but first things first. Bring the boy Israel before me.'

Enoch and Jasper shoved Israel forward.

'Do you know me?' Lud asked.

'You appeared to me in my dreams,' Israel replied. 'You're my Master.'

Lud seemed pleased with the answer. 'And you will raise an army to serve me.'

'I will?'

'That's right.'

Israel's brow furrowed. 'But how do I do that?'

Lud's phantom form seemed to envelop the boy. 'Are you still having the nightmares?' he asked. 'Do you still dream of the walking dead?'

Israel felt the creep of unease. 'You know about my nightmares?'

'Why, of course,' Lud said. 'I am unable to walk on solid ground so I must inhabit another realm. I stalk the back streets of your minds. It's always the same dream, isn't it?'

'Yes.'

'Every night you see a corpse come to life and rise from its grave. Am I right?'

Israel nodded.

'This is no nightmare,' Lud told him. 'It is a premonition. When the time arrives to fulfil your destiny, you will find the power within you. Just follow your instincts. Samuel will guide you in what you must do. The time approaches when you will do me a great service, Israel.'

Samuel nodded. 'I have a meeting with the Resurrectionist this very night.'

Lud seemed satisfied. The apparition started to fade.

'Wait!' Noah cried. 'The renegade, Master, we don't know his name.'

Lud turned towards Samuel. 'Have you not told them?'

Samuel smiled. 'I wanted it to be a surprise.'

'Ah, that's my Samuel,' Lud said, 'always the mischief maker. Tell them now.'

Samuel nodded. 'The renegade is called—' he permitted himself a brief pause. 'He is called Paul Rector.'

The name drew a gasp all round.

'Rector,' Jacob said, 'you don't mean . . . ?'

'Didn't you listen to the Master?' Samuel said. 'The renegade and I share direct lineage from Lud. We are his descendants. Paul Rector is the sole stain on my blood-line. When I kill him, the shame will be erased.'

'Fine talk,' Lud said, as he faded from the room. 'Just make sure it's matched by deeds. I will be disappointed if you fail.'

Once the demon master was gone, Samuel addressed his Rat Boys.

'You heard the Master,' he said. 'I want you to start

143

a storm in the East End. Hand out beatings. Give bribes. Do what it takes.' He thought for a moment. 'Keep an eye on the newspapers too. Look for any unusual events that may give you a clue to his whereabouts.' He glanced at Betsy. 'You'll stay with me.'

The Rat Boys hesitated.

'Well, what are you waiting for? Get to it.'

Ethan Lockett was following the others out of the door when Samuel caught his sleeve. 'On second thoughts, I want you to stay behind too. I've got a special job for you tonight, Licker.'

'I hope it's something important, guv'nor,' Ethan said.

'Oh, it's important,' Samuel said. 'You're the one who's going to clear the way to the crypt.'

He explained what he wanted. Ethan was more than happy with his mission and left without a word.

'What about us, Samuel?' Betsy asked nervously. 'What do you want me for?'

'There ain't nothing to worry about,' Samuel told her as he slipped his arm round her waist and guided her to the door. 'Didn't I tell you, you're my princess now. I need somebody pretty on my arm when I go to see Smethwick. He has an eye for the ladies, does old Olly. It will help the negotiations to proceed without a hitch.'

'Who is he, this Smethwick?' Betsy asked. 'I don't recall meeting him.'

'That's because you ain't,' Samuel told her. 'I don't include you in all my dealings, Bets. Do you really want to know?'

'If it ain't too much bother, Sammy.'

Samuel indulged her. 'Oliver Smethwick's only the

most notorious Resurrectionist there ever was. That's right, my dear girl, he's the finest grave robber that ever split a coffin lid.'

Samuel and Betsy found Smethwick in a beer hall in Bethnal Green. They crossed the sawdust-strewn floor to a corner where a tall, rake-thin man was holding forth to two gaudily-dressed women. They greeted his every word with raucous laughter that was as forced as it was loud. The moment Smethwick saw Samuel, he lost interest and waved them away.

'Sit down, Samuel,' Smethwick said, 'take the weight off your plates of meat.' His eyes ran over Betsy, making her feel uncomfortable. 'Who's this, Sammy? How do you manage to attract all the tastiest morsels to your table?'

'It's my natural animal charm,' Samuel said with a chuckle. He dropped a few coins into Betsy's hand. 'But shove them eyes back in their sockets, Smethwick. Bets is my girl, got that? Anybody makes a play for her, I'll tear his face off.'

'Whatever you say, Samuel,' Smethwick said.

Samuel smiled. 'Get yourself a drink, Bets, and don't go far. This won't take long, then we'll take in a show at a penny gaff.'

Betsy wandered over to the bar attracting interested looks from some of the customers. A scowl from Samuel warned them off. There wasn't a man in the East End who would cross the guv'nor lightly.

'So what can I do for you, Sammy boy?' Smethwick asked.

'It's your expertise I need,' Samuel said. 'You used to be a Resurrectionist, I hear.'

'Resurrectionist?' Smethwick repeated. 'Now, that's a word I haven't heard in a long while.' He mimed wiping away a tear. 'Why Sammy, I'm starting to come over all nostalgic.'

'I aim to revive the trade,' Samuel said. 'I need to know where the richest pickings are.'

'You're behind the times,' Smethwick told him. 'There's no profit to be had from bodysnatching no more, not even if you find a fresh cadaver.'

'Trust me,' Samuel said. 'I'll give a dying profession a new lease of life.'

'I don't see how,' Smethwick replied. 'There's been no market for stiffs since the Government passed the Anatomy Act. That killed the trade stone dead, it did.'

'Why's that?' Samuel asked.

Smethwick set about his tale. 'You see, at the height of the trade there was a problem. Surgeons were only allowed to practise on the cadavers of convicted criminals. Now there weren't that many about, even in London town, so our great healers had to come by their corpses illegally. That's where the likes of me came in.'

'You dug up the bodies.'

Smethwick grinned. 'I did. It was eight guineas for a ripe one, twenty if it was fresh. Great days they were, Sammy. If you had a strong stomach and you didn't mind being up to your knees in dirt at dead of night, you could earn yourself a decent income. I miss those times.'

Samuel interrupted him. 'You've no need to lecture me about the fleshmarket, Smethwick. I get the picture. Let's get down to practicalities. I need cadavers, lots of them. I want you to tell me where to find the best.'

He was about to press Smethwick about his knowledge of the graveyards and burial grounds when he noticed Betsy hovering nearby. 'Do you want something?' he asked frostily. 'I hope you're not trying to eavesdrop.'

'Of course not, Sammy,' Betsy answered, though eavesdropping was exactly what she'd been doing. 'I was just wondering how long you were going to be. I want to see that show. I love a good sing-song.'

Samuel slipped an arm round her waist and pulled her closer. 'Ain't she a regular angel, Smethwick?' He winked. 'She ought to be up there on the stage. What a combination, pretty and talented.'

'Oh absolutely, Samuel,' Smethwick answered. 'She's like a little porcelain doll. You're a lucky man.'

The retired grave-robber didn't say that he could see things in Betsy's eyes. He could see her pain, her humiliation, her fear of Samuel.

Samuel laughed. 'No, Betsy here's the one who's lucky. She's bagged the future King of London. Ain't that right, darling?'

Betsy gave a faltering smile. 'Sure Sammy, I'm . . . lucky.'

Samuel patted her on the hip. 'You occupy yourself just a little bit longer, my little nightingale. You'll get your sing-song by the by.' He waited until Betsy was out of earshot then continued. 'I'll give you thirty shillings for your knowledge, Smethwick.'

'Why don't you make it a round forty?' Smethwick asked. 'I've got expenses.'

Samuel's eyes blazed. 'What did you say?'

Smethwick remembered why the man across the table was called the Satan of Spitalfields. He realized his mistake and faltered. 'I thought there was room for negotiation. I didn't mean anything by it.'

Samuel slapped his palm on the table. 'Don't you get greedy, Olly my old cove.' He started to rise. 'There are other former Resurrection Men out there that can give me all the information I need.'

Picturing his thirty shillings vanishing into thin air, Smethwick rushed to placate Samuel. 'Thirty's fine. Please sit down.' He gestured at the chair. 'Come on, Samuel. Forget I ever said it. Let nobody say Oliver Smethwick's greedy. Here's the lowdown.' He nodded encouragingly. 'Don't go off in a huff.'

Samuel nodded. 'That's more like it.' With a satisfied smile, he sat down again.

From the bar, Betsy strained to hear their conversation. It wasn't easy to make sense of the whispered exchanges but she was able to get the gist of it. But what did Samuel want with dead bodies?

148

Seventeen

Paul started his day by calling in at a public wash house where he paid six shillings for a 'first class, warm bath'. He went past the entrance three times before he plucked up the courage to go in. The need to feel clean overcame his worries about seeming odd and unfamiliar with the ways of the time. Though he'd scrubbed his head and shoulders at Mrs Flaherty's, that basin of hot water had done little to erase the stench of the streets. In the wash house he sank into the warm, soapy water and just lay there, allowing the warmth to envelop him. Now he felt clean for the first time in many weeks.

Refreshed, he walked across town, following the instructions given him by the staff at Hummums. He was almost ready for battle. Soon, he would take his stand against Samuel Rector and his attempt to break the first seal that held King Lud in chains. Paul knew where the enemy would strike. He knew the identity of the general who would lead the assault. He was about to locate another piece of the jigsaw. He had to know *how* Samuel was going to do it.

He walked briskly towards his destination, pausing only to make some purchases. He was learning to pass as a young gentleman. Assuming an air of authority, he ordered that the shirts, trousers, jackets and shoes be delivered to his room at Hummums and enjoyed the expression on the counter staff's faces when he paid in cash on the spot.

He had one more stop-off. This was to send a letter to Chaim Wetzel, informing him of his whereabouts. Paul knew that Israel Lazarus had an important part to play in Lud's plans. Soon, he was enjoying the challenge of finding his way round 1830s London. He arrived at the house he was seeking just after noon. He'd seen the building before but in a different time and under different circumstances. Straightening his cuffs, he climbed the steps to the front door of number thirteen, West Cromwell Place. The maid who answered the door looked suspicious. Paul knew from observing other young men that he was both well turned out and fashionable. It had to be because of his age.

'I would like to speak to Mr Arthur Strachan,' Paul said.

'May I ask your name, sir?' the maid asked.

Paul told her.

'I'm afraid Mr Strachan is out on business,' the maid said. 'You will probably find him at the construction site. He is supervising work on the new Minories railway station.'

'Do you have any idea when he might be home? Your master wouldn't want to miss me.'

These words had the desired effect.

'If you please, sir,' the maid said, thinking she might

get into trouble if her Master missed the young gentle-man, 'I can consult his diary.'

'Thank you,' Paul said.

The maid gestured towards an anteroom. 'Would you like to take a seat in here, sir? I won't be a minute.'

Paul sat down. The house was both familiar and strange to him. He had seen its future. The rooms were laid out just as they would be a century from now. The house differed in its atmosphere. Tragedy was yet to strike and transform it from the bright, sunlit family home to a kind of sepulchre whose desiccated inhabit-ants relived the horrors of history. Paul was seeing the house in its final few days of happiness. After several minutes the maid returned.

'The master will be in for lunch. Would you like to wait?'

'Please.'

The maid frowned. The young caller might be dressed like a gentleman but there was something very odd about the way he spoke. She even worried he might be foreign.

Ten minutes later, Arthur Strachan opened the front door. Paul heard the maid talking to her master. Strachan walked down the corridor and the maid reappeared.

'Follow me please, sir,' she said.

Paul could tell from her manner that Strachan must have reacted sharply to the name Rector. She ushered him into the drawing room where Strachan was stand-ing by the fire. He gave Paul a hostile stare.

'Your name is Rector, sir,' he said. 'I am sadly familiar with the name. Would you be related in any way to one Samuel Rector?'

151

'Unfortunately, yes.'

His answer seemed to mollify Strachan a little. 'You say "unfortunately",' he observed.

'That's right,' Paul replied. 'There's no love lost between Samuel's side of the family and mine.' His every word was calculated to neutralise the engineer's wariness of him. Trying to copy Strachan's way of speaking, Paul said, 'I can see, from your reaction, sir, that my relative has displeased you.'

'Displeased me!' Strachan snapped. 'That is an understatement. The man's nothing but a blackguard, a criminal.'

'That's why I'm here,' Paul said, slipping back into his own speaking style. 'He's dangerous. We should work together to defeat him.'

Strachan consulted his fob watch. 'You have exactly one minute to convince me that you have nothing in common with your relative. If I am not convinced by that time, I will have you thrown out on your ear.'

Paul didn't wilt before Strachan's anger. 'May I speak frankly, Mr Strachan?'

Strachan nodded.

'My family,' Paul began, choosing his words carefully, 'is a respectable one.' He pressed on, seasoning the stew of invention with a light sprinkling of truth and, all the while, trying to sound like a gentleman in a Victorian novel. 'Samuel is a distant uncle. He has brought shame on the family name. It is in our interests to expose him for what he is and recover our reputation. I am here to warn you about him.'

'I need no warning,' Strachan said. 'He has already subjected me to threats and menaces.'

'May I enquire as to the nature of these threats?' Paul asked.

'He wants me to re-route the railway, leaving him in complete control of the company's land in the Aldgate area. I refer to the Minories to Blackwall Line.'

'I know of it,' Paul said.

'Your uncle has a scheme to defraud the Railway,' Strachan said, 'as far as I can make out his intentions. He is attempting to bribe me. He wishes to take exclusive control of the site for the next two weeks. I told him that was quite impossible.'

'Why?' Paul asked, though he knew very well what Samuel wanted to unearth.

Strachan examined Paul's face. 'I don't know what to make of you, Mr Rector.' He paused. 'You're very young.'

'I can help you,' Paul said. 'You do need help, don't you?'

Strachan was unsure how to respond. After a few moments, he answered. 'I think it has to do with an ancient wall we have uncovered. That is the only part of the site he is interested in.'

'What did you say to Samuel?'

'If it's any of your business,' Strachan said, 'I sent him away with a flea in his ear. That's when he issued his threats.'

'What exactly did he say?'

Again, Strachan hesitated before answering.

'You think me young, sir, but I can see that you are troubled by my relative's behaviour.'

'I am,' Strachan said. 'He warned me that he was going to find some way to change my mind. That's the gist of it.'

'You've done the right thing standing up to him,' Paul said, 'but I am here to give you some advice.'

153

'Are you, by Jove?' Strachan said. 'That's just what I need, advice from a boy.'

Undeterred, Paul pressed on. 'Samuel will not stop. You must be vigilant because he will do anything to get his way.'

'You don't surprise me,' Strachan said. 'I took an immediate dislike to the fellow. I felt that there was something . . .' He hesitated. 'I felt that there was something of the macabre about him.' He frowned. 'Though I don't know why I'm telling you that.'

'You were right to be suspicious,' Paul said. 'You must know what you're dealing with. My relative is a thief-trainer in the Spitalfields area. There isn't an area of criminal activity in which he doesn't have an interest. If he says he is going to change your mind, you can be sure he is going to try his damndest and his methods will be unscrupulous.' Paul wished he could say more but he knew that Strachan would show him the door if he told the truth. 'You're a widower, aren't you?'

Strachan searched Paul's face. 'How the Devil do you know that?'

'That doesn't matter,' Paul said. 'You have a child.'

'I do,' Strachan said, still wondering where Paul got his information from. 'I have a daughter called Victoria. She looks about your age.'

'I am convinced,' Paul said, 'that Samuel intends to use your daughter to bring you to heel.'

'Victoria?' Strachan said. 'Surely he wouldn't stoop so low. She is an innocent young woman.'

'Believe me,' Paul said, 'he would. Samuel has no scruples about hurting anyone who stands in the way of his plans – be it man, woman or child, guilty or innocent. You must watch over your daughter night and day.' He

154

handed Strachan one of Hummums' printed cards. 'You can contact me at my hotel if you need me.'

Strachan gazed sceptically at the card.

'Please,' Paul said. 'Nobody else can help you.'

Eventually, Strachan took the card and slipped it into his jacket pocket. It was at that moment Victoria entered the room. She was blond and pretty and dressed in a sumptuous crinoline.

'Are you going to introduce me to our guest, father?'

'This is Mr Rector,' Strachan said, still digesting what Paul had told him.

'It's a pleasure to make your acquaintance, sir,' Victoria declared. She squeezed her father's arm. 'Whatever were you whispering about, Papa? It sounded very intriguing from the hall.'

'Victoria!' Strachan snapped. 'I will not have you eavesdropping on my conversations.'

'I'm sorry, father,' Victoria said, 'but curiosity got the better of me.'

'A surfeit of curiosity is a dangerous thing,' Strachan said stuffily.

Paul chose the moment to take his leave. 'I have to go now, Mr Strachan,' he said. 'Remember. I'll be at Hummums if you need me.'

Strachan seemed to gaze past Paul. 'I'm sure I can handle this myself, thank you.'

Paul nodded towards Victoria. 'Miss Strachan.'

As he stepped out onto the street, he glanced back. Paul feared for Victoria. She was Strachan's Achilles Heel. Don't lose that card, Paul thought. You might not know it yet, but you do need me.

Eighteen

M rs Rector doesn't seem surprised to see Netty standing on her doorstep.

'Come in,' she says.

Netty perches on the end of the couch. The flat seems very empty without Paul. She wonders how Mrs Rector is coping.

'I had to come,' Netty said. 'We're the only ones who understand, *really* understand. Have the police been back?'

'DS Hussein calls now and then,' Mrs Rector replies. 'They're going through the motions, treating Paul as a missing person. They know they're not going to find him. She *knows*.'

An image of DS Hussein transfixed by fear as Redman, whose killing spree Paul had brought to an end, approached her flashes into Netty's mind. She sits with her hands clasped in her lap. 'Mrs Rector . . .'

'Go on,' Mrs Rector says.

She looks tired. Netty finds it hard to imagine how

she carries on. Her husband walked out years ago. Her elder son John is dead. The other is lost.

'Do you have any idea where Paul is?' Netty asks.

'I know the same as you,' Mrs Rector says stiffly. 'I saw the photograph.'

'I think you know more than you're letting on,' Netty says. 'Paul told me you burned some documents. Can you tell me what was in them?'

Mrs Rector sighs. Part of her wants Netty to leave. Part wants to share what she knows. 'I looked at them. I know his destination.'

'Where is he?'

'I'll tell you where he is,' Mrs Rector says, 'if he's still alive . . . Oh, what a terrible thing to say! He's alive. I know he is. I feel it in every atom of my being.'

'But where is he?'

'There were some newspaper clippings from the year 1839,' Mrs Rector says, dabbing at her eyes with a tissue. 'It mentions somebody called Samuel Rector, a notorious villain. He ran a gang, the Rat Boys. One headline calls them Satan's Children.'

'Was there any mention of Paul?'

'No, none.'

It is some time before either of them speaks. Finally, Mrs Rector breaks the silence. 'You care about Paul, don't you?'

'Yes,' Netty says, 'I do, though . . . well, sometimes I wish I didn't.'

'I understand,' Mrs Rector says. 'There was a girl in the photograph.'

'It's not just that,' Netty says. 'He must be so lonely. It's selfish really. I want to get on with my life but I don't know how. I mean, I don't even know how I feel about him. We didn't go out for that long, did we?'

'You need to forget him,' Mrs Rector says.

'That's easy to say,' Netty retorts. 'Can you do it?'

'I'm his mother,' Mrs Rector says simply. 'He's the first thing I think about every morning, the last thing on my mind every night. I don't have any choice. You do. Forget him, Netty. Go and live your life.'

Netty lets herself out. She wants to take Mrs Rector's advice. She just doesn't know how. As she jogs down the bleak stairwell she doesn't see Mrs Rector watching her from the kitchen window, nor does she know that Mrs Rector was holding something back, the most terrible secret of all.

Nineteen

From the diary of Arthur Strachan
Sunday, 10 February, 1839

Victoria is not feeling well today. She rose late and appeared listless and pale all morning. The change is rather sudden. I asked Dr Wade to examine her. He could find nothing wrong but recommended a tonic to fortify her constitution. Though I immediately sent one of the staff for the tonic, it has done little to improve my daughter's condition. It is not just that she appears tired and frail. There is a fractiousness about her that is most unsettling.

What disturbs me most is the expression in her eyes. Normally such a loving and obedient child, Victoria watches me much as a mistreated animal might its master. I cannot for the life of me think of a reason for this abrupt change of character. It is at times like this that I miss my dear wife most. She was a sweet-tempered creature and a wonderful mother. She would have wasted

159

no time getting to the bottom of Victoria's change of temperament. But here I am alone and quite at a loss how to proceed.

I have never been a demonstrative man or one who can communicate his emotions easily. I am desperate to express my feelings to Victoria but I don't know how. In a low moment this afternoon I actually wondered if my daughter's condition was in some way related to Samuel Rector's threats, but surely that is impossible. What could the blackguard possibly do to engineer such a dramatic change in my child's well-being?

Twenty

Chaim was missing from school the following Monday. He'd asked David Marks to say he was ill. David, like his teachers, had been surprised. As a reliable pupil-monitor, working closely with the teachers and entrusted with some of their duties, Chaim was the most unlikely student to skip school. David knew there had to be a good reason and readily covered for his friend, taking care to discourage Moses' enquiries.

To his parents Chaim said nothing at all. He felt guilty but he decided to follow the advice he'd given to Paul: sometimes you have to do a little wrong to achieve a greater good.

Chaim's renewed surveillance of the house in Flower and Dean Street paid off just after ten o'clock when Israel appeared in the company of the other boys. They set off mob-handed towards the West End. What Chaim found most intriguing was the transformation undergone by Jacob Quiggins and Noah Pyke. Samuel Rector had issued them with more respectable outfits than they were accustomed to wearing. They looked quite the young gentlemen about town. What are you up to? Chaim wondered. Why the sudden change of appearance?

The group split in two at the top of Piccadilly. Chaim, of course, stayed with Jacob Quiggins' group, which included Israel. Jacob stopped outside one fashionable shop and proceeded to give the younger boys their instructions. He was pointing to something in the *Morning Post*, an act which in itself raised Chaim's curiosity. Leaving the other Rat Boys out on the pavement, Jacob entered Hatchett's Hotel. That set Chaim's nerves jangling. He knew, from the recent letter inquiring about Israel, that Paul had a room at Hummums. Now here were the Rat Boys starting to call on city centre hotels. It was no coincidence. How had they got on to him so quickly? Jacob called in at three more hotels, the last being the Burlington in Old Burlington Street. He seemed frustrated not to have made an early breakthrough and tossed the copy of the *Morning Post* on the ground.

Chaim waited until they reached the street corner then scooped it up. He followed them at a distance with the newspaper tucked under his arm. It was only when Jacob stopped to call in at Fenton's Hotel that Chaim got his chance to read it. Immediately, a headline jumped out at him:

Daring break-in at Bloomsbury house
Metropolitan Police mystified

Metropolitan Police sources admitted to being baffled this morning as they investigate the theft of a large amount of money from the safe of Mr James Ludlum, merchant, of 9, Harker Terrace. Mr Ludlum discovered the theft on Saturday morning. The burglars had somehow broken open the lock of a Chubb safe of a new design. One of the most curious features of the robbery is that the thief left another substantial sum in cash and many bonds and promissory notes worth considerably more. There were no signs that he had been disturbed while committing his crime though there was some evidence that he had tried to start a fire on the premises. He also ignored Mr Ludlum's cheque book and Mrs Ludlum's jewellery.

Detective Superintendent Maurice Perryman said, 'This is a new kind of crime. We are still trying to discover how it was done.'

Refusing to be drawn on the thief's decision to take only a portion of the money and valuables available, DS Perryman concentrated on the nature of the crime itself. Commenting further, he said that its sophistication indicated that it had been committed by a professional thief, maybe even somebody masquerading as a gentleman.

Fear and fire, Chaim thought to himself, that's what Paul had told him. They were his powers. So you did it, my friend. You're the gentleman thief, aren't you, a regular Robin of Locksley. You took from the rich and gave to the poor, meaning your good self. Chaim smiled. I'll bet you're not wearing some old *shmutter* now. There'll be no rags for the renegade any more. Then the smile faded from his face. If he'd guessed the burglar's identity from the article, then so had the Rat Boys. That's what had got them scouring the hotels.

What if Noah Pyke's group was even now checking the guest list at Hummums? Chaim was torn. What was he to do? Stay here and keep an eye on Israel or go to warn Paul? He turned the idea over in his head for a while then made his decision. Paul said he could defeat Samuel. Maybe he was Israel's only hope. Casting a last glance in Israel's direction, Chaim started to run towards Covent Garden.

His heart sank the moment he approached the hotel. The second group of Rat Boys was gathered in a huddle across the road from the main entrance. That meant Noah was already inside. He was still trying to decide on a course of action, when he heard a familiar voice from behind him.

'What are you doing here?'

Chaim spun round to see Paul standing there. He immediately grabbed Paul by the arm and dragged him round the nearest corner.

'What are you doing?' Paul repeated. 'Is something wrong?'

Chaim jabbed a finger at the group opposite Hummums.

Paul's eyes widened. 'But how . . . ?'

'How did they find you?' Chaim said, finishing Paul's sentence. 'It's simple. They read the piece in the newspaper about the gentleman thief of Bloomsbury and put two and two together.'

'And you did the same?'

Chaim shook his head. 'To be honest, no. I was following Israel. I only discovered what they were up to when Jacob started calling in at every hotel along the way.' He handed Paul the crumpled copy of the *Morning Post*. 'It even mentions the fact that there was

164

a fire in the merchant's study. That's how you got through the lock, isn't it?'

Paul read the article intently, then glanced at Chaim. 'You have my gratitude. They won't discover me. I used a false name when I signed the hotel register. If they are looking for a single occupant, they will be disappointed. The manager thinks I'm waiting for my father to arrive to convey me to my new school. I even paid for two rooms in advance, just in case somebody came looking for a single person.' He put on a posh accent. 'My family has been living abroad for some time and we've just returned. I have a place at Eton, don't you know?'

Chaim smiled at the impersonation of a toff. 'You're enjoying this, aren't you?'

Paul gave a non-committal shrug but Chaim was right.

Chaim glanced out at the street. 'That should throw them off the scent for a while. You'd better leave the surveillance to me. You don't want to be seen.'

'What about you?' Paul asked.

Chaim frowned. 'What about me?'

'I'm not stupid,' Paul said. 'I know why you're here. You're going to try to snatch Israel back, aren't you?'

'Of course.'

Noah emerged from the hotel and crossed the name off his list. A few moments later Jacob's group appeared. The reunited Rat Boys huddled together, dividing up the next lot of hotels. Chaim was about to resume his pursuit of Jacob's group when Paul restrained him.

'What are you doing?' Chaim demanded, trying to pull away.

'I've got a better idea,' Paul said.

'But we're going to lose them,' Chaim cried despairingly.

'No, we're not,' Paul said. 'I know where they're going. We can take a different route and beat them there.'

Chaim paused, head cocked. 'How can you know where they're going?'

'I heard every word that passed between Noah and Jacob,' Paul told him.

Chaim estimated the distance to Hummums' front door. 'That's impossible.'

'Not for a renegade demon,' Paul told him. 'Something is happening to me. All my senses are becoming more acute.' He explained his plan. 'Even if you succeed in snatching Israel away from them, how do you know he's going to stay? The demon seed casts a powerful spell over its victim.'

Chaim didn't interrupt which gave Paul the confidence to go on.

'Then there's the danger to his mother and your own family. Samuel would be bound to go after him. Do you really think you could fight off the Rat Boys? You've seen what they can do.'

Chaim took a few moments to consider his options.

'Very well,' he said, 'you've persuaded me that my plan isn't going to work. That doesn't mean I can just give up.'

'I'm not asking you to,' Paul said.

'So what are you going to put in its place?'

'The only way Israel has any chance is if we break Samuel's power for good,' Paul said as they followed the route taken by Jacob and his companions. 'I know he's about to attack Aldgate, but it's protected by powerful magic. Samuel has only eight Rat Boys at his disposal. They could all die trying to attack the seal which protects the gate. To stand any chance of breaking through, he needs dozens of warriors at least. I have to know where he's going to get them.'

Chaim understood. 'So you want Israel to remain with the Rat Boys?'

'That's right,' Paul said. 'He's torn. He hates Samuel but he can't break free of him. I've seen enough to believe he wants to do the right thing. If you can talk to him, I think he might be our eyes and ears inside the Rats' Nest.'

'We'd be taking a terrible risk,' Chaim said. 'I don't know how strong he is.'

The Rat Boys came into view round the next street corner.

'There's only one way to find out,' Paul said. 'Now listen, once Jacob is inside the hotel, I'll occupy Ethan, Enoch and Malachy. You've got to get Israel away.' He laid his right hand on Chaim's shoulder. 'But when I give the signal, you must let your friend go.'

'You're asking a lot,' Chaim said.

Paul nodded. 'I know you're capable of great things.'

Chaim lowered his eyes. 'Then you know more about me than I do myself. I don't know if I can send Israel back to them.'

'You must,' Paul said. 'This is our best chance to destroy the demon infestation. Are you ready?'

'Yes.'

Paul smiled and turned his attention to the Rat Boys. Jacob entered the hotel. Paul counted to five then made straight for the remaining members of the gang.

'It's him,' Ethan cried, 'the renegade!'

No sooner had Ethan raised the alarm than he, Malachy and Enoch transformed. Their dark eyes flashed and they raced forward, claw-like fingernails slashing. Paul's hands glowed but he didn't use the full extent of his powers. He was content to keep them at bay and draw them away from the startled Israel. While Paul drew the Rat Boys away, Chaim seized his chance. Paul skirmished with the attacking Rat Boys, leading them a dance. Chaim sprinted across the road and dragged a struggling Israel to one side, hastily explaining Paul's plan. After a minute or so Jacob, alerted by Ethan's shout and the sounds of battle, emerged from the hotel.

'Where's Izzy?' he yelled.

Paul glanced across at Chaim who gave the briefest of nods to tell him the job was done. He'd got their intentions across to Israel. Jacob followed the direction of his stare. He advanced on Chaim.

'You've got to get away!' Paul yelled.

As Chaim made his escape, Paul clapped his hands together unleashing a spray of fire. Under the cover of the fog of smoke and flame he too fled the scene. Now he had to pray that the ruse had worked.

Twenty-one

The church bell tolled midnight as Samuel led the way into the burial ground. The white spire of Christ Church loomed high above them, stark against the racing clouds. It was a night of high wind and squally showers and there were few people on the street. Jacob and Noah, having changed out of their gentlemen's outfits, slipped through the gate followed by the rest of the Rat Boys. They started their search for the newly-dug grave on the north side of the churchyard by Heneage Street. From time to time, they were startled by the hollow shriek of a bird, but under Samuel's watchful gaze they didn't let up. It was Ethan who found the new arrival.

'Here he is,' he hissed. 'The earth's fresh and dark, just like Smethwick said it would be.'

The Rat Boys gathered round. Only Israel hung back, revolted at the thought of opening a grave. From time to time, flurries of rain swept over him, making him shiver violently. Samuel said this was the night he would begin to understand his unique power. But what was he expected to do? He felt only the bleak fear stirred by the darkened graveyard.

'Well, get to it,' Samuel said. 'The stiff won't dig itself up.'

Jacob and Noah started to turn the soil. Soon their spades struck the wooden lid of the coffin.

'Ain't it shallow?' Jacob said. 'I thought they were supposed to bury them six feet under.'

'Not in Spitalfields, they don't,' Samuel said, 'or any other poor area of London. Space is at a premium, so Smethwick says. They stack them one on top of the other here, like slices of bread on a plate. There can be up to a dozen in one plot.'

'Don't seem right though, do it?' Ethan observed. 'Where's the dignity in that?'

'It ain't going to bother a stiff when he's popped his clogs, Licker,' Samuel said. 'What difference does it make when you're cold and gone?' He peered over the freshly-turned earth around the grave. 'So who's going to open up the coffin?'

Malachy volunteered. 'I'll do it, guv'nor.'

'Then get to it, Play Dead,' Samuel said.

Malachy drove his spade into the lid, making a jagged split in the wood. 'This is a poor construction to carry a man to the afterlife, Samuel. I thought there'd be a polished casket and shiny steel screws.'

'Now where did my Rat Boys get all these grand ideas?' Samuel wondered out loud. 'Polished caskets and shiny screws indeed!'

'It's the way you're supposed to go, ain't it?'

'If you're the Duke of Wellington or one of your Kings and Queens of England maybe,' Samuel said, 'but there's no polished casket for the likes of this poor cove. He snapped his neck in a fall at St Katherine's Dock.'

Malachy levered up a section of the lid. The cheap wood splintered and creaked open. Enoch and Jasper tugged at the split and succeeded in heaving it open, exposing the body wrapped in its crumpled cloth. Malachy grinned and drew back the burial shroud.

'Just look at him,' he said. 'He's a right Sleeping Beauty and no mistake.' He leaned forward. 'Phew, he don't half pong for somebody newly buried.'

'That ain't him, you numbskull,' Samuel said. 'Didn't I just explain? It's all the noxious gases from the stiffs laid beneath him.' It was his turn to chuckle. 'Smethwick said he was digging up a stiff once and he cut down too far. The corpse beneath was bloated with gases. The moment the spade sliced it open, the whole shebang exploded. He said there were organs and scraps of flesh everywhere. He could have made a pair of earrings out of the kidneys.'

The Rat Boys roared with laughter. Israel felt quite queasy. Once they'd settled down, Samuel held his shaded lantern over the coffin. Through the ruptured lid, it was possible to make out the dead stevedore's features. 'Will you look at his face? He looks so peaceful.' He followed with a mischievous grin. 'It's a shame to wake him.'

'Wake him!' Enoch exclaimed. 'What do you mean?'

Ethan scrambled to the edge of the grave to take a look. 'Don't tell me they buried him alive.'

Jacob and Noah chuckled. 'You're wide of the mark there, Licker. You're talking about Israel's power, ain't you, guv'nor? He can raise the dead.'

171

Israel remembered his dream and felt the creep of dread through the marrow of his bones.

'Come here, Izzy,' Samuel said. 'We're ready for the laying on of hands.'

'You want me to touch *that*?' Israel croaked. 'You don't mean it!'

'Don't tell me you haven't seen your destiny when you dream,' Samuel said. 'Your whole life has been a preparation for this moment. You, my lad, are the gate-keeper of the afterlife.'

'But I can't do it,' Israel said, still averting his eyes from the corpse.

'Oh, but you can,' Samuel said. He laid his hands on Israel's head. 'I want you to cast your mind back a few months. Do you remember that blackbird you found, the one that cat killed?'

Israel's eyes widened. 'How do you know about that?'

Samuel gave him his answer. 'You've been watched almost every waking moment for months now.'

Israel felt a chill curl round his heart.

'The Master was perched on your shoulder when it happened,' Samuel continued. He tapped his forehead. 'He tells me things and I store them away in here.'

'What about the bird?' Israel asked. 'Why did you bring it up?'

'You were upset, weren't you?' Samuel said. 'You didn't like seeing it broken and bloody. You willed it to come back to life.'

'Did it?' Malachy asked, intrigued by the tale. 'Were you able to make it as good as new?'

'Yes,' Israel answered. 'It healed as if by magic. It fluttered away the moment I held it in my hands.' He

172

remembered the way it was forlorn and broken one moment and urgent with new life the next. 'It was a little miracle.'

'That's your power,' Samuel said.

'So is this stiff going to start talking to us?' Malachy asked.

'No, that's too much even for our miracle worker here,' Samuel said. 'It's like this. Lay hands on a creature in those first few minutes after its death and there's every chance it will be right as rain.' He gestured towards the grave. 'It ain't the same with this fellow, of course. He's had time to go cold. His body will revive but his mind's done for. You'll have to do the thinking for him.'

'But what do I do?' Israel asked.

Samuel guided him. 'Just crouch forward and place your hands on his chest.'

Israel was tempted to protest but one look into Samuel's eyes and he thought better of it. Trembling, he laid his palms on the exposed rib cage of the cadaver. Its skin felt cold, like a side of beef hanging in Smithfield market.

'I don't know how,' he said.

'Then don't think about it,' Samuel said. 'The first time a member of the demon brotherhood uses his powers, he doesn't think about it. He lets his natural instincts flow to the surface. Training comes later, to sharpen your abilities.'

'But I don't feel anything,' Israel protested it.

'You're fighting it,' Samuel said, 'just like you've been fighting me. Close your eyes. Remember the first time you saw Lud.'

Israel did as he was told. He relived the blast of heat,

the whipping debris, the glow of the white chapel. He felt the darkness stirring within him, recognizing Lud, reaching out for him.

'That's it,' Samuel said. 'Now, picture the Master's face.'

Israel allowed Lud's blazing, soulless eyes to enter his mind. He felt a curious energy starting to pulse through his veins and flow towards his fingertips. Simultaneously, though he had his eyes closed, the white spire of Christ Church seemed to burn through his lids and a brilliant light slashed into his brain.

'No!'

'Don't struggle,' Samuel told him. 'Let the white chapel enter your soul.'

The spire started to change shape, dissolving then reconstituting itself into a second, whitewashed structure, immense and guarded by four gates.

'Do you see it?' Samuel asked.

'Yes,' Israel said excitedly. Then his voice changed. 'What are those cries? Somebody's in pain.'

'It's only the Master's enemies,' Samuel told him. 'Now, press your fingers harder.'

Israel followed instructions and felt a faint but unmistakeable thump in the corpse's chest. 'There's a heartbeat,' he murmured. His eyes flickered open.

'No,' Samuel said, 'don't look. Close your eyes and guide your power into his flesh. You've seen this moment in your dreams. Soon it will happen for real.'

The cadaver spasmed.

'There,' Samuel said. 'It's begun.'

Israel could feel the connection with the corpse as the heartbeat drummed unnaturally through its inert flesh.

174

'Press deeper,' Samuel ordered. 'Don't relax your grip. That's it. *That's it.*'

Israel felt the body's movement. It underwent a series of violent convulsions then Israel sensed a cold grip on his arms. His eyes flew open. The corpse was sitting up, holding onto him. The boy wanted to scream or vomit or pull away but Samuel was by his side.

'Now stand,' Samuel said. 'Get to your feet and he will follow.'

Israel stood, legs trembling. The corpse followed.

'Step away,' Samuel instructed.

Israel took two steps back and Samuel peeled the corpse's fingers from his arms.

'Tell him what to do,' Samuel said. 'He's no use to us if we can't control him.'

Israel glanced at Samuel. 'What do I say?'

'There's no need to speak,' Samuel said. 'Just think what you want him to do.'

Israel saw a rat scuttering by. At his silent bidding, the living corpse thrust out a hand and seized it. Caught by surprise, the rodent squealed.

'You're not a Rat Boy until you eat a rat,' Israel said.

His companions looked on as the corpse crushed the living rat into its mouth and crunched it, fur, skin, bone, muscle and tissue. Once the corpse had chewed the animal into a bloody pulp, it swallowed, the hairless tail vanishing between its grey lips.

Samuel laughed out loud then clapped his hands. The Rat Boys joined in the applause.

'You did well, Israel,' he said. 'Put him back to bed.' He watched the walking cadaver return to his coffin. There was satisfaction in his eyes.

'What's going to happen now?' Malachy asked.

'Old Corpsey here's just going to take forty winks till we need him. We'll cover him up for now. He's the first soldier in our army.'

'The first?' Malachy said, as Jacob and Noah shovelled earth back into the grave. 'You mean there's going to be more?'

'Oh yes,' Samuel said, 'many more. Israel's going to raise them in their tens, their scores, their hundreds if need be. Our coffin dodgers will break the first of our Master's shackles. The trumpet of his freedom is about to sound.' He clapped Israel on the back. 'Let's go home. We deserve a good night's sleep after this.'

But Israel could still feel his hands on the corpse's dead, cold chest. He wondered if he would ever sleep again.

Twenty-two

From the diary of Arthur Strachan
Tuesday, 12 February, 1839

My fears for Victoria are growing. Something unnatural is happening to her. I was woken in the early hours and crossed the landing to check on her. I found her sprawled across the counterpane, her sleeping form arranged in a kind of victim-like abandon. My gaze was drawn immediately to her right wrist where there was a pronounced wound. It reminded me of a bite mark but how could that be? There has never been any sign of vermin in this house. I inspected the entire room. The sash window was tightly fastened and the door closed.

That is when I lit the gas jets and was disturbed to see the first evidence of an intruder. There were damp footprints on the carpet. Needless to say, after that I explored the household with a fine toothcomb, in search of the interloper. The servants were all asleep in their quarters and there was no sign of forced entry from *outside. When I examined the footprints closer, I found traces of soot mixed into the fibres of the carpet. That led me to an obvious but unsettling conclusion. But what kind of creature can make its way down the chimney? It would have to be thin and extremely agile.*

Returning to my daughter's room, I sat with her for the rest of the night, snatching a few hours of uneasy sleep in the armchair. More than once, I was woken by her groaning. It was incoherent and difficult to decipher. I finally managed to interpret snatches here and there. What I heard gave me great cause for concern. One of the words that fell from her lips was Rector. Dear God, what did I do when I repudiated the fellow? It seems that his threats were far from empty.

Twenty-three

Paul was just finishing his breakfast when the waiter approached his table to tell him he had a visitor. 'Who is it?'

'The gentleman asked me to give you this,' the waiter said, placing a monogrammed card on the table next to Paul's place setting.

Paul read the details: *Mr Arthur Strachan. B.Sc. Edinburgh University. Civil Engineer.*

'Show him in,' Paul said, 'and would you mind bringing us a fresh pot of tea please?'

With money in his pocket and the kind of status wealth conferred, he felt more alive than he had for weeks. Privilege was proving seductive indeed. Waiting for his guest, he felt as if he was holding court here in his Covent Garden hotel. Strachan joined him at the table a few moments later.

'Would you like something to eat, Mr Strachan?' Paul asked.

'Nothing, thank you,' Strachan said in his

179

Edinburgh burr. 'I wish to speak to you about a most serious matter.'

'You mean Victoria?' Paul asked, getting straight to the point.

'I do, Mr Rector,' Strachan said. 'My daughter has taken a turn for the worse. Last night I found damp footprints on the carpet in her room. More disturbingly, there are lacerations to both her wrists.'

This news cast a shadow over Paul's good mood. The tendrils of King Lud reached into every corner of the city. 'What do they look like, these lacerations?'

'By the closest approximation,' Strachan answered, 'I would describe them as . . . bite marks.'

'Are you quite sure?' Paul asked.

'That's what I said,' Strachan replied. 'Some creature, some fiend has entered my daughter's bedroom.' He glanced at the other guests breakfasting around them and lowered his voice. 'Please accept my apologies. I'm beside myself with worry. I'm not a superstitious man, but I cannot ignore the evidence of my own eyes. Something is feasting on my poor child in the night.'

'How deep are these wounds?' Paul asked.

'Not very,' Strachan said. 'The family surgeon thought they might be accidental. He also suggested that, during her hysteria, Victoria might have harmed herself. I was on the point of throwing him out.'

'How is Victoria's health in daylight hours?' Paul asked. 'You told me the last time we met that she was tired.'

'It is not just tiredness,' Strachan said. 'There are long periods of lassitude but she is subject to wild rages too. There are moments when she unleashes the vilest

180

stream of invective at me. I have never heard such foul and abusive language from the lips of a common labouring man, never mind an educated young lady. When I attempt to restrain her, she is liable to spit and scratch and scream until she is hoarse. Sir, I am at my wit's end.'

'May I see her?' Paul asked. 'I don't think any doctor will be able to help her.'

'That is my view entirely,' Strachan said, 'and the reason I am turning to you. I think we both know who is at the root of this matter. Victoria's illness has to have something to do with your relative. I would be in your debt if you would accompany me to the house immediately. I have a carriage outside.'

Paul finished his tea and followed Strachan to his carriage. Twenty minutes later, they were standing outside Victoria's room.

'Prepare yourself, Mr Rector,' Strachan said. 'You are sure to be appalled by the change in my daughter.'

On entering, Paul and Strachan were greeted by the sight of Victoria being restrained by two of Strachan's maids.

'You may go now,' Strachan told them.

Paul could see the relief in the servants' eyes. Their bonnets were askew and their hair had come loose. Victoria had scratched one of them just under her left eye. Paul guessed that they'd been struggling with her ever since their master left the house. When Victoria sat up, spewing insults, Strachan went as if to remonstrate with her.

'No,' Paul said, 'let her speak.'

'Sir,' Strachan said, 'I object. It is an abomination.'

'And one I have to hear,' Paul told him.

Victoria turned towards his voice. Her eyes flashed recognition. 'I know you. I was told you would come.'

'Who told you?' Paul asked.

'One who will destroy you,' the girl snarled in a voice that was deeper and coarser than the last time Paul had met her. 'One who will split your ribs asunder and rip out your heart.'

'Somebody has visited you, Victoria,' Paul said. 'Who was it?'

'Renegade,' she snarled, ignoring the question. 'My Master will devour you, boy.'

'Your Master?' Paul said. 'What's making you so coy? Speak his name, Victoria.'

'You know his name,' Victoria sneered.

'Then you won't mind me hearing it from your own lips.'

'I serve King Lud,' Victoria said, 'once and future lord of all you see about you.'

'Then I'm confused,' Paul said. 'The brotherhood does not admit females to its ranks. They think you're inferior. The demon seed is only found in the male line. Why do *you* serve Lud? How has this happened?'

Victoria's eyes burned with madness. 'Renegade!' she shrieked.

'You haven't given me an answer,' Paul said, continuing to probe.

He made a sudden grab for her hands. She fought him for a moment then he allowed fire to seep from his flesh. Victoria screamed.

'You're hurting her!' Strachan protested.

'Don't interfere,' Paul said. 'I'm not going to do her any lasting harm. I need to get her attention.'

He was becoming more confident of his abilities

every hour. He had judged the intensity of the flame perfectly. It would leave no marks on her hands, no blistering, but the moment of searing pain served to subdue Victoria.

'Who gave you these scars on your wrists?' Paul demanded. 'Was it Samuel? Was it one of his Rat Boys? Who did it, Victoria?'

'He comes each night,' Victoria said, smiling as she savoured the memory. 'My body is wracked with torment until he visits me.' Her eyelids fluttered. 'He is my saviour.'

'Who comes?' Paul cried.

'He presses his lips to my flesh,' Victoria answered dreamily. 'Presently, I feel such a balm of peace.'

Paul glanced at the anxious Strachan, warning him not to interrupt. He lowered his voice.

'Who comes, Victoria?' he asked. 'I need a name.'

'Licker,' Victoria said. 'Licker visits me.'

Paul remembered hearing the nickname. 'Does Ethan Lockett come to you?' he asked.

Victoria gave a blissful smile. 'Ethan. Yes, that's his name. Ethan's the one. He heals me.'

'He doesn't heal you,' Paul said. 'He pumps venom through your mind and soul. Listen to me, Victoria. Lud is evil incarnate. He is using you to threaten your father. You have to resist him.'

Victoria started to twist and turn, snatching back her hands from him. 'Resist my Master? Why should I do such a thing? I am only alive when the divine fire burns in my veins.'

'You don't understand,' Paul said. 'You can never join the demon brotherhood. Lud is using you. When

183

he's finished, he will cast you aside. The seed will destroy you.'

'Liar!' Victoria screamed. 'Leave me be, renegade.' She glared at her father. 'And take that fool with you.'

'Victoria!' Strachan cried. 'I'm your father.'

'You're my enemy!' Victoria retorted. 'I despise you, old man.'

She was about to spring at Strachan. Instinctively, Paul placed a hand on her forehead. Intense heat pulsated from Paul's fingers, flooding her mind with a sudden wave of energy. Her eyes widened in shock then she fell back against the mattress unconscious.

'What did you do to her?' Strachan cried. He swept the limp Victoria up in his arms. 'What did you do to my poor child?'

'Believe me,' Paul said. 'I did nothing. Is she all right?' He leaned forward, stunned to discover another facet of his emerging power. To his relief, Victoria was at rest. 'She will sleep now,' Paul said. He drew Strachan to one side. 'Listen to me. One of Samuel's boys has been visiting your daughter, tasting her blood. He is the cause of her condition.'

Strachan recoiled in horror. 'Dear God!'

'That's his power,' Paul continued. 'That's why they call him Licker. He bends people's minds so that they will serve Lud.'

Strachan stared in horror.

'I have no way of knowing how deep-rooted the infection is,' Paul explained, 'or whether it's reversible. Of this I'm sure, if you allow Ethan to get to her, sooner or later she will be lost to you for ever. You must mount a vigil night and day by her bedside.'

184

'My poor child,' Strachan murmured like an automaton.

'Listen to me,' Paul said. 'You must find a way of securing her to the bed so that she can't go to Ethan. Always make sure that there are at least two of you in the room. One person on his or her own will never repel the intruder. Another thing, whoever keeps vigil must avoid meeting the demon's eyes. If you maintain your vigilance, she may yet be saved.' He snapped his fingers in front of Strachan's face. 'Are you listening to me?'

Strachan finally made eye contact.

'Yes,' he said, 'I'm listening. I will do as you say. She'll not be left alone.'

'There is much that I have to do,' Paul said, 'but I'll be back tomorrow. Don't forget. There must be at least two people in here at all times. They must not meet the intruder's stare.'

Strachan nodded. 'I will ensure everyone understands your instructions. I'm in your debt, Mr Rector.'

'Just call me Paul.'

'Paul, I am in your debt.'

Twenty-four

hat night, Samuel Rector gathered his boys around him in the Rats' Nest. Shadows played on the walls and the wind howled outside.

'Do you want me to call on the daughter, guv'nor?' Ethan asked.

'Not tonight,' Samuel said. 'Let's give Mr Strachan some time to decide what he's going to do. If he doesn't surrender soon, you can call again.'

Ethan looked disappointed.

'Don't be so downcast,' Samuel said. 'If Strachan doesn't do as I say, I will let you pull your little puppet's strings soon enough.'

Israel saw the look of disgust from Betsy. He felt the urge to tell on her well up inside him. He wanted to rip that part of him that was demon from his living flesh and burn it. He tried to resist the voice in his head. I don't belong to you yet, Lud, he thought. He relived the moment the cadaver's heart started beating. What am I, he wondered, to possess such a power? What will

I become if I stay here? Then he thought of his promise to Chaim. He would not succumb to the dark thoughts that raced through his mind. He was going to play his part in Samuel's downfall. For the next hour he had to be content with looking on while the Rat Boys talked and squabbled in their usual manner. Then Samuel said something that made his heart leap.

'I'm going over to the Ten Bells,' he said. 'I'm meeting Smethwick there. He's found some new recruits to my army. Are you ready to use your gifts again, Israel?'

Israel flinched visibly. 'Tonight?'

'No,' Samuel said, 'not tonight. It'll be soon though.'

Israel nodded grudgingly. 'Whatever you say.'

'That's what I like to hear,' Samuel said. 'Now, is there anyone who'd like to accompany me?'

Jacob, Noah and Malachy all stepped forward.

'That's enough,' Samuel said. 'The rest of you will have to keep an eye on our little Izzy.' He glanced at Betsy. 'Don't you want to join us, Bets?'

'No,' Betsy answered, who had been absent-mindedly tinkering with the precious locket where she kept a curl of Molly's hair. 'I'm tired, Sammy. I'm going to turn in if you don't mind.'

'It's a lady's prerogative,' Samuel said.

Then, pulling his greatcoat around him, he led the way downstairs. Betsy listened for the slam of the front door, then she relaxed. At first, the Rat Boys kept a close eye on Israel but it wasn't long before their attention started to wander. Enoch dozed off to sleep while Ezra and Jasper started helping themselves to Samuel's brandy. Once he was satisfied they weren't listening, Israel crept over to Betsy.

'I want you to do something for me, Bets,' he whispered.

'I can't help you,' Betsy answered, darting a glance at the Rat Boys. 'I daren't, Izzy. Have you forgotten what happened to Molly?'

'She would have wanted you to help me,' Israel said. 'Please, Bets. I just want you to take a message to Chaim.'

Betsy's flash was crawling. She willed Israel to keep his voice down. 'No, it's too dangerous.'

'What are you pair whispering about over there?' Jasper slurred.

Betsy could barely breathe. Then Ezra unwittingly came to her aid. 'Give over, Bets,' he chortled, 'Israel's a bit young for you, ain't he?'

Betsy's pounding heart settled. Israel waited until the boys had drained the bottle of brandy completely and were lolling drowsily on their beds before he spoke to Betsy again. 'Chaim's got to know about my power,' he said.

Bets grimaced. 'What, bringing the dead back to life? It ain't right, Israel. Ungodly's what it is.'

'Maybe it's all of that,' Israel said. 'I don't do it out of choice, Bets. In that cemetery I felt like a devil, making that corpse walk around like some cold, obedient machine.' He paused. 'But there's another side to it.'

'There's only one side, if you ask me,' Betsy countered, still desperate for him to leave her alone. 'Bad is bad and that's all there is to it.'

But Israel refused to believe it. 'There's beauty there too. My nature is full of darkness, but there's a spot of light. I can't forget the little bird I brought back to life. That was different.'

Betsy could barely believe her ears. 'How was it different?'

'It didn't have a chance to go cold. I wasn't raising a dead thing. You should have seen it. Its little breast was still warm. When I revived it, it was as good as new, singing and fluttering away into the sky. That can't be wrong, can it? Maybe I can do good, as well as evil.'

Bets shook her head. 'It's for God to say who lives and who dies, not the likes of us, and certainly not the guv'nor.'

'Please, Bets. I've written it all down on this piece of paper. You've just got to put it into Chaim's hand. Samuel don't have to find out.'

'I don't know,' Betsy said. 'What if somebody follows me?'

'You can take care of yourself,' Israel said.

'That's what Molly used to say,' Betsy answered. 'Bold as brass she was and as brave as a Staffordshire bull terrier and look what happened to her. Samuel snapped her like a twig.' Betsy looked at Ezra and Jasper watching from under heavy lids. 'No, I won't do it.'

Israel didn't get a chance to say another word because Betsy crossed the floor to the room she shared with Samuel.

'I'm going to get some kip,' she said. 'The bed's a lot better without him in it.'

Samuel returned some two hours later.

'It's Bethnal Green next,' he announced. 'Smethwick says there's at least a dozen fresh corpses to be had. We're going to add to our army, Izzy boy.' He

189

dropped into his armchair. 'We're on the verge of great things. Ain't that true, Jacob?'

'Of course it is, guv'nor,' Jacob said.

'And what do you say, Noah?' Samuel asked.

'You're the next King of London,' Noah said, not wanting to be outdone.

'That's right,' Samuel said, 'some day soon, I'll climb to the top of St Paul's and gaze across my realm. Imagine it, all those people dancing to the devil's hornpipe. We're going to have so much fun, my lads. Now where's my brandy? I'm going to drink a toast.' He saw the look of panic in Jasper's face. 'What's this? Have you been at my liquor again, Jasper?'

Jasper jumped up. 'It wasn't me, guv'nor. It was Ezra.'

'You lying wretch,' Ezra yelled. 'It was you. I only had but one sip.' He spun round to plead with Samuel. 'He used his power guv'nor. He moved the drink out of its cupboard, then made the cork pop itself.'

'Now who's lying?' Jasper cried. 'You was guzzling it down like a fish.'

They were about to come to blows when Samuel boxed both their ears.

'Which one was it, Izzy?' he asked. 'I know they've both been at my brandy. I just want to know who got the idea first.'

Israel had no wish to see anyone chastised. 'I don't know, guv'nor. I must have dozed off.'

Samuel looked about drunkenly. 'So where's my Betsy? She'll know who the culprit is.' He staggered to his feet. 'Where are you at, Bets?' He pounded on the door to his room. 'You come out here. I want to ask you something.'

Israel heard Betsy's sleepy voice. 'Please, Samuel,' she said, 'I'm trying to get some shut-eye.'

But Samuel wasn't in the mood to take no for an answer. 'Don't talk back to me, girl. You get out here right now!'

'But Sammy . . .'

That was enough to throw Samuel into a fierce rage. He burst into the room and dragged Betsy out in her nightdress. Her bare feet skidded across the floor as he hauled her out. With one powerful hand he lifted her off the floor and snarled in her face. Her eyes were wide with terror.

'Don't you ever say no to me, girl!' he bellowed, shaking her until her teeth rattled. 'I plucked you from the streets and raised you. You belong to me body and soul and don't you forget it.' He leered into her face. 'Have you started remembering your place yet?'

Betsy was terror-stricken. 'I'm sorry, Sammy,' she wailed, quaking before him. 'I didn't mean to upset you.'

She searched his face, willing him to go easy on her. After a few moments, Samuel's face broke into a smile.

'You didn't upset me,' he told her, stroking her hair. 'Even if you did, now's the time to remedy it. You've been here all night. Tell me, which of these two lousy young ruffians got the idea of drinking my brandy?'

Betsy's heart sank. What could she say? 'I don't know, Samuel. I didn't see a thing. I turned in early, didn't I, Izzy?'

Samuel's mood changed once more. 'Liar!' he shouted. 'When did you ever have an early night?' Then, without warning, he struck Betsy across the face. 'Don't you ever defy me, Bets, or you'll suffer for it.' For a moment his fist hovered over her then he stamped over to his room. 'You should be my eyes and ears when I'm out. You've let me down, you idle creature. As a reward, you can doss in the big room with all these boys. There'll be no comfy mattress for you tonight.'

With that, he threw her to the floor and retired to his room. She lay there, chest heaving with fright. Just moments later, he could be heard snoring away. Relieved, Israel went to comfort Betsy. He dabbed the trickle of blood from her nose.

'Thanks, Izzy,' Betsy whispered, 'you're the only human being in here.'

Israel was about to go when she caught hold of his sleeve.

'Let's have that note,' she said. 'I ain't got nothing to lose. I'll get it to Chaim somehow.'

Twenty-five

From the diary of Arthur Strachan
Wednesday, 13 February, 1839

I have been visited by Samuel Rector again. I was walking back from Aldgate this afternoon when a hansom drew up alongside. The door opened and there was Rector. He told me to get in. I decided to listen to what he had to say.

'How's family life?' he asked, exuding the foulest menace any man can imagine.

How I wanted to wipe that leering smile from his face but he is threatening my child's life. I had to bite my tongue and hear him out. When I said that Victoria was unwell, he laughed in my face.

'That's a bit of an understatement, ain't it?' he said. 'I think "possessed" is the proper word for it.' He leaned forward. 'That's right, I'm the one who's behind your trouble. I can decide whether she's mad or sane.'

A week ago I would have thrown his words back in his

face. Now I could only sit in silence while he boasted about his power over me.

'Now,' he said, 'are you going to carry out that work for me as I asked?'

I told him that it was beyond my power to authorize the excavation in defiance of Mr Stephenson.

'That's the wrong answer, Mr Strachan,' the creature said. 'You think Victoria is bad now, but she can get worse, much worse.'

I don't know where I found the courage to defy him but I met his threats with some of my own.

'You won't get near her,' I told him. 'I have taken advice from your relative.'

'Relative?' Rector said. 'If you mean the renegade, I'll be dealing with him presently.'

I wondered what he meant by that. 'We're watching Victoria night and day,' I told him. I remembered the family motto. 'Vince Malum Bono. Good conquers evil.'

'You can quote all the Latin you like,' the blackguard snarled. 'I'll still get to her, you see if I don't.' His eyes flashed. 'As for the renegade, he'll get his just desserts soon enough.'

At that, I demanded to be set down. But, as I descended from the cab, he leaned forward.

'You're a fool, Strachan,' he said. 'I'll get my way in the end. But if you want me to turn the screw again, I'm happy to oblige.'

Then the hansom clattered away into the fog.

Twenty-six

An hour after Samuel Rector picked up Arthur Strachan in his hansom, Paul was sitting in a coffee house, treating Chaim and Betsy to a meal. He'd chosen a rendezvous outside Samuel's home territory. The fact that Betsy was in unfamiliar surroundings, several miles beyond the usual reach of the Rat Boys, didn't stop her casting anxious glances out at the street. She knew that Samuel's brutality had long and poisonous tendrils.

'You look uneasy,' Paul said.

'I just keep thinking about the Rat Boys,' Betsy answered. 'They could come along any time and catch me talking to you.'

Paul noticed that a pair of hawkers had just left a booth in the far corner by the stove.

'Would you be happier sitting over there?' he said. 'There's a wooden partition. Nobody will be able to see us from the street.'

Betsy gave a grateful nod and they changed tables.

'Can you imagine what Samuel will do to me if he knows I've gone behind his back?' she said. 'He got in a terrible rage last night and that was just because I went to bed and didn't keep an eye on the boys.'

'You'll be safe here,' Paul said. 'Try to relax.'

'That's easier said than done,' Betsy told him. 'I've lived in fear most of my life. There are times I wonder whether I'll live to see another dawn.'

'I can imagine,' Paul said. 'I wish I could take you away from him. I'm not going to lie to you and tell you there's a happy ending just around the corner. We're all in great peril. But it will be worse for us if we do nothing. What have you got to tell me?'

Betsy glanced at Chaim. 'Show him the note I gave you,' she said. 'I'll do my best to answer any questions when he's read it.'

The door swung open and two workmen strode in. One stared at Betsy.

'I should go,' she said. 'I can't just sit here letting the day go by. Samuel will want to know what I've been doing.'

'You can spare half an hour,' Paul said. 'Do you still want something to eat?'

'Not half,' Betsy said eagerly. 'Samuel never allows any of us enough to eat. He says we're better for being lean and hungry. I'm always starving in this cold weather.'

Paul smiled. 'You can have anything you want.'

Betsy's eyes lit up. 'Anything?'

'Yes,' Paul said, 'you can eat the whole menu if you wish.'

They ordered mutton stew and a halfpenny cup of tea each, with a plate of sweet buns to follow. While

196

Chaim and Betsy ate, Paul read Israel's note. When he'd finished, he folded it and handed it back to Chaim.

'Were you there when this happened?' Paul asked Betsy. 'Did you see Israel demonstrate his ability?'

Betsy swallowed a mouthful of stew before answering.

'No,' she said, 'Samuel wouldn't allow that. He said it was man's work. He won't involve his girls in this kind of business.' She looked across the table at Paul. There was bitterness in her voice. 'He don't think females are properly human.'

'That's the seed at work,' Paul said. 'The demon is always male.'

'Do you think it's true what Izzy says?' Betsy asked. 'Can he really make the dead walk?'

'I've read his note,' Paul said. 'I've no reason to disbelieve him.'

'That's unnatural,' Betsy said with a shudder.

'Everything about the Rat Boys is unnatural,' Paul said.

'But what's Samuel going to do with a load of walking stiffs?' Chaim asked.

'When Lud was buried,' Paul explained, 'the priests who bound him invested his tomb with protective powers. They were determined to imprison Lud for many centuries. As I understand it, anyone who approaches its walls will face the wrath of their ancient curse. They will be burned alive or, at the very least, driven insane.'

Betsy's eyes widened. Chaim seemed less surprised.

'Don't you see?' Paul continued. 'That's the reason for this army of the undead.'

'To attack the crypt?' Chaim asked.

'Exactly that,' Paul confirmed. 'Samuel is going to hurl all his legions of the undead against the gate until he breaches the seal,' Paul said. 'By using the walking dead as cannon fodder, he won't have to sacrifice his inner circle.'

'How many of these walking cadavers will he need?' Chaim asked.

'I don't know,' Paul said. 'Tens at least, hundreds maybe.' He was repeating what Cormac had told him. 'I can only guess how strong the magic is within those walls.'

Betsy listened then said her piece. 'If I hadn't lived alongside the Rat Boys all these years, I'd have thought you were mad.' She finished her stew and drained her cup of tea. 'But you ain't.'

'Are you ready for this?' Paul asked.

'Half scared out of my wits is what I am,' Betsy answered. 'But I do feel better for a good plate of food.' She picked up a bun and took a bite. 'A girl shouldn't be kept half starved.' She closed her eyes and savoured the sweetness of the bun. 'Oh, that's gorgeous, that is. You're a real gentleman, Mr Paul.'

He grinned. 'It's just Paul.'

'I've got to go now,' Betsy said. 'It's been a pleasure sitting here, remembering what proper human company is like.'

'You're thinking of Molly, aren't you?' Chaim asked.

'Yes, I miss her terribly.' Betsy's eyes took on a faraway look. 'I had a family once. I was happy. Imagine that, I was happy.' She showed them the locket that contained Molly's hair. 'My mother gave me this trinket. It's all I have to remember those days.'

'What happened?' Chaim asked.

'My father made a terrible mistake,' Betsy explained. 'One winter it looked like we were going to end up in the workhouse. He agreed to take part in a robbery. He was only acting as the look-out but the Beak said he was as bad as the others.'

'What happened to him?' Chaim asked.

'He was transported halfway across the world, leaving Ma and me to scrape an existence any way we could. He never did come home. God alone knows where he is now. I don't even know if he's dead or alive.'

'And your mother?'

'She never got over it. She died the next winter of the cholera.' Betsy wiped a tear from her eye. 'You probably think I'm a weak, pathetic creature, but I didn't want to end up like this. Sometimes people look at me like I ain't worth a brass curtain ring. But that ain't true.' She pulled out a handkerchief and blew her nose. 'Me and Molly used to dream of going into service, keeping house for some kind master.'

Paul marvelled at Betsy's narrow horizons. Compared to her present lot, even working as a domestic servant seemed like Heaven.

'We tried to run away once,' Betsy said, resuming her tale. 'We got as far as Epping Forest but Samuel caught us.' She shuddered. 'He put us through Hell for that.' She took a moment to compose herself then added one last comment. 'Here's a funny thing. You've never tried to judge me, neither of you. I'm grateful for that.'

'Why would we judge you?' Paul asked.

'None of this is your fault,' Chaim said. 'Samuel took you in when you were a helpless child. You don't have a thing to be ashamed of. You're a person I'm proud to know, Betsy. You're brave and true. Molly was the same.'

Betsy swallowed hard to hold back the tears. Without a backward glance, she hurried to the door. Paul and Chaim watched as she made her way back towards Spitalfields.

'I fear for her,' Chaim said, 'and Israel too. Tell me we're going to save them.'

'We'll try,' Paul said. 'That's all I can say. We face almost insurmountable odds.'

'You've fought these monsters before, haven't you?' Chaim asked. 'I can hear it in your voice.'

'Yes, I've faced Lud's disciples.' Paul swallowed a mouthful of tea. He didn't say that he was also fighting the monster within every day of his life and that he sometimes feared for his own sanity. 'I'm still learning how it's done.'

'There's so much horror,' Chaim said. 'How do you cope with this life, Paul? You must be forever looking over your shoulder.'

'I don't know if I do cope,' Paul said. 'Every day I want it to be over. I want to go home.'

'So you do have a family?'

Paul nodded. 'Friends too, but they're a long way from here.' A long way distant in the labyrinth of time. 'I can't return to them until Lud is destroyed for good and all.'

'You must be lonely.'

'Yes,' Paul said, 'sometimes I am.'

His eyes travelled over the lost souls sitting or standing in every corner of the coffee house. Chaim sat there in silence, turning his fork over and over between his fingers. He seemed preoccupied. The longer he remained silent, the more Paul got the feeling he had something to say.

'What's on your mind?' he asked. 'If something's bothering you, then you need to get it off your chest.'

Chaim sighed. 'You won't like it.'

'I won't know until you tell me.'

'Sitting here with Betsy, I realized just how much is at stake here,' Chaim said. 'We're all depending on you: me, Betsy, Israel, all of us.'

'I know that,' Paul replied.

'I'm just worried . . .' he set his jaw. 'No, you should forget I said anything.'

'Come on, what's on your mind?'

Chaim finally spoke out. 'I'm worried that you might be losing sight of why you're here.'

Paul frowned but he didn't interrupt.

'Well, we don't seem any closer to defeating Samuel, do we?' Chaim said. 'Just look at you. You've taken to wearing toffs' clothes while Israel and Betsy live in fear. The money you're spending, it's more than poor families earn in a year.' He changed tack. 'You say you're homesick. You say you want the horror to end.'

'Yes?'

'What if King Lud offers you wealth, power?' Chaim asked. 'He's turning Israel. What if he does the same to you?'

'Are you saying I'm going to let you down?' Paul demanded. 'Is that it? For goodness' sake, Chaim, just think what you're saying. You're the one who told me to steal if I had to.'

'I was trying to save your life,' Chaim retorted. 'I thought you'd put some clothes on your back and find somewhere to doss that was better than the streets. Just look at you. You're staying at Hummums and enjoying the good life. I didn't think you would enjoy your new-found wealth so much.'

Paul was shocked to hear such doubts. 'You've no need to worry about me,' he said frostily.

'Then I'll say no more on the matter,' Chaim said, looking away.

Paul immediately regretted the quarrel and wanted to break the tension between them.

'I really won't forget what I'm doing here,' he said. 'In fact, I'm going to take a look at the works around the Minories. I need to see Lud's tomb for myself. Will you come with me?'

Chaim nodded and they walked out onto the street.

Half an hour later, they were picking through the trenches. To their left there was the Tower of London. To their right they could see Aldgate High Street and Houndsditch beyond. The fog had gathered. It was foul-smelling, opaque and yellow. But for once it was welcome, disguising them as it did from the prying eyes of the watchmen. Paul was guiding the way with a lantern he had bought from a chandler's on the way. He half-shielded it with his coat, so as not to attract the attention of anyone who might still be about.

'Over here,' Chaim said. 'I think I've found it.'

Paul joined him at the opening of a deep shaft. From deep within there came a luminous glow. Paul had seen it in so many dreams and visions.

'The white chapel,' he murmured, 'or part of it.'

Chaim rubbed at his forehead.

'I don't understand it,' he said. 'I've broken out in a sweat, and on a cold night like this one.'

'Are you feeling all right?' Paul asked.

'Yes,' Chaim said, 'I think so.' He staggered slightly. 'I just seemed to come over all faint.'

'It's the gate,' Paul said. 'It's warning you to keep away.'

'Why isn't it affecting you?' Chaim asked.

'I think it recognizes me,' Paul said. 'It knows I'm trying to protect it against intruders.'

'You mean the wall *thinks*?' Chaim asked. He blinked rapidly, trying to focus his mind.

'Yes, in a way.'

'There's something else I don't understand,' Chaim said. 'Just before, you called it a chapel.'

'It's many things,' Paul said, 'a chapel, a temple, a crypt, a prison too.' He gave Chaim another long look. His friend was swaying on unsteady legs. 'I think you need to get away from here.'

'I'll wait for you over there, on the corner of Petticoat Lane,' Chaim said. 'How long will you be?'

'Not long,' Paul said. 'I'm going to get a bit closer. I need to see the gate for myself. I want to know how the seal works.' He spotted a sleek, black rat scampering over an iron rail and made a grab for it. 'I'm going to use my rodent friend here to test it.'

He gripped the rodent by the back of its neck. It squirmed and twisted but Paul kept hold of it. There were a series of wooden ladders so he started his climb down the shaft. He'd gone some way when the glow became stronger, each pulse of light striking deep into his brain. In flashes he could just about distinguish the shape and dimensions of the gate. It was a solid slab of pure white rock some ten feet tall and six feet wide. By now, even Paul was beginning to be affected by its power. He shielded his eyes and edged a few rungs further. It took a huge effort to go on. He was disoriented by the strobing light. By now, there was a second distraction as bird-like shrieks filled his head. The echoes of scores of nightmares crashed in his head.

'This will have to do,' he told himself. 'I can't go any further.' He held the squirming rat firmly. 'Let's see what it does when you get too close, my little friend.'

He threw the rat towards the gate. Immediately the creature was enveloped in a ball of liquid fire and reduced to dust. In the darkness Paul could trace the flame's shape. It formed a band that stretched all the way round the gate and the surrounding walls as far as he could see. This had to be the seal. Within moments, the heat died down and the ribbon of fire was lost in the darkness. He could no longer make out the seal. Satisfied with his experiment, he scrambled back to the surface and rejoined Chaim.

'What did you see?' Chaim asked.

Paul did his best to explain. 'Flesh and blood would never survive such sorcery,' he said. 'Only a supernatural army could hope to storm the gate.'

'And Samuel is assembling such an army,' Chaim said, thinking out loud. 'He's using Israel to raise regiments of the undead. Paul, how can we resist such a force?'

Despair seized Paul as he gazed down Whitechapel. 'I only wish I knew.'

Twenty-seven

From the diary of Arthur Strachan
Thursday, 14 February, 1839

My mind is in turmoil. I am tormented by the condition of my poor, tortured child. I have done as Paul bade me, ensuring that Victoria is supervised every moment of the day and night. Dear God, what am I doing? Young Mr Rector is little more than a boy himself. My staff and I are working in four-hour shifts. It is exhausting. Victoria barely sleeps and the invective she pours out quite overwhelms those who have to hear it. One of my maids has already taken to her bed, unable to continue her duties. Two more are threatening to resign their positions. I don't know how long I can go on. I swear, if the monster who calls himself Samuel Rector were to appear this very moment and put his offer to me again, I would probably agree to it.

My pen nib hovers over the page. No, what I have written is not a true statement of my feelings. Sheer tiredness is clouding my judgement. I must not succumb to despair. Samuel Rector is my nemesis and his intentions are evil. I hardly dare imagine what nefarious end would ensue if he were to gain control of the site. But how long must I endure Victoria's dementia? I have decided to consult Paul again. He alone has been able to control Victoria's moods, even if it was only for a few minutes. There must be something we can do to break the spell Samuel has over her.

I will post a letter to him at his hotel this very afternoon.

Twenty-eight

Paul arrived at West Cromwell Place just after eight o'clock that evening, carrying Strachan's letter in his pocket. He jogged up the stone steps to the door of number thirteen, oblivious to the curious eyes. Ethan Lockett was standing in a doorway. The moment the door closed behind Paul, Ethan scurried round the corner to tell Jacob Quiggins what he'd seen. 'Does it change the plan?' Ethan asked.

'That's up to you, Licker,' Jacob said. 'Are you feeling lucky?'

'What do you think?'

Jacob slapped him on the back. 'So you fancy a challenge then?'

Ethan grinned. 'Try to stop me.' With that, he scampered round the back of the house and started scaling the chimney stack.

As before, the maid showed Paul into the drawing room. Gone was the warmth, the air of purposeful activity. Despair now seeped out of the walls.

Strachan too had undergone a transformation. He seemed thinner and less robust than before. His former confident air had been replaced by a deep weariness and lassitude.

'Have you continued to protect her from the demons?' Paul asked.

'She is always under guard,' Strachan confirmed. 'I have also ordered that there is to be a roaring fire in every fireplace. I believe the creature entered my house down the chimney. Is that possible?'

Paul thought of the way the Rat Boys could scuttle up and down the walls of buildings. 'It's possible.'

'Dear God!' Strachan murmured.

Paul nodded. 'May I see her?'

The scene in Victoria's room was profoundly disturbing. Her bedclothes were torn. The headboard of her bed was criss-crossed with scratches where she had clawed at the wood in an attempt to break free of her bonds. Victoria herself was a skeletal shadow. Her cheeks were sunken and her eyes were deep, dark pits.

Paul examined the scars on her wrists. They had scabbed over. Licker hadn't returned.

'Renegade!' Victoria spat, straining against the straps that held her down.

'She isn't eating, is she?' Paul asked.

Strachan shook his head. 'She's starving herself to death. She just keeps asking for this creature called Licker.'

Paul glanced at the other people in the room, a manservant and a maid and drew Strachan to one side.

'I hardly know what to say,' he murmured. 'I have no cure to give her. All I can tell you is that you must not surrender to Samuel.'

'Is that the only advice you can give me?' Strachan cried. 'You were my last hope. Sir, I am resisting him body and soul, but Victoria is all I have. I can't go on watching her suffer like this.'

All Paul could do was stick stubbornly to his point. 'No matter how intense your anguish becomes, you must not permit Samuel to control Lud's crypt. The consequences would be incalculable.'

He knew that he must sound unfeeling but what else could he do?

Strachan glanced again at the servants. 'Can we discuss this somewhere else where we're not going to be overheard?'

He guided Paul into a long gallery, bare except for a desk and a rack of rolled-up plans. Paul stiffened. He had been in this room, a hundred years hence, in another age. He saw the Strachan family motto: *Vince Malum Bono*.

'So tell me,' Strachan said, hostility crackling in his voice, 'how am I to continue to refuse your relative's demands when I am being forced to witness the slow death of my child?'

Just as Paul was about to answer there was a loud crash.

'Victoria!' Strachan cried.

He ran from the room. Paul followed. They saw the manservant hurrying towards them from the opposite end of the corridor.

'What are you doing out here?' Strachan demanded. 'Why did you leave the room? Did I not give you express instructions?'

'I was tired and thirsty,' the man answered. 'I'm sorry, sir, but nobody has relieved me for eight hours.

209

It's only supposed to be four. I had to get out of the room. I thought it would be all right.'

'Does it sound as if it's all right?' Strachan cried.

They burst into Victoria's room. It was a scene of devastation. The maid was lying sprawled on the floor, unconscious. The window was shattered, shards of glass covering the bed and the carpet. Worst of all, Victoria was gone.

'No,' Strachan groaned, 'oh dear God, no.'

While the manservant tended to the maid, Paul vaulted over the window sill and dropped down into the garden. He saw three pairs of footprints leading to a back gate. There was also a scrap of Victoria's nightgown hanging from the post where she must have snagged it. Paul tried to give chase but Victoria and her abductor had already vanished into the night. It was with a heavy heart that he returned to the house. In response to Strachan's pleading look, he simply shook his head.

'I know that you must be in despair,' he said, 'but you can't do what Samuel says. It won't get Victoria back and it will place the lives of many more in danger.'

It wasn't what Strachan wanted to hear. His eyes blazed with fury. 'You told me you could help. Now the monster has stolen my daughter from under your very nose. What earthly good are you?'

'You feel as if your life has been torn apart,' Paul said. 'But you have to listen to me—'

Strachan interrupted. 'No, I don't have to listen. I will do whatever is necessary to secure her safe return.'

Paul's heart gave a panicky thud. 'What do you mean?'

'Exactly what I say, even if it means acceding to the monster's demands.'

'You can't do that,' Paul protested. 'Don't you understand? She's lost to you already. If we can only find a way to break Samuel's power, we may yet recover Victoria.'

'Damn you!' Strachan shouted. 'What have you brought me but more grief?' He sank his head in his hands. 'How am I to know you're not in league with the villain?' A change came over him and he glared through his fingers. 'I was suspicious of you from the very beginning. How could a mere boy save my daughter from that blackguard, especially one who carried the Rector name. Yet I trusted you. Well, no more!'

Paul saw eyes full of hatred staring back at him.

'You've been part of this conspiracy all along. You wheedled your way into my house. You got me out of the room so they could take her.'

'Mr Strachan,' Paul objected. 'Grief is making you say these things. It was you who asked me to leave the room.'

Strachan was no longer listening. 'Get out!' he yelled. 'Leave my house this instant.'

'But—'

'Get out!'

Paul stared helplessly at him, then turned and walked away down the corridor. There was no more to be done. Paul had just reached the door when he heard someone call his name. Strachan's manservant caught up with him. 'Don't go, Sir. He didn't mean it.'

'You're probably right,' Paul said. 'It doesn't alter the outcome of this evening. Our enemy has your mistress in his possession. Your master is going to do anything he says.' He let himself out. 'Goodnight.'

Paul stepped onto the pavement. A thin mist hung around the streetlamps. As he walked towards Hummums, he was overwhelmed by hopelessness. The Rat Boys had Victoria. It was only a matter of time before Strachan surrendered to Samuel's will and handed him control of the ground around the gate to the crypt. Once it was done, Samuel would assemble his army of the undead for the assault. Then time itself would begin to unravel. Lud could remake the future. He had all but won.

'But what can I do?' Paul wondered.

Then he remembered that he had an ally.

Twenty-nine

The following afternoon there was a knock at the
door in Flower and Dean Street.

'That's my visitor,' Samuel said. 'Run down and
let him in, Betsy.' He lay back in his armchair and
stretched. 'I'm going to enjoy this.'

Betsy did as she was told and descended the stairs
to admit Samuel's guest. Noah wandered over to
Samuel.

'Don't take this the wrong way, guv'nor,' he said,
'but are you quite sure you can trust her?' He watched
from the landing as Betsy answered the door.

'What's that you're saying?' Samuel growled.

Noah flinched under his master's stare. 'I was only
thinking out loud. I didn't mean nuffin' by it.'

But Samuel's initial anger had been replaced by
curiosity. Could there be something in Noah's suspicions? 'If you've got something to say about Betsy, let's
hear it.'

'It's just the way she's been acting,' Noah said. 'She's

been looking at everybody very strangely of late. I catch her eye sometimes and I don't see the same Betsy. I ain't imagining it, guv'nor. She's different.'

He had Samuel's attention. 'Different how?'

Betsy was returning with the guest. A man's voice could be heard.

'Haven't you noticed?' Noah asked. 'You know Betsy better than any of us. She's always done everything you tell her, meek as a lamb. She used to come across real spineless, like she needed someone to think for her all the time. She ain't been the same since Molly died.' He realized what he was saying. 'That's it. When I look Betsy in the eye, it's as if it's Molly who's staring back. Does that make any sense, guv'nor?'

Samuel held Noah's gaze for a few moments then he watched Betsy enter the room, followed by Strachan. Molly's eyes? It gave him food for thought. It was a moment or two before Samuel's stare shifted to his visitor.

'Well, well,' Samuel said, 'if it ain't Mr Strachan. Does this mean you've had a change of mind?'

Noah examined the newcomer. 'Lor,' he said, 'will you look at his fine togs!'

'You must excuse Noah,' Samuel said. 'Where's your manners, you jolter-head? Get the gentleman a seat.'

'That won't be necessary,' Strachan said. 'I prefer to stand.'

'Have it your own way,' Samuel said. He affected a yawn. 'I was wondering how long it would be before you turned up at my doorstep. Have you got something to say?'

214

Strachan looked around the room with an obvious expression of distaste. 'I want my daughter back,' he said.

'You can have her any time,' Samuel said, 'on one condition.'

'What's that?'

'Don't play games with me, Mr Strachan,' Samuel said. 'You know what I want to hear.'

Strachan cleared his throat nervously. 'I have conceded to your demands, sir. I have ordered excavation work to begin this very day. The first gang of tunnellers are already at work. The ground is yours, sir.'

'And the gate won't be disturbed until I've finished my work there?'

'I give you my word.'

Samuel was enjoying his moment of triumph. 'Now, ain't you a sensible gentleman, Mr Strachan?' he gloated. 'Do I take it that you've dispensed with the services of my relative?'

'I shall have nothing more to do with Paul Rector,' Strachan said. 'I have instructed that he be refused admission to my home.'

'That's good,' Samuel said. 'You've made me a very happy man.'

'I've kept my side of the bargain,' Strachan said. 'You must keep yours. Where's my daughter?'

'Go and get her, Bets,' Samuel said. 'May I introduce my business colleagues, Mr Strachan? Over here we have Jacob and Noah.'

'Charmed, I'm sure,' said Noah, doffing his cap and bowing.

Jacob just laughed.

'This is Jasper,' Samuel continued, 'and over there

you've got Ethan, Ezra and Enoch. Finally, these two young rogues are Malachy and Israel.'

Strachan didn't say a word. After a few moments Betsy returned with Victoria. Strachan appraised her condition. Gone were the demonic tantrums. She was subdued and some of the colour had returned to her face.

'As you can see,' Samuel said, 'Victoria's on the mend. My Betsy made her some broth last night. It's done her the world of good.'

'Let's dispense with the pleasantries,' Strachan said, scowling. 'You're no friend of mine.' He kept his gaze averted from Samuel's. 'You've got what you want. That doesn't mean I have to stand here and listen to you. I just want to take my daughter and leave.'

'Nobody's stopping you,' Samuel said. 'The door's open. You can go whenever you like.'

'Come with me, Victoria,' Strachan said, holding out his hand.

Victoria glanced across at Ethan. He nodded and she joined her father. Strachan led her down the stairs.

'It's been a pleasure doing business with you,' Samuel called.

A moment later the front door slammed so hard the whole house shook.

'Is it something I said?' Samuel asked.

The Rat Boys sniggered. Betsy and Israel swapped glances. The exchange of looks wasn't lost on Noah. He resolved to keep a close eye on the pair.

The next two hours were typical of the Rats' Nest. There was some drinking and squabbling. Samuel discovered that Malachy had held back a shilling and gave

216

him a brutal beating for his pains. About seven o'clock Betsy gathered her shawl from a peg by the door.

'Where are you off to, Bets?' Samuel asked.

'You wanted me to collect off the shopkeepers,' Betsy answered. It was his new task for her now. The shopkeepers paid him a weekly amount for protection, though the only person they needed protection from was Samuel himself.

Remembering what Noah had said, Samuel put a question to her. 'Early though, aren't you, Bets?'

'Whatever do you mean?'

'Exactly what I say,' Samuel drawled, observing the nervous tic in Betsy's eye as she tried to disguise her fear. 'You seem in a hurry to leave our little abode.'

'Well, maybe I am going out a little bit early,' Betsy conceded. 'I need a breath of fresh air.'

'Fresh air,' Samuel scoffed, 'in the East End? Wherever do you go walking, my dear? All I can smell is animal dung, slaughterhouses and open sewers. Have you taken to going up West for your constitutionals perhaps?'

At the mention of the West End, Betsy swallowed hard. Did he know something? Try as she might, she was unable to disguise her anxiety. 'You don't catch me going all that way. She knows her place, does Betsy and that's right here in her own back yard.'

Samuel walked over to her, drawing Israel's attention. He laid his hands on Betsy's shoulders. 'I do like you, Bets,' he said. 'I wouldn't be happy if anything was to happen to you.'

Betsy's eyelids fluttered nervously. 'You've no cause to worry on that, Sammy. I'm your girl now. Who's

217

going to hurt me when they've got you to account to?' She grabbed her shawl. 'I'll be back presently.'

With that, she fled into the early evening dark. Samuel gestured to Noah who leaned forward to receive his instructions.

'Follow her,' he said. 'You're right. She's up to something.'

Soon Betsy had reached Osborn Street. She glanced right towards Brick Lane then crossed the road. Noah was in high spirits. He couldn't wait to see the fireworks when he reported back on Betsy's little expedition. It wasn't long before his sense of excitement reached fever pitch. Another ten minutes' walk brought Betsy to St Botolph's Church. Noah watched her enter, then transformed so that he could scamper up the walls and watch from a window.

Betsy entered the church, glancing at the carved ceiling and decorative plasterwork. She glimpsed Paul sitting in one of the front pews, staring straight ahead. Instinctively removing the shawl from her head, she went to join him.

'You came.' Paul glanced around. 'Are you sure you weren't followed?'

'I didn't see nobody,' Betsy replied.

'Do you have any news?'

'I should say,' Betsy answered. 'It's that engineer.'

'Strachan? What about him?'

'He came to the house this afternoon,' Betsy said. 'He's started clearing the earth from around the crypt or temple or whatever it is.'

Paul rubbed wearily at his temple. 'So Samuel's got his way at last.'

'What are we going to do?' Betsy asked. 'It can only be a matter of days before the way is open to this gate of yours.'

Paul considered her words. 'You're right. Listen, Betsy, you're taking a terrible risk coming here. I've got to get you out of that house.'

'What about Israel?' Betsy asked. 'I'd leave tomorrow if it wasn't for him. And where are you going to get your information from?'

'I don't like it,' Paul said. 'We both know what happened to Molly.'

'I won't be persuaded,' Betsy told him. 'I can't leave Israel to those vultures.'

'You won't be deserting him,' Paul said. 'I'll be watching the house. Chaim's lending a hand too. He's been keeping an eye on Israel when he visits the graveyards.' The church bell tolled. 'In fact he should be on his way to the house now. Just don't acknowledge him if you happen to see him.'

'I won't,' Betsy assured him.

Paul took her hands. 'Are you sure you want to go back?'

Betsy shook her head. 'I don't want to go nowhere near Samuel Rector ever again,' she said. 'I feel mortally sick when he touches me. But I won't rest till Molly's avenged.'

'Fine,' Paul said, 'you can go back this once but I'm getting you out of there as soon as I can. Don't meet me here again. I'll find you next time.'

Betsy nodded. 'It's going to be all right,' she said, getting up and heading for the door. 'Some day soon you, me and Chaim are going to sit down in some fancy restaurant reminiscing about these times.'

Paul smiled. 'Yes, some day we'll do that.'

He watched Betsy slip away into the night. He allowed her five minutes then he walked to the door himself. He had more questions for O'Shaughnessy, his informant in the underworld. He smiled as he imagined the look of horror on the warehouseman's face.

Up at the East window, Noah smiled too, though for a different reason. He would be well-rewarded for his night's work.

Not half an hour later, Noah broke the news to Samuel.

'So that's her game, is it?' Samuel growled. 'She's working for the renegade. Don't these wenches ever learn, Noah? Didn't she see how Molly ended up?'

'What are you going to do to her, guv'nor?' Noah asked.

'Why, I'll strew her worthless brains on the street, so I will!' Samuel paced the floor, watched by the other boys. 'I'll rip out her heart. Nobody takes liberties with Samuel Rector.' He was working himself up into a rage. 'I put a roof over her head and food in her belly. I trusted her and made her my girl. Now this is how she repays me.'

'It's a crying shame, guv'nor,' Ezra said.

'It's worse than that,' Noah said, stirring the pot. 'It's treachery.'

'That's the very word,' Samuel agreed. 'Treachery.'

'Do you want us to go looking for her?' Jasper asked.

'There's no need,' Samuel said. 'She'll come crawling back when she's good and ready. I'm a patient man. I can wait.'

Thirty

From the diary of Arthur Strachan
Sunday, 17 February, 1839

*T*he monster has broken his promise. My men completed the work yesterday, digging out a ramp to the
white gate. But what is my reward? I was woken in the
night to be informed that Victoria had been spirited
away once more. Both of my daughter's carers were
found in a state of hypnotic trance, as if half scared to
death. Of Victoria, there was no sign.

She returned to her bed this morning. Sad to say, my
spirits remain as low as they were when she vanished.
Her hair is wild and tangled with twigs. Her legs are
smeared with mud. Strangest of all are her fingers. The
fingernails are gone entirely. At first I screamed in
horror. Had the demons torn them out? Were they
torturing poor Victoria in her madness? But there is no
sign of blood or any damage to the flesh. For all that, I
am not content. I ran my fingertips over the skin where

her fingernails ought to be. There's something there. I'm not imagining it. Buried within the flesh is some new growth. It feels claw-like. I have not spoken of it to anyone. They would commit me to Bedlam for even speaking of it. Yet every moment my sense of apprehension grows. What foul metamorphosis has begun?

As to the scars on her wrist, always ugly, they are now livid and seeping. There is something else. She smells of rotten wood. All around her there is an air of decay. Yes, there is something of the graveyard about her. Where has she been all night?

Thirty-one

Betsy made her way back to the Rats' Nest about eight o'clock that night, weaving through the drunken revellers who were spilling from the Ten Bells. The rain was drumming on the pavements and it was getting heavier. She was already quite soaked through. She paused by Fashion Court at the far end of the Flowery and looked up at the dirty, decayed house that had been her home since she was nine years old. She glimpsed a blurred shape in a doorway and a chill swept her slight frame. That's when she realized it must be Chaim. By way of confirmation, he gave her a brief wave. His presence cheered her a little.

Drawing a deep breath, she opened the door and started to climb the stairs. Her tread had never been as heavy as it was since Paul, Chaim and Israel had come into her life. The more tantalising the promise of escape from this life of slavery and fear, the greater her dismay each time she entered the oppressive house. As she approached the top landing, the door to the Rats' Nest swung open. Noah was silhouetted against the light of a tallow candle. The whole place seemed strangely silent. Betsy couldn't help but think that the expectant hush was for her. She gripped the banister and forced herself forward. Her heart was pounding and her throat tightened as she brushed past Noah. Something was wrong.

'The guv'nor wants to see you,' he said.

Betsy forced a smile. 'Ain't it nice to be welcomed home?' she said, as brightly as she was able.

Noah followed her inside.

'Have you been waiting for me?' Betsy asked.

When Noah didn't answer, she felt the creep of apprehension grow stronger. She saw Samuel and his Rat Boys seated around the room watching her, as if in judgement. There was hostility in every face except Israel's. But there was no comfort there either. He looked utterly terrified.

'What's going on, Sammy?' she asked. 'Why's everyone so quiet?'

She noticed that the window was open. Samuel rose from his armchair and gazed outside.

'Where've you been, Bets?' he asked.

His voice was low, though no less menacing for that. The wind howled in behind him, spraying the floor with freezing droplets of rain.

'You know where I've been,' Betsy said. 'I've been collecting your protection money.'

Samuel held out his hand. 'Let's be having it then.'

She handed over the two shillings she'd collected on the way back from her meeting with Paul. The rain gusted in, peppering both of them with its icy touch.

224

'You've been gone a long time to bring back just two shillings,' Samuel observed.

Betsy frowned. The pulse in her throat was thudding violently. 'Whatever do you mean, Sammy?'

'You're wearing a new perfume,' Samuel said. 'You smell of renegade.' He glanced at Noah. 'What do you think?'

Noah gave a humourless smile. 'You've got a sharp sense of smell, guv'nor. You're right though. I think I recognize it. She reeks of the boy Rector.'

A rush of panic welled up from deep inside Betsy's chest.

'Why, guv'nor,' Noah exclaimed, in mock astonishment, 'I do think she's in league with your sworn enemy.'

Betsy looked away from Samuel but she could feel his gaze upon her, suspicious and cold.

'I don't know what you're t-talking about,' she stammered.

Samuel latched onto her frightened stutter and mimicked it cruelly. 'I'm t-talking about a stupid, wayward girl who don't know which side her b-bread is buttered. I'm talking about a girl who heads up West for a meeting without telling the man who's put a roof over her head all these years.'

'Sammy,' Betsy said, 'I only went as far as Coulston Street. You know I'd never stray all the way up West. You've got this all wrong.'

'No, he ain't,' Noah interrupted. 'When did you turn all religious, Bets?'

They were the words that finally confirmed to Betsy that she was lost. Her voice shrunk to less than a whisper.

225

'What did you say?'

Israel was sitting on the edge of his seat, desperate to do something to put a halt to the interrogation.

'You heard,' Noah said. 'I saw you go inside St Botolph's. I saw you walk to the front pew and sit down next to a cove I knew only too well.' He grinned. 'Yes, I saw you talking to the guv'nor's worst enemy.' He turned the screw. 'You had your heads together all lovey dovey.' He challenged her with a stare. 'I don't hear you denying it.'

'Stop this!' Israel cried, rising to his feet. 'I had to watch Molly die. I won't sit in silence while you kill Betsy too.'

Samuel turned round. 'What's this, Izzy? Found your voice at last, have you? Now you're telling me what you will and won't do. When did you get so bold as to go giving orders? I've let you have my protection so far. Don't push your luck. Ezra, Jasper, get hold of him.'

Ezra and Jasper pinned Israel against the wall. Israel struggled but they were too strong. 'Don't hurt her,' he cried.

Samuel wasn't listening. He marched across the room towards Betsy. She retreated onto the landing, thrusting out her hands in a feeble attempt at self-defence.

'Noah says you've got Molly's eyes,' Samuel said. 'Now I know what he means. When I look at you I see nine parts deception and one part defiance. Yes, you've learned Molly's troublesome ways.' He gave the open window a sideways glance. 'Well, you can have her fate too, if you like. Come here, Bets. Take your punishment like a good girl.'

Betsy had retreated as far as the top of the stairs, her hands thrown out in self defence.

'Get away from me!' she cried.

Samuel kept on coming.

'Run, Betsy,' Israel cried. 'It's your only chance.'

But Betsy was too paralysed with fear. She pounded her fists against Samuel's powerful chest in a vain attempt to protect herself. For a moment she struggled with him then he let go and she tumbled backwards down the stairs.

'No!' Israel cried, as he heard Betsy's skull crack against the stairs.

'Now ain't that a shame,' Samuel said, turning round. 'She's taken a tumble all the way down to the bottom. And there's me wanting to drop her out of the window like I did Molly. I had it all planned. I do like symmetry. Look at that. She's quite spoiled my night.'

'You're a monster!' Israel cried as Samuel sauntered back into the room.

Ezra and Jasper had relaxed their hold on him. He struggled free, and ran from the room. What followed was the tortured sound of him sobbing over the dead girl. The Rat Boys stared at Samuel. Few of them had protested when he killed Molly. With her fiery temper, she had always been an irritant. Betsy was different. Demons that they were, they still remembered her caring nature, the way she had comforted them when they first came to the Rats' Nest.

'What are you looking at?' Samuel barked.

They lowered their heads. 'Nothing.'

'Bring Izzy back,' Samuel said.

Ezra and Jasper set off after Israel. They weren't in any hurry. There was no chance of him bolting. They knew Lud's hold on Israel was too strong. He would never be able to break free of the Rat Boys. Samuel opened a bottle of brandy and downed a third of it in one swallow.

'It's a pity about Bets,' he said when he'd finished. 'She was a pretty little thing. Why can't these girls be more obedient? Why, I'd—'

He was interrupted by the sounds of struggle followed by Ezra's voice. 'Guv'nor, she's gone.'

'What do you mean *gone*?' Samuel ran to the top of the stairs. His face was white with rage and disbelief.

'You've got to see this,' Jasper shouted.

Samuel joined them in the hall. The front door was wide open and the wind was gusting in. Israel had his back to the wall and his body was convulsed with laughter.

'What did you do?' Samuel roared. He was already thinking of Lud's wrath. Israel continued to laugh. 'I asked you a question,' Samuel repeated. 'What did you do?'

'Remember that blackbird?' Israel answered, mustering what defiance he could. 'That's right, you're the one who gave me the idea in the first place. If a creature's still warm, you said, I can make it as good as new. Well, that's what I've done, guv'nor.' He pointed at the open door. 'I revived her and sent her on her way and there ain't a thing you can do about it.'

Samuel stared.

'You've lost,' Israel laughed. 'You won't hurt Betsy any more.'

'You're lying,' Samuel said. 'You wouldn't dare defy me.'

'No guv'nor,' Jasper told him. 'Israel's telling the

truth. We was halfway down the stairs when we saw her rise up and stagger into the arms of the Wetzel boy. Then Israel fought us tooth and nail while Betsy made her getaway with him.'

Samuel was beside himself. 'You defied me!'

'That's right,' Israel said. 'I know I can't get away from you. Lud would find me wherever I ran. But Betsy's got a chance.'

'Find her!' Samuel cried. 'She can't have got far.'

'I wouldn't be so sure,' Israel retorted. 'Chaim had a hansom waiting. That's right, Paul paid for it.'

'The renegade!'

'Yes,' Israel said, 'the renegade. He got one over you this time, didn't he?'

The Rat Boys poured into the night but Chaim and Betsy were long gone.

Thirty-two

Samuel Rector sat brooding well into the night, waiting for Lud to appear. If any of Samuel's many victims had seen him then, they would have been astonished at his transformation from the brutal bully they had known. He was sitting hunched, eyes darting fearfully to left and right. He had good cause to be afraid. His Master was bound to be displeased by Betsy's disappearance, but mainly by Israel's continuing defiance. The clock had just struck when Samuel felt the familiar rush of air. Dust started to whirl around him. He turned to face the direction of his Lord's approach. Soon, Lud's dark vortex started to swirl before him and the light of the white chapel radiated around the room.

Samuel swallowed hard and greeted his Lord. 'Master.'

'You seem troubled, Samuel,' Lud said. 'Why so?'

Samuel grovelled, head and shoulders bowed. 'I have failed you, Master,' he answered in a broken voice. 'I have encountered my first obstacle and I don't know what to do.'

There was no emotion in Lud's voice. 'Explain.'

'It's Israel,' Samuel said. 'He is resisting us. He helped Betsy get away.'

'Ah,' Lud said, 'so he spirited away your little plaything. No wonder you're upset.'

Samuel blurted out a hasty explanation.

Lud was not surprised by the turn of events. 'I half expected something like this. The renegade is growing in strength and confidence and Israel has more courage than you imagine. You need not worry. I won't punish you.'

Samuel's spirits lifted. Where was the fury he'd been expecting? Where was the retribution?

'Climb up onto the roof, Samuel,' Lud commanded. 'We will talk in private. I won't have the boy eavesdropping on us.'

Samuel was sure Israel was fast asleep but he obeyed anyway. He shoved open the skylight and clambered outside. He gazed at the storm clouds as they raced past the towering spire of Christ Church. Soon Lud reappeared.

'The powers of the demon brotherhood are many and varied,' he said, raising his voice above the howl of the wind. 'But Israel is unique. The nature of his talents was always going to pose a problem for us, Samuel. To reach through the dark curtain between life and death is to challenge the very fabric of time itself. Israel, like the renegade, is one of the mavericks of demon kind. His abilities have given him a bargaining counter in his dealings with us.'

'I agree,' Samuel said. 'He isn't our usual kind of

231

recruit. He doesn't easily fall under your spell. There is little appetite for mischief in him.'

'Almost none,' Lud said. 'That makes him difficult to control by our usual methods.'

'But he has obeyed us until this moment,' Samuel said.

'He is weaker than the renegade,' Lud said. 'He lacks the willpower to break away and chart an independent course. For all that, he is not proving as pliable as my other disciples. I had hoped to make him my willing pawn by now but he continues to find ways to oppose me.'

'Can you overcome his resistance, Master?' Samuel asked.

'In time I believe I can,' Lud said. 'Once we have destroyed the renegade and the boy Chaim, Israel will break too. He is sentimental. That's his weakness.'

'I am still concerned, Lord,' Samuel said. 'Don't we depend on him to deliver the undead? What if he refuses to attack the gate?'

'I'm sure that's precisely what he has in mind,' Lud said. His image shimmered. 'Israel has defied us. In the greater scheme of things, we will still prevail.'

'We will?' Samuel asked. 'Israel holds a powerful advantage. Without him, we will not raise the undead.'

'Israel is over-confident,' Lud explained. 'He is beginning to master his powers. Have you noticed how he's revelling in his new-found abilities? This is the most dangerous moment for the apprentice demon. This is when he can over-reach himself.' The demon master's translucent form floated around the chimney stack. 'Believe me, he is no match for us.'

Samuel didn't understand. Why was the Master so

untroubled by the setback? What was the boy's Achilles' heel? Lud anticipated the question.

'Let him think he's got the better of us,' Lud said. 'You must play your part well, Samuel. I expect you to be all suppressed rage.' He nodded to himself. 'That shouldn't be difficult. But there's one thing Israel doesn't know. Think, Samuel, where is my power at its strongest?'

'At the gate to your crypt, Master.'

'Well done, Samuel,' Lud said. 'That's where Israel will be broken.' The demon master's image glowed with joy. 'I have permitted him to believe he has exclusive power over the undead.'

'And he doesn't?'

'Samuel, Samuel,' Lud growled, 'what have I done to make you doubt me so? Of course he doesn't. When he reaches the gate, I will show him who is the true master of the creatures.' There was a moment's silence when the wind tore and clutched at Samuel's clothes. 'Because of the confinement of my physical form,' Lud said, 'the graveyards and burial grounds of London are beyond my reach. I need the boy to raise the army and deliver it to me. But once they reach the precincts of the white chapel, I will assume control from the boy. That will be your opportunity, Samuel. Israel will be helpless before you. Find the girl and make sure she is present to witness my triumph as the first seal is broken. Then you can do with them what you will. You will have your revenge.'

Samuel was silent for a few moments as he imagined the agonies he would inflict upon Israel and Betsy.

Lud waited for several moments before he spoke

233

again. 'You can make it as slow and painful as you wish. Are you happy now, disciple?'

Samuel smiled. 'Yes, Master.'

He turned to go but Lud's translucent form enveloped him. 'Don't be too quick to retire to your bed, Samuel,' Lud told him. 'I have another piece of news for you. It is equally as good as the first, maybe better.'

Soon Samuel was swept by an overpowering sense of triumph. When he did climb into bed it was with a cruel joy in his heart. His Master had outwitted the renegade. One by one, Samuel conjured the images of his enemies: Israel, Betsy, Chaim and the renegade Paul Rector himself. Soon every one of them would perish.

He would enjoy prolonging their death agonies.

Thirty-three

From the diary of Arthur Strachan
Tuesday, 19 February, 1839

The nights are always long and dark. I sit alone at Victoria's bedside, waiting for the demons to come. Samuel was never going to return my beloved daughter to me. The servants will no longer keep vigil. They are too afraid of what will appear once the sun has set. What a fool I was to vent my anger upon Paul. He was a true ally and I drove him away with my show of temper. It is days since I have snatched more than an hour's troubled sleep.

This evening I tried to get some work done. I retired to the study and started to examine my plans. I have always felt at home in the long, low-ceilinged room. Seated at my desk beneath the family motto, I have felt protected. *Vince Malum Bono. Good conquers evil.* A few hours ago something happened to destroy that sense of security for ever. About eight o'clock the door swung open.

I saw Victoria's gaunt, skeletal form silhouetted in the doorway.

I duly rose to guide her back to bed but, as I had feared, she struggled. Such was her inhuman strength, I found myself unable to restrain her. She threw me roughly to the floor. As I rose to my feet, my blood ran cold. I had an explanation for the mysterious hardness beneath her fingertips. Like a cat unsheathing its claws, Victoria produced a set of lethal talons that glinted in the candle-light.

'What are you going to do?' I asked fearfully.

She crossed the floor to the wall facing the family motto and started slashing and cutting, her talons scoring a satanic response to my question. This is what it read: Ut Malus Sim, Vince Bonum Male. *Evil conquers good.* Even then, the horror wasn't at an end. Blood started to foam from the deeply-gouged lettering and the room filled with the most awful stench. It was like brimstone. Victoria stood smiling a while, taking pleasure in the look of revulsion on my face. Then, still barefoot, she padded from the room and closed the door. During the entire macabre performance, she didn't say a single word.

Is it any wonder I dread each new day?

Thirty-four

Paul dismissed his carriage and walked over to the grass verge. The driver had dropped him at a crossroads in the countryside two miles outside London and was turning the horse around. Paul's meeting with Mrs Flaherty and O'Shaughnessy had been fruitful. They knew London's underworld inside out. Paul was about to meet the man Mrs Flaherty had recommended for the next stage of his plan.

'Be sure to return at five o'clock precisely,' he told the driver. 'I'll be here waiting for you.' He paid the man in silver coins. 'I will give you the remainder on our return to the city.'

The driver nodded and flicked the reins. Paul watched the carriage as it disappeared over a hill. He found a milestone and perched on it. He hoped the man he was due to meet would be on time but he wasn't. It was another half hour before Paul heard the crunch of gravel.

'Mr Kidd?' Paul enquired as a lean, dark-haired man in his late forties strode into view.

'I'm Kidd,' the newcomer said. He neither smiled nor made any attempt at small talk. 'And what's your name . . . boy?'

'My name is irrelevant,' Paul said, overlooking the comment. 'I'm told you were a soldier.'

'Did O'Shaughnessy tell you that?' Kidd demanded.

'Yes, he did. He told me all about your military career,' Paul said. 'He said you could provide me with enough gunpowder for my purposes.'

'What does a young pup like you want with gunpowder?'

'That's a private matter, Mr Kidd,' Paul told him, 'just like my name. You're going to be well paid for your services. In return I expect you to be the soul of discretion.'

Kidd looked unimpressed. 'I'll be having a word with O'Shaughnessy. He shouldn't go blabbing about my past, especially to a mere boy.' He blew his nose. 'What about the money? Have you got it?'

Paul produced a fat wallet. 'Does that answer your question?'

'Yes, I reckon it does,' Kidd said, eyeing the wallet greedily. 'Now it's my turn. Can I ask you something?'

'Ask away.'

'Does anybody else know you're doing business with me?'

Paul shook his head. 'Only one.'

Kidd's air of self assurance slipped for the first time. He looked panicky. 'His name wouldn't be Samuel Rector, would it?'

238

Paul moved to reassure Kidd. 'No, I don't have dealings with Mr Rector. I meant Mrs Flaherty, of course.' Kidd relaxed visibly. 'It's between you, me, O'Shaughnessy and his mistress. None of us are going to say anything.'

'How do you know neither of those two will let it slip?' Kidd asked. 'They ain't exactly the most reliable of people either.'

Paul shrugged. 'You'll find we can rely on them. I'm a good judge of character.'

Kidd squinted against the sunlight. 'You'd better be right, boy. The guv'nor doesn't like unauthorized transactions in his territory. I'll stand toe to toe with most any man, but not the Satan of Spitalfields.' He grimaced. 'No, not him.'

'That's why I chose to meet you out here,' Paul said. 'To ensure your safety and make payment away from the prying eyes of Rector's spies.' He was gambling that Kidd was more motivated by greed than by fear. 'Do you have the material I requested? I don't see a cart.'

'Precautions,' Kidd said, 'I left it nearby and walked the rest of the way. I ain't no mug. I need to see the colour of your money first.'

Paul opened a white vellum envelope and flicked through the notes. Kidd reached for it but Paul slipped it back into the inside breast pocket of his frock coat.

'You'll be paid when our business is complete,' Paul said. He handed Kidd a folded piece of paper. 'I've hired a warehouse to store the barrels.'

Kidd ran his eyes over the note. 'I know the place.'

239

He looked suspicious. 'What's to stop you clearing off without paying me?'

'I'll pay you one third now,' Paul said, 'one third on delivery to my premises and one third on transportation from the warehouse to . . . to its final resting place.'

'I'll do it if you pay the lot up front,' Kidd said.

Paul peeled off the first instalment and handed it over. 'I won't haggle with you, Mr Kidd. We do it our way or we don't do it at all. Do we have a deal?'

Kidd thought it over for a considerable time then nodded. As he tucked the bills inside his jacket, Paul felt his senses tingling. There was movement in a coppice over to his right. They weren't alone. There was something else. There was a sheen of sweat on Kidd's brow. He was nervous.

'You sound pretty cocksure,' Kidd said. 'How are you to know I don't have an accomplice creeping up on you at this very moment?'

'You do,' Paul said, enjoying the look of astonishment on Kidd's face, 'two in fact.'

He pointed at some winter undergrowth and it caught fire. The man who'd been hiding in the tangled bushes stumbled clear, beating the flames from his sleeve.

'Does that explain why I'm so sure of myself?' Paul asked.

Kidd gave his second accomplice a low whistle. 'You can come out,' he said. 'He's rumbled you.'

A second man emerged from a clump of trees, looking sheepish.

'How did you do that?' Kidd asked. 'How did you make that scrub catch fire?'

Paul shrugged. 'Do you really think I'm going to tell you?'

'There's still three of us,' Kidd said.

'Are you thinking of robbing me?' Paul asked.

Kidd had his eye on the pocket where Paul had put his wallet. 'We might be. Who's going to stop us, you?'

'I'd advise against it,' Paul said. 'Let me demonstrate why.' He seized Kidd's wrist. Instantly, the man's skin started to blister.

'Let go!' Kidd cried.

Paul maintained his grip, revelling in the man's suffering. His dark passions were rising again.

'For pity's sake,' Kidd pleaded, 'I won't give you no trouble, honest I won't. Just don't hurt me no more. Please let go.'

Paul did as he was asked. 'You see,' he said, 'I made sure Mrs Flaherty gave me an address where I could find you if you failed to deliver the merchandise. The pain you have just suffered is nothing compared to the agony I could inflict if I wished.'

'I ain't going to try anything,' Kidd grumbled.

'I'm glad to hear it,' Paul said. 'Let's get on with the demonstration.'

Kidd exchanged glances with his companions and led the way to a small paddock. Kidd's cart was waiting. It was shielded by trees to one side and deserted outbuildings to the other. The gunpowder was stored in barrels under a tarpaulin.

'Most people have the wrong idea about gunpowder,' he explained. 'It's mainly used as a propellant. It fires things. If it's an explosion you want, you'll have to pack it tight with other material. It might help if you told me what you want to do.'

'I want to cause the maximum confusion,' Paul said. 'I want lots of fire and smoke.'

'I can arrange that,' Kidd said, glancing across at his accomplices. 'Do you want a demonstration?'

'That's what we're here for,' Paul said.

Kidd and the other men buried a barrel beneath the smallest of the jumble of outhouses.

'You don't need to worry about a fuse,' Paul said. 'I can take care of that.'

Kidd finished his preparations and came over to stand by Paul.

'It's ready,' he said.

Paul concentrated all his attention on the spot where Kidd had buried the barrel. Soon the ground started to smoulder. Unleashing a final blast of energy, Paul triggered an ear-splitting roar that tore up the ground and set the building on fire.

'Is that powerful enough for your purposes?' Kidd asked.

Paul smiled. 'I'm quite satisfied, thank you. Please transport it to my warehouse.' He waited until Kidd reached his cart before adding a warning. 'Oh, there is just one thing. Don't think about trying to cheat me. Samuel isn't the only monster in Spitalfields.'

Kidd gave him a wary glance. 'I'll keep that in mind.'

Pleased with his afternoon's work, Paul returned to the crossroads to wait for his carriage. After a few minutes he started to tug at his collar. Dark spots started to gather at the edge of his field of vision. A wave of heat rushed over his skin. Hellish visions poured through his mind.

'No,' Paul gasped, 'no!'

But the attack overwhelmed him. By the time his driver came to collect him, he was curled up semi-conscious on the road. As he rocked to and fro in the back of the carriage, he knew he was paying for using his powers. He had fed the demon seed. Now he was feeling the potency of its dark venom.

Thirty-five

From the diary of Arthur Strachan
Wednesday, 20 February, 1839

I *have made my decision. Sometimes a man's family has to come before his work. I must get Victoria away from this city and the malign influence of Samuel Rector. If we were to stay, Victoria's future could be only death or madness. Her condition deteriorates by the hour. As a result, I have requested an emergency meeting with Mr Stephenson. He already had wind of developments at the construction site. He is demanding to know what's going on and why I have ignored his express instructions.*

The trunks are packed and all the arrangements made. Soon we will embark on our journey north. I hope that this will be the saving of my poor child. Normally, I would be anxious about my meeting. Frankly, I no longer care what happens to me. My professional life is over. Only one thing matters now and that is Victoria's health. I pray I am not too late to save her.

Thirty-six

The following evening, Samuel Rector strode through the tap room of the Frying Pan pub, enjoying the way people cleared a path for him. The air was foetid and laced with tobacco smoke. He soon discovered Tobias Gumm and Albert Murray sitting in a corner opposite the door. They both looked up expectantly.

'Good evening to you, guv'nor,' Tobias said.

Samuel pulled up a chair. 'Good evening, gentlemen. Do you have any news for me?'

The opening gambit came from Tobias. 'The way to the gate is clear.'

'That's old news,' Samuel said. 'You don't get paid for that.'

Tobias looked disappointed. Albert spoke next. 'Would you be interested in Mr Strachan's latest plans perhaps?' he asked.

Samuel glowered. 'What plans?'

Albert announced, 'He intends to take his daughter

out of the city to recover from her illness. In a day or two he will no longer be in charge of the project.'

'Strachan's clearing out?' Samuel asked. 'How do you know?'

Albert leaned forward conspiratorially. 'He had a meeting on site with Mr Stephenson,' he said. 'As you know, it's Stephenson who's in overall charge. I made sure I overheard what passed between them.' He gave a wry smile. 'Mr Stephenson was tearing a strip off old Strachan, I can tell you. You could hear their raised voices all over the site.'

Samuel got straight to the point. 'What are the implications for the construction of the line?' he demanded.

Albert held out his open palm and Samuel dropped half a crown into it. 'Well?'

'Mr Stephenson is taking over complete control of operations in a couple of days,' Albert told him. 'He has some business to conclude first.'

'What about Strachan?'

'I told you,' Albert said. 'He's finished. Rumour is he's jumping before he's pushed.'

'Where's he going?'

'Back to Scotland, I think.'

Samuel pondered the news for a moment or two. 'What's Stephenson going to do about the gate?'

'What do you think?' Tobias said. 'He's going to bury it and get on with laying the line.'

Samuel looked put out by the news. 'When's this meant to happen?' he asked.

Tobias held out his hand just as Albert had done before him. This time Samuel was in no mood to bargain. He seized the younger man by the throat.

'I asked a question,' he spat. 'I want an answer.'

'Give over,' Tobias begged. 'You're throttling me.' Then he saw the shadow of madness rise in the guv'nor's eyes.

'Just tell me!' Samuel hissed.

Tobias felt the cold passage of fear right through him. 'Two days,' he answered hurriedly, 'three at most. If you want to enter that crypt of yours, you'd better get to it, and sharpish.'

Samuel released him and a self-satisfied grin spread across his features. 'Two days,' he repeated. 'Do you agree with that, Albert?'

Albert nodded, at the same time flicking an uncertain glance in the direction of Tobias who was tenderly rubbing his throat.

'Let them do whatever they want,' Samuel said. 'It doesn't matter any more. I'm ready.'

'Ready for what?' Albert asked.

'No questions,' Samuel told him, pointing a thick, gnarled forefinger. 'I thought I made that clear.' He rose to his feet. 'This is our final meeting. I no longer require your services. I'd like to say it's been a pleasure.' He spat on the floor. 'I'd like to but I can't. You boys would sell your mothers for a few shillings.'

With that, he marched out onto Brick Lane and set off down Chicksand Street. He knew what to do.

Thirty-seven

Ethan Lockett was scampering across the roofs of East London, approaching its outer suburbs. Soon the boy known as Licker spied a familiar chimney stack. Scrambling up the steep, sloping tiles, he vanished into the flue and was soon emerging from one of the many fireplaces built to warm thirteen, West Cromwell Place.

Ethan had chosen well. Strachan would be probably be so exhausted he was still in bed. The boy glanced at the conflicting Latin inscriptions on the walls then he listened. A maid was laying a fire in the drawing room. A second one was preparing breakfast. Other than that, the house was largely quiet. Ethan grinned. Yes, Strachan and Victoria must still be asleep.

'Time to wake you, princess,' he murmured.

He eased open the door a crack and peered down the hallway. The maid had lit the fire in the drawing room and a flickering glow was dancing along the bottom of the door. Ethan watched it for a moment then he padded across to Victoria's room.

The first thing he noticed was the fireplace. Strachan had had it boarded up to protect his daughter from intruders. Ethan had expected as much, hence the entry through the study.

Victoria was lying awkwardly against the headboard, propped up on a heap of pillows. It looked as if she had collapsed from exhaustion after a long night of torment. Strachan was sitting in an armchair, fast asleep.

'Now ain't that touching?' Ethan observed. 'You've never left her bedside.'

He approached Victoria, keeping his footsteps light lest he wake Strachan. The moment he pressed his lips to her wrist, she stirred. When she opened her mouth to speak, Ethan killed the words with a stare. Victoria glanced at her father and nodded her understanding. Ethan gestured in the direction of the door and they left together.

Strachan woke a few minutes later to discover his daughter gone from her bed. 'Victoria,' he groaned.

Finding her bed abandoned and the room empty, he hurried to the door and started to search the house. The study was the fourth room he entered. He gazed at her squatting in the far corner. She had her back to him and didn't answer. Relieved to discover that Victoria hadn't left the house, he addressed her in a quiet, patient voice.

'Victoria, my child,' he said, 'what am I going to do with you? I begged you to stay in your room. Can't you indulge me in even this one request?'

Still she didn't speak. When she failed to respond,

249

Strachan approached her, unaware of Ethan emerging from behind the door.

'We're leaving tomorrow morning,' he said. 'We only have one more night in this house then we will embark on a new life. You love Edinburgh, don't you, my darling? There you will recover your strength and we will forget everything we have been through.'

He stood in the middle of the room, willing her to answer, but she maintained her silence. 'Victoria?' he said.

There was still no answer. Strachan reached her and knelt down, gently placing a hand on her shoulder.

'You must speak to me,' he said.

At that moment he noticed a dark blur in the periphery of his vision. He half-turned and saw the Rat Boy.

'Get away from her, demon!' Strachan commanded.

'I'm afraid I can't do that,' Ethan said. 'It was your daughter who invited me. Ain't that right, Victoria?'

Strachan turned back to his daughter and a gasp of horror caught in his throat. She was looking straight at him, her eyes metallic and cold. Worse still, a strange, leathery tongue was flickering from her beak-like mouth.

'What have you done to her?' Strachan cried.

'Don't she make the prettiest little bird you ever did see?' Ethan asked.

Strachan seized Victoria's shoulders. 'You must fight him,' he sobbed. 'Don't let him turn you into this hell-creature.'

But Victoria's answer was as swift as it was deadly. She raised her hands and unsheathed the talon-like

250

claws that Strachan had discovered lurking under the flesh of her fingers.

'What are you doing?' Strachan asked. 'Victoria, no!'

At that moment the world dissolved into a frenzy of screeching and tearing. Talons ripped through skin, flesh, organs, bone, tendon and gristle. Strachan twisted and turned, writhed and squirmed, yet he did little to resist the creature his daughter had become. The attack continued until, after a couple of minutes, Strachan slumped, lifeless, to the floor. Then Victoria reached for Ethan. But there was no solace. He stepped away from her.

'You won't be seeing me again,' he said, then scrambled up the chimney.

'Come back,' she screamed. 'Come back!'

Victoria's bird-like deformities faded, leaving a broken, disoriented child gazing down at the body of her father. Then, as human understanding returned, she screamed. She was still screaming when the servants burst through the door.

Thirty-eight

Paul slept for eighteen hours back at his hotel. When he woke, he felt terribly weak, as if the attack had drained him of every ounce of strength he had. It was a warning. Day after day, he had revelled in his growing power. Now he had paid the price. But he had survived the onslaught.

Now he had work to do. He changed carriages three times on his way to the smart, clean house in Holloway he had found for Betsy. Satisfied that he hadn't been followed, he knocked to be admitted. He noticed a peep hole in the door. A curtain also twitched at one of the front windows. The door was opened by a tall, angular woman. A bonnet covered her severely pinned back grey hair. She didn't smile but there was something in her eyes that told Paul she had great compassion.

'Mr Rector?' she said. 'Do come in.'

'Good morning, Mrs Mayhew,' Paul said, following her inside. 'How is Betsy?'

'Last night I made sure she washed and bathed

before she retired,' Mrs Mayhew reported. 'It is an old adage, but a true one, that cleanliness is next to Godliness. Our young charge slept for a good eight hours between clean sheets. She is much recovered from her ordeal.' She screwed up her face. 'I have had the garments in which she arrived burned, as you requested. You want to help her forget her past life, I assume?'

'Of course.'

But that wasn't the reason. Paul knew that Lud would want to seek Betsy out. He was keen to destroy anything that connected her to the Rats' Nest. Imprisoned in his crypt Lud might be, but his evil reached far across space and time. Any object, however tiny, however commonplace, might lead him to his prey.

Mrs Mayhew nodded. 'I have furnished her with new attire.'

'How much do I owe you?' Paul asked.

'Eight shillings should suffice for now,' Mrs Mayhew told him.

Paul handed her the coins.

'Is your family wealthy, Mr Rector?' Mrs Mayhew asked.

'If you're asking whether the money is going to dry up,' Paul replied, 'then the answer is no. It isn't a problem.'

Mrs Mayhew knew when she was being told to change the subject. 'I have examined Betsy, Mr Rector. Her body is covered in bruises. She wouldn't tell me how she got them.'

Paul knew all about the brutality Betsy had suffered. He remembered the things Mrs Flaherty had told him about her time with Samuel Rector. He understood the depths of intimidation and horror to which the guv'nor could sink.

'I'm sure she will answer all your questions in time,' he replied. 'The man who made her a virtual slave is a monster. That is all you need to know. Where is she now?'

'She is finishing her breakfast,' Mrs Mayhew replied. 'There are three other girls under my roof at the present time. They are keeping her company. You have done a good thing placing her under my protection, Mr Rector.'

'When I was seeking a refuge for Betsy,' Paul said, 'I visited the Magdalen Hospital. They recommended you.'

'I am gratified that they hold me in such high regard,' Mrs Mayhew said. 'The Magdalen recovers women from a life of vice. It does a fine job. As you will have discovered, I specialise in hiding victims of violence from the men who would do them harm.' She led Paul indoors.

'I wanted to ask you about that,' Paul said. 'What if one of the men came here? How would you protect your charges from harm?'

'My husband Bill fought in the Peninsula campaign with Wellington,' Mrs Mayhew said. 'He was wounded at Waterloo. Believe me, he has a strong right arm and the heart of a lion. With the support of my brother James, he is all the security they need. Does that answer your question?'

Paul wondered how the pair would fare against the Rat Boys but at least the house had some sort of protection. 'It goes some way to allay my fears,' he replied.

254

'I'm gratified,' Mrs Mayhew said. 'This way please.'

When Paul followed Mrs Mayhew into the breakfast room, Betsy's face lit up.

'I'm sure you would like some privacy,' Mrs Mayhew said. She turned to the other girls round the table and clapped her hands. 'Upstairs with you now and make your beds. I want those corners done correctly, remember.'

Paul couldn't believe the way Mrs Mayhew had transformed Betsy. Her hair was in ringlets and she was wearing a crisp, clean dress and white gloves. 'Mrs Mayhew is a harsh taskmaster,' he observed.

'She's a wonderful woman,' Betsy answered. 'I can't remember the last time I laid my head down to sleep in a house where I felt safe.'

Paul smiled. 'So you're comfortable here?'

Betsy nodded eagerly. 'It's a dream come true. You should see my room. It's clean and tidy and there are ornaments on a dresser.' Then her face clouded. 'I'm just afraid I'm going to wake up and discover that a dream is all it ever was.'

'It's no dream,' Paul told her. 'I've paid for your lodgings here for three months. Mrs Mayhew has offered to educate you, so that you will have the skills to find yourself employment.'

'I ain't afraid of hard work,' Betsy said. 'I'll do anything just so long as I don't have to go back to Samuel.'

'You won't,' Paul said. 'That chapter of your life is closed for good.'

'But what about the guv'nor?' Betsy asked. 'He'll never stop looking for me so long as I live. He thinks I

255

belong to him. And what about Lud? Samuel used to tell us he never slept. He's got eyes that never blink.'

'Leave them to me,' Paul said. He sounded more confident than he felt. A battle was coming for which he was ill-prepared.

'I heard the news about the murder,' Betsy said, dropping her voice. 'The Rat Boys did for old Strachan, didn't they?'

'How do you know that?' Paul asked. He'd hoped that, even if it was only for a short while, she would be quarantined from the horrors of the world outside.

'One of the other girls heard Mrs Mayhew's cook discussing it. There were two more murders. Were they the guv'nor's doing too?'

'It looks like it,' Paul said. 'They were both workmen on the Minories site. It's too much of a coincidence. Samuel's tying up all the loose ends before he launches his attack.'

'Lor,' Betsy said, her face draining of blood, 'there's no hiding place. Him and Lud are going to kill us all.'

'I will do everything in my power to protect you,' Paul said. 'The only thing you have to do is recover and accept Mrs Mayhew's guidance.' He leaned closer. 'Chaim tells me Israel revived you.'

'I don't remember a thing about it,' Betsy said. 'One minute I was teetering at the top of the stairs, trying to fight off Samuel, the next I was coming to in Israel's arms. Chaim swears I was quite lifeless until Israel laid his hands on me.'

'Do you still think his powers are ungodly?' Paul asked.

Betsy smiled. 'Maybe there's something good in it after all.' She took Paul's hand. 'There's something I've

256

always wanted to know,' she said. 'Do you mind me asking you now?'

When Paul didn't answer, Betsy pressed on. 'Where are you from, Paul? And I don't mean Mile End. There's something about you, something different. Chaim told me he felt it too.'

At first, Paul didn't know how to reply. Should he tell her he was destined to roam the tunnels of time until his mission was complete? Should he even tell her about the nightmares that had tortured him all the previous night?

'I don't belong anywhere,' he said. 'I'm rootless, homeless. The only home I have is the struggle against the demon master. Wherever he strikes, that's where I must be. Does that answer your question?'

Betsy's gaze lingered on his face for a few moments. 'No, I don't think it does.' Then she grinned. 'But it's the best I'm going to get, ain't that right?'

Paul squeezed her hand between both of his, then rose and walked to the door. 'Yes, it's the best you're going to get. If I triumph in this struggle, I'll be back to see you.'

'And if you don't?'

'If I don't,' Paul replied, his voice suddenly subdued, 'then we're all lost.'

He left the house without another word. He had great confidence in Mrs Mayhew. But there was something he didn't know. When Betsy had thrown away everything else that linked her to her former life, there was something she couldn't bear to destroy, the precious locket her mother had given her. It contained the lock of Molly's hair.

Thirty-nine

The Rat Boys were gathered before their Master. They were all kneeling, heads bowed while Lud's dark image floated before them.

'Four priests bound me,' Lud told his disciples. 'Four priests suffered and died. But their ghosts haunt me still. All these centuries later, the seals they made bind me in my tomb. Tomorrow you will break the first of them.' He saw the eagerness in the boys' eyes. 'Be patient, my young friends. It will take a fierce battle to break each succeeding seal. When the seal is broken, you will feel my power surge from the white chapel and pulse through every fibre of your being. Your strength will be doubled. Imagine the mayhem you will unleash on these streets.' His eyes roamed over them. 'Who knows, when the renegade tastes defeat his despair may be so great that he surrenders his very soul to me. Then there will be no obstacles to my return. Are you ready?'

His question was met by a chorus of shouts. Just one

of the boys remained silent. 'You do not share your brother demons' joy at my impending victory, Israel?' Lud asked.

Israel averted his gaze.

'Look at me!' Lud roared.

Israel obeyed.

'You still long for your human life, don't you?'

'I serve you because I have no choice,' Israel murmured in a voice made small by fear. 'You can't ask for more.'

'I ask only that you raise the undead and march them to the white chapel,' Lud said.

'I will obey you,' Israel replied. 'You know that I don't have the will to resist.'

Lud seemed satisfied with his answer. 'Leave us if you wish, Israel. Go into the kitchen and get some sleep. You will need to be strong to raise the army of the dead.'

Samuel and the Rat Boys watched him go.

'Close the door, Ethan,' Lud said.

Ethan did as he was told.

'You wanted him out of the way, didn't you?' Jacob asked.

'Clever boy,' Lud said.

Jacob glanced at the door. 'Won't he hear us?'

Lud chuckled. 'I have sealed the door tight. He hears nothing.' He turned his gaze on Samuel. 'I don't see the girl.'

'Betsy is still missing,' Samuel said. 'The boys have searched high and low. She has vanished off the face of the earth. It's the renegade's doing.'

'It would be such a shame not to exact your revenge,' Lud said, his voice rich with malice. 'I have been so looking forward to the spectacle. Do you have something belonging to her? I'll soon sniff her out if you do.'

Samuel disappeared into the room he'd shared with Betsy and returned with one of her handkerchiefs. 'I have this.'

Lud's apparition floated around it. 'If the renegade has his wits about him, he will have destroyed everything that links her to this place. But I am not sure he has learned his lesson. He lacks the ruthlessness the rest of demon kind have in abundance. He made a mistake once before and lost a friend because of it.' He remembered with relish the last moments of Cotton, a man who had paid the ultimate price because the renegade underestimated the power of the demon master. 'We may be in luck.'

'No, he's bound to have taken everything from her,' Samuel said, grinding his teeth. 'She's lost to me.'

'Not necessarily,' Lud told him. 'Mortal kind are sentimental creatures. If I understand the female heart and I'm sure I do, the girl will be clinging to her memories through some precious keepsake. I fancy your little songbird may have held something back from her rescuer.'

Samuel leaned forward eagerly. 'Do you really think so?'

Lud chuckled.

'Then find her, my Lord. I will be forever in your debt.'

'You already are, Samuel,' Lud chuckled. His dark form pulsated against the fluorescent gleam of the white chapel. His gaze roamed round those present. 'You must remain quiet while I seek her out.'

A hush fell over the room. Lud's shape, already translucent, became so wispy and gossamer-thin that it was hardly visible. Then it blazed black once more.

'A locket,' he murmured. 'I see a locket.'

'Yes,' Samuel said, 'Betsy had one. It belonged to her mother.'

'Didn't I tell you,' Lud declared. 'I have her!'

Samuel leapt to his feet. 'Where is she?'

Lud gave him the address. 'You understand that some of your boys harbour a certain affection for Betsy, don't you, Samuel?'

Samuel glowered at the Rat Boys. 'Is that true?'

For a few moments, they cowered before his gaze. Then, one by one, the boys swore their loyalty. Malachy was the last one to speak. 'She was good to us once, guv'nor, a real gem, but that was before she walked out and took up with the renegade. We don't feel nuffin' no more.'

'Is that the same for you, each and every one?' Samuel demanded. There were nods all round and Samuel's eyes glowed with a primal hunger. 'She'll wish she'd never heard the name Rector.' He dispatched his underlings to find Betsy then turned to face the demon master. 'Let all your enemies tremble. Tomorrow they will perish and your march to freedom will quicken.'

There was a hot snarl of wind and Lud was gone.

At the house in Holloway, Mrs Mayhew was playing the piano while her brother James turned the pages of the music. Her husband Bill sat by the fire, warming his toes on the fender. Betsy and the other girls sat

261

together on the settee listening. When Mrs Mayhew finished, they clapped.

'You can't half tinkle the ivories, Mrs M,' one of the girls said.

'It was beautiful,' Betsy added. 'I never did hear the like of it.'

'I will introduce you to the pleasure that music gives us,' Mrs Mayhew said. 'I will introduce you to books too.'

'That won't be easy,' Betsy said. 'My mother taught me the basics of reading when I was little but I ain't hardly had a book in my hand since.'

'I will guide you,' Mrs Mayhew said. 'From what I've seen of you, Betsy, you're a most intelligent young woman. You'll soon pick up where you left off.'

She was about to say something to one of the other girls when there was a knock at the door. Mrs Mayhew frowned.

'Who can it be?' she said.

'Come with me, James,' Bill said.

They stood in the hallway while Mrs Mayhew and her girls listened fearfully.

'Who's there?' Bill asked.

A muffled voice answered from the street. 'There's a boy out here, sir. He looks stone dead. Is there somebody here perhaps who can help me.'

'What did he say?' Betsy asked.

Mrs Mayhew gestured to her to be quiet and stole to the window. She peeped through the curtains. 'There's a boy lying on the pavement. It's true. He is quite senseless.'

'Tell Bill not to open the door!' Betsy cried.

'But what if I can revive him?' Mrs Mayhew said.

'It's a trick,' Betsy screamed. 'Don't answer the door.'

'Why, whatever's the matter?' Mrs Mayhew asked.

'That boy,' Betsy said, 'I think I know who it is.'

'But you haven't even seen him.'

'I don't need to,' Betsy insisted. 'They call him Play Dead.' Her eyes were wide with terror. 'It's the Rat Boys. They've found me. Please don't let them in.'

Mrs Mayhew hurried into the hall. 'Keep the door bolted, Bill. Betsy thinks it's a deception.'

When Bill failed to slide back the bolts and turn the key, the boy at the door changed his tune. 'Open this bleedin' door before we tear it down.'

'Get out of here,' Bill yelled. 'I'll have the law on you.'

The sound of running feet followed as the besiegers fanned out around the house. Betsy and the other girls clung to each other.

'It's them,' Betsy sobbed. 'They've found me.'

Mrs Mayhew picked up a poker from the fire. 'Finding you is one thing. Taking you away is quite another.'

Betsy shook her head. 'That poker won't be any good against the Rat Boys. You don't know what you're up against, Mrs Mayhew.'

Her new friends discovered exactly what they were up against moments later.

'Quick,' James cried, 'you've got to see this!'

Bill ran to his side and stared in disbelief as the bolts slid back by themselves.

'It's Jasper,' Betsy cried, 'he can move things with his mind.'

Simultaneously, the key that had been in the lock

263

wriggled free and dropped onto the hall floor. Betsy fell to her knees and made a grab for it. She was too late. It slid under the door and into the hands of the dark forms besieging the house.

'Dear God!'

The door opened to reveal two of the Rat Boys, Jasper and Ezra. At the sight of them, the girls clustered together on the settee screamed. Mrs Mayhew lashed out with the poker but Jasper snatched it from her.

'I should lay about your wizened old body with this,' he told her.

Bill and James stepped forward, arming themselves with whatever was at hand, a candlestick and a cane.

'Get back, whatever you are,' Bill commanded.

His words were followed by another crash from the rear of the house and Ethan, Enoch and Noah scampered into the room. Finally, Malachy and Jacob made their entrance, following Jasper and Ezra through the front door. They fell upon their victims, forcing their eyes open so that fear flooded into their souls. Betsy knew all about the Rat Boys' power, the ability to kill with a stare.

'Please don't kill them,' she said. 'I'll come quietly if you'll just let them live.'

The younger boys hesitated.

'Oh, wasn't I good to every one of you once?' Betsy pleaded. 'Didn't I treat you kindly when you were crying for your families? Wasn't I like a mother to you?'

Jacob saw the hesitation all around him and shrugged. 'Unconscious will do. We're in a hurry anyway. The guv'nor can't wait to see you again.'

Leaving the rest of the house's occupants sprawled senseless on the floor, the Rat Boys led Betsy away.

Forty

Paul was roused from his sleep later that night by the sound of raised voices outside on the landing and fists pounding on the door. There had been nightmares, but fewer than the night before. He swung his legs off the mattress and slipped on the expensive dressing gown he'd bought in the West End.

'Who's there?' he demanded.

'It's Mayhew,' a man's voice answered.

Paul opened the door and saw Bill Mayhew standing on the threshold. The hotel manager was standing behind him, tugging at his elbow.

'Please accept my apologies, young sir,' he was babbling. 'This man just barged his way in.' Two more hotel employees arrived. 'I will have him evicted immediately.'

Bill spun round and fixed all three men with a stare. He clenched his gnarled fists and growled a warning. 'The first of you likely lads that tries to haul me away will be picking his teeth up from the carpet.' His eyes blazed. 'I fought Boney's boys in the Peninsula and I faced them Frenchies again at Waterloo. I've got a bayonet wound in this leg and a musket ball went through my shoulder here. See, when I've been through all that, I don't think I've anything to fear from you lot, you lousy bed wetters. Do you take my meaning?' Bill's defiance stopped the hotel staff in their tracks.

'It's all right,' Paul said, stepping between them. 'I know this man. You can leave us now.'

The hotel manager looked relieved. 'Sir, if you're sure.'

'I'm absolutely certain.' Paul watched the manager as he walked back to the top of the stairs, followed by his porters. He turned up the gaslight. 'I can only assume you have some news for me.'

Bill nodded. 'Yes, and it's all bad. Your enemies have taken Betsy.'

The news tore Paul's composure. 'How could this happen?' he demanded.

'I'll tell you how,' Bill answered. 'Damn you, why didn't you tell us what we were up against? Why didn't you warn us? Those creatures weren't human.'

'You're right. But Bill, would you have believed me if I had?'

Bill rubbed at his fleshy nose. 'Maybe not.'

'I've let you down though. Was anyone hurt?'

Bill shook his head. 'No thanks to you,' he grunted. 'We were lucky.'

'It's not the first time I've underestimated my enemy,' Paul said. He voiced his thoughts out loud. 'But how did Lud find her?'

Bill looked confused. 'Lud? Who the Hell's this Lud? It sounds to me like you've been keeping a lot of secrets from us.'

Paul evaded the question. 'Tell me everything, Bill. Don't leave out a single detail.'

Bill stumbled through his tale, trying to make sense of the supernatural events. Paul listened. He didn't interrupt once. When Bill had finished, it was Paul's turn to speak.

'If I'm to save Betsy,' he said, 'I will need help. I understand if you want to walk away. What do you say, Bill?'

'You won't find me wanting, Mr Paul,' Bill said. 'Those creatures took me by surprise once. It won't happen again. Let's go.'

He made for the door but Paul held him back. 'Now what are you up to?' Bill complained.

'If you're thinking of trying to mount a rescue,' Paul said, 'I'd advise against it.'

'Would you now?' Bill said. 'Are you telling me you're going to leave that poor girl where she is? What if they hurt her, or worse?'

'No,' Paul said, 'I'll never let her down again. The thing is, Bill, right now I can't guarantee her safety.' That earned him a ferocious glare. 'Just trust me. I swear to you, we will save her.'

'You'd better be right about this,' Bill snapped. 'If you ain't, if they hurt a hair on Betsy's head, I'll take it out of your hide mister.'

'If I've misjudged Samuel's state of mind,' Paul said, 'you can do anything you want to me. I won't stop you. Try to believe me. However much it pains me to say it, we have to be keep our powder dry for now. The first shots have been fired in a war that will decide the fate of London. The battle will not be joined tonight but it's coming soon. For now,' Paul told him, 'there's nothing you can do. Go back to the house and await my call.'

Forty-one

Jacob dragged the struggling Betsy into the Rats' Nest.

'Here she is, guv'nor,' he announced.

With that, he shoved the terrified girl forward. She stumbled and fell to her knees. For a brief moment, she crouched there on all fours. Then a shadow fell over her. Slowly, fearfully, she raised her eyes.

'Now who gave you these pretty clothes?' Samuel wondered out loud. 'Just look at our Bets, boys. Ain't she a picture?' He ran his thick, powerful fingers over her hair. 'Somebody's put her hair in ringlets. She looks just like a princess.'

When he touched her cheek, Betsy flinched.

'What, ain't I good enough for you now?' Samuel demanded. 'Have you forgotten your guv'nor already? We were a perfect couple once.'

'We were never a couple,' Betsy retorted, finding her voice. 'I stayed with you because I was scared.' Her voice broke over the last word.

'Scared of me?' Samuel murmured. He looked around at the assembled Rat Boys. 'Now, what's to be scared of? Do any of you boys find me in the least bit frightening?'

Noah was the first to answer. 'Never. You're a regular philanthropist, Mr Rector, a man who devotes himself to good works.'

'There,' Samuel said. 'Did you hear that, Bets? I'm a philanthropist. I take in the wretched and the lonely and I put a roof over their heads. I even give them gainful employment.' He gestured at the walls of the Rats' Nest. 'What's this but a charitable institution?'

'It's a prison!' Israel cried, unable to listen for another moment.

Samuel offered Betsy a hand. Shrugging it away, she got to her feet by herself. Instinctively, she felt for something in the folds of her dress. A lock of hair wasn't the only thing she'd kept of Molly's. She still had the small knife Molly had always carried. You ain't going to humiliate me no more, Sammy, she thought. She traced its shape with her fingertips.

Samuel circled her slowly, examining her appearance with cruel relish. 'Are you a prisoner, Betsy?' he asked. He traced a line down her spine with his finger. 'Is this a prison dress?'

Betsy was trembling, rendered speechless by Samuel's lowering presence.

'Don't you hurt her,' Israel pleaded.

Samuel continued to pace out a circle round Betsy. 'Now why would I hurt such a pretty little songbird, Israel?' He ran his finger over her nose and lips, down over chin and throat until he rested his hand on her thudding heart. 'You should feel her heart fluttering away here. She's so excited to be back among her friends.'

Betsy held her breath, waiting for the first blow to fall. She gripped the knife's handle.

'It's all right, Bets,' Samuel said, slowly withdrawing his hand. 'You've no need to fear old Samuel.'

When he turned his back and walked away, Betsy released the knife, leaving it concealed in the folds of her dress. She almost crumpled to the floor with relief. Israel rushed forward and she leaned against him, shallow breaths shuddering out of her.

'Don't taunt me, Samuel,' she sobbed. 'If you're going to kill me, the way you killed Moll, just get on with it. I'm ready.'

'You might be ready,' Samuel said, keeping his back to her, 'but I ain't.'

The Rat Boys were as nonplussed as Betsy and Israel. Every one of them had expected him to exact swift retribution on her.

'What kind of trick is this?' Israel demanded.

'No trick,' Samuel replied. 'I've got these two little birds in my cage. Neither one of them seems very happy without the other and I do miss their singing.' He turned to face Israel and Betsy. 'So I got to thinking, how do I get the best song out of my birds? Why, it's simple. I let them sit on the same perch.'

Israel frowned.

'You want me to spell it out in simple English for you?' Samuel asked. 'I've got a great deal of stiffs to raise tomorrow night. If I give you Betsy to take care of, I reckon you'll raise no protest when I ask you to put my army together for me. I'm right, ain't I?'

The tension fell from Israel's face. 'Anything, guv'nor, I'll do anything you say. Just don't hurt her.'

Samuel held out his hands in a gesture of magnanimity. 'It's a deal then, Izzy. You give me my army, and I give you your pretty little friend. That way we're both happy.'

With that, he strode into his room, gesturing to Jacob and Noah to follow. Noah closed the door.

'You're a real, diamond, guv'nor,' he said, 'letting Bets off like that.'

Samuel spun round. 'Let her off, did you say?'

Noah saw the ferocious fire burning in Samuel's eyes and swallowed hard.

'I ain't letting her off,' Samuel continued, his voice low but no less terrifying for that. 'No, I won't touch a hair of her head until we've broken the seal. But once we have . . .' he made a gesture as if he were ringing a bird's neck '. . . once we have, I'll snap our songbird's spine like a twig.'

Noah and Jacob exchanged glances.

'All you two have got to do is keep an eye on them until then,' Samuel said. 'Tomorrow night, when all the preparations are complete, the Master begins his march to freedom.'

Forty-two

O'Shaughnessy answered the door to Mrs Flaherty's house. The wind blew in, stinging his eyes. Finally he was able to recognize the new arrival. He scowled. 'What brings you back here?'

'What's the matter, O'Shaughnessy?' Paul said. 'Aren't you pleased to see me?'

Hatred oozed out of Mrs Flaherty's gatekeeper. 'We was all right here, me and Kit, before you came along.' But O'Shaughnessy saw the tell-tale scarlet glow eddying over Paul's hands.

'If you know what's good for you,' Paul said, 'you'll quit your whining right now and tell your mistress I want a word.'

O'Shaughnessy stepped back to let Paul enter. 'I'll get her.'

While Paul leaned against the mantelpiece, surveying the room, O'Shaughnessy skulked away to rouse Mrs Flaherty. She returned five minutes later wearing a nightgown. Her hair tumbled over her shoulders in an unruly tangle.

'I wondered when you'd turn up again,' she said, a twinkle in her eyes. 'Can't stay away, eh?' She flicked a glance at O'Shaughnessy. 'What have you been saying to him, Paul? You've put my friend here all out of sorts.'

Paul held out his hands in mock-innocence. 'I was pulling his leg. He's too sensitive for his own good, that's his problem.'

Mrs Flaherty patted O'Shaughnessy's cheeks. 'Find yourself something to do. I want to talk to Paul.'

O'Shaughnessy dithered for a moment, then stamped out of the room.

Paul waited for the door to close. 'This isn't a social call,' he told her. 'It's business.'

'And what kind of business can you put my way?' Mrs Flaherty asked. She curled up in an armchair by the fire and watched him with intelligent, brown eyes.

'Samuel must have made a lot of enemies over the years,' Paul said.

Mrs Flaherty poured herself a tumbler of whisky. 'Some,' she said. 'Would you like a tipple?'

Paul glanced at the bottle. It might ease the ache of loneliness and apprehension. 'Yes, pour me one.' He gulped it down. For a moment he almost retched then he felt the heat sweep through him. 'Now, as I was saying, Samuel must have made enemies.'

'Of course he has,' Mrs Flaherty said, refilling both glasses. 'Every gang of miscreants across the East End would like to settle accounts with the guv'nor. But there ain't a living soul would dare go up against him.

Besides, the gangs hate each other as much as they hate Samuel.'

'What if I showed them they could defeat him?' Paul replied.

Mrs Flaherty looked at him over the rim of her glass. 'You want them to put aside their differences for a day?'

Paul nodded.

'And what's going to convince them they can crush Samuel?' Mrs Flaherty demanded. 'Those few barrels of gunpowder Kidd got for you? It'll take more than a fireworks display to shake old Sammy off his perch.'

Paul finished the second whisky and held out his glass for more. 'Organize a meeting of the gangs and I'll demonstrate.'

Mrs Flaherty chuckled. 'Cocky, ain't you?'

It was Paul's turn to smile. 'I'm cut from the same cloth as Samuel. I share his abilities, but not his cruelty.'

Mrs Flaherty swallowed a gulp of whisky. 'Are you sure there isn't a little bit more devilry in you than you've been letting on, Paul?'

Paul remembered the way he'd wanted to hurt O'Shaughnessy. What did Kit know of the demons that haunted him? His eyes flashed. 'What do you mean by that?'

'Oh, nothing.'

'Speak your mind, Kit. I've admitted there's a dark side to me. Is there any more to say?'

Mrs Flaherty rose from her chair and stroked Paul's face. 'I lived with Samuel for six years. In that time I got to know him pretty well. You try to make out that, for all your "dark side", you're opposites, you and him.

But that ain't so, is it Paul?' She took a step nearer. 'You'd like me to believe you've got the demon seed under control. But I've seen you up close. I've seen the doubts. I've got an inkling what goes on in that mind of yours. You hide it deep but there's an awful lot of Samuel in you.'

Paul scowled. 'Do we have an agreement?'

'To bring down Samuel?' Kitty asked. She grinned. 'Why not?'

forty-three

Betsy crouched in a corner far from the others. She had cared for every one of them once. But any warm feelings she had had towards them had evaporated. They'd been like a pack of wild animals with blood in their nostrils. Every one of them belonged to Lud, body and soul. Israel was the only one she would allow near her.

'We've got to do something,' he said.

'Like what?' Betsy hissed. 'You saw Samuel. I've seen him in one of his rages but this was worse. It was like waiting for a dam to burst. I don't want to be there when it does.' She ran her fingers through her hair. 'I swear, I'm just grateful I'm still breathing. Thank God you're here. He's only keeping me alive so you'll do what he wants.'

'That's true,' Israel said, 'but there's got to be more to it. Think about it Bets, even if he'd . . . even if he'd done for you, I'd still have had to serve Lud. This voice in my head, it's too strong. There's got to be something else.' He thought for a moment, then the frown of confusion cleared from his face. 'There's only one thing it can be. I always give in eventually but—'

Betsy leaned forward. 'What?'

'Well, I keep fighting him, don't I? I make everything difficult. I think Lud needs me to obey him immediately and without question.'

Betsy was listening intently. 'That means he's in a hurry.'

'Exactly,' Israel said. 'If I read him right, the attack on Aldgate has to be soon.'

Betsy nodded. 'But if we're to be of any use to Chaim and Paul, we've got to tell them when. *Exactly* when.'

'I don't see how we're going to find out,' Israel said. 'It ain't like they're going to tell us.'

Betsy was still turning this over in her mind when she caught Noah watching her.

'I think I know how to get it out of them,' she said. 'It's a risk, but it's one worth taking.'

Israel followed the direction of her stare. He saw the hungry look in Noah's eyes and understood instantly.

'It's dangerous,' he said.

Betsy suppressed a snort of bitter laughter. 'Of course it's dangerous. But what choice do we have? Do nothing and Lud will triumph.' She squeezed Izzy's hand. 'Just imagine what Samuel will do to us then.'

Reluctantly, Israel agreed to her plan. 'You'll have to bide your time,' he said. 'The only way it'll work is if you get him on your own.'

Noah saw them looking and scowled. 'What are you staring at?' he snarled.

'Nothing,' Israel said.

Betsy didn't speak. She let her eyes do the talking, expressing an interest in Noah that she didn't feel. He saw the look and the hostility left his face. She'd given him food for thought.

Forty-four

For most of the evening, the Rat Boys occupied themselves drinking. But they were subdued. There was none of the usual carousing and squabbling. Soon, most of them had lapsed into a drunken stupor, except Noah who had drunk less than the others and wanted to know what that look from Betsy meant.

'He keeps watching me,' Betsy whispered to Israel.

He nodded. 'He ain't exactly subtle, is he? It's a wonder Samuel didn't cotton on weeks ago.'

'Samuel's too full of himself,' Betsy said. 'He'd never dream one of his boys would dare challenge him.'

Still aware of the attention Noah was paying Betsy, Israel decided. 'I'll make myself scarce.' He had only gone a couple of steps when he half-turned. 'Just be careful, Bets.'

Once Israel had wandered off in the direction of the Rat Boys, Noah made his way over to her.

'I saw you giving me the eye,' he said.

Betsy was determined to take her time before reeling

him in. 'That's wishful thinking, that is, Noah. You've been doing the same to me for months.'

'Yes,' Noah pouted, 'and you turned me down flat.'

'What do you expect?' Betsy replied. 'I knew what the guv'nor would do to me.'

'It ain't fair,' Noah said. 'I don't see why the guv'nor should have you all to himself. You know how I feel.'

'You might be in luck,' Betsy said. 'I'm not sure Sammy cares for me all that much. I don't think he looks at me the same way no more. Maybe he's getting bored of me.'

'Is that it?' Noah demanded, his eyes gleaming with pleasure. 'Is that why you was giving me the eye? The guv'nor's lost interest so you're looking for somebody new?'

Betsy was revolted by Noah's presence, especially by his eagerness to step into Samuel's shoes. She wanted to scrub her skin where he was touching her. She still managed to force an encouraging smile. 'Might be.'

'Let's away,' Noah said, 'you and me, right now.'

'Out of the Rats' Nest?' Betsy asked eagerly. This was too good to be true. She might be able to break away and run to Paul.

Noah hesitated.

'Well no,' he said, 'I daren't let you outside. I thought we might slip downstairs, to that room on the second landing.' He grinned. 'Yes, I've been keeping an eye on you, girl. I know where you go when you want to be alone.'

The thought of his eyes following her all the time sent prickles down Betsy's spine.

'Noah,' she said, making light of it, 'you're a wicked

280

devil, you are! You shouldn't rush a girl. No, you'll have to be a bit more patient.'

'But it's got to be tonight,' Noah said.

Betsy's pulse quickened. Her eyes narrowed with interest. 'Why has it?' she asked.

'Because tomorrow . . .' Noah began, before breaking off.

'Tomorrow?'

Betsy rested her hands on Noah's chest. 'What happens tomorrow?'

But Noah wasn't deceived. Even he could read the signs this time. He pulled back, as if she'd struck him a blow.

'I know your game,' he gasped. 'You've been playing me, ain't you? You ain't interested in me at all.'

Betsy chanced a triumphant smile. 'Of course I'm not interested in you, Noah Pyke. I'd rather kiss one of Israel's stiffs than kiss you. You're vermin, you are. You make me sick.'

Noah made a grab for Betsy's arm. Before he could lay hands on her, a door slammed. He glanced across the Rats' Nest. Samuel had just emerged from his room. Betsy took a chance.

'What are you going to do, Noah?' she hissed. 'Are you going to tell the guv'nor I know when he's going to strike?' She shoved her face in his. 'Oh, it'd be bad for me, but what do you think he'd do to you? His right hand man goes flirting with his girl then gives away his plans? You know how he hates people who go behind his back.'

'You wouldn't say nuffin',' Noah said uncertainly, suddenly very aware of Samuel's presence in the room.

'Wouldn't I?' Betsy said.

'No, you ain't got the guts.'

'What have I got to lose?' Betsy asked. 'I know he's going to kill me when he's finished with Izzy.'

Noah flinched visibly.

'Oh yes,' Betsy said, 'I keep my eyes and ears open. I'm not stupid.'

'You're bluffing,' Noah said. 'You're the same pathetic, frightened creature you always was.'

'Maybe something of Molly has rubbed off on me,' she said, keeping her voice low. Her heart was banging. She could feel the pressure of pure terror behind her eyes. But she was going to see it through. 'Do you want to take the risk, Noah? Well, do you?'

Noah stared at Betsy then followed Samuel's progress over to the fire where he stood, warming himself.

'So what if you do know about tomorrow night?' Noah spat. 'You can't do nuffin' to stop it, can you? I tell you what, Betsy Alder, if the guv'nor doesn't rip your lousy guts out, you can be sure I'll do it.' He whispered a final threat into her ear. 'You'll wish you'd never taunted Noah Pyke.'

He was about to continue when Samuel barked an order. 'Come away from her, Noah. I made Izzy a promise. Him and Bets go unmolested and he does what I say. I don't want you upsetting them.'

Grudgingly, Noah edged away, leaving Betsy trembling but proud. Noah wasn't going to say a word to Samuel. When she had steadied her breathing, she caught Israel's eyes. She'd done it. Now all they had to do was get a message to Chaim.

Forty-five

Paul emerged from breakfast to find Chaim waiting for him.

'I can smell perfume on your suit,' he complained. 'You've been to see that Mrs Flaherty again, ain't you?'

'So what if I have?' Paul asked, shoving past.

'Just listen to me,' Chaim begged. 'You can't trust her, Paul. Her name's a byword for all sorts of wickedness round here. She's nearly as bad as Samuel.'

'That's enough,' Paul said, hesitating at the door to the hotel, 'I'm not going to argue with you. I don't want to hear it.'

'Well, I'm going to make you hear it,' Chaim retorted. 'I'm risking my neck for you. So are Izzy and Bets. And what are you doing, Paul? You're putting your trust in someone who was once Samuel Rector's woman.'

The mention of Izzy, and especially Betsy, stopped Paul in his tracks. 'All right, you've got my attention, Chaim. Why are you here?'

'I've heard from Izzy,' Chaim said. 'He threw a message down from the Rats' Nest. All that time keeping vigil has paid off.'

'Is Betsy all right?' he asked.

'Care, do you?' Chaim asked scornfully. 'All the while she's been in Samuel's clutches, you've been talking to that woman.' He shoved a piece of paper into Paul's hand. 'Read it.'

Paul took the crumpled note and read the strange scrawl. The letters were russet brown. 'Is this blood?'

Chaim nodded. 'Looks like it. Israel tossed the note into the alley wrapped round a piece of coal. He's had to use his own blood as ink.'

Paul read the single word: *tonight*. He screwed the note up in his fist.

'Well,' Chaim demanded, 'what are we going to do?'

'We're going to fight,' Paul said simply. 'I have allies.'

'You'd better not be talking about Mrs Flaherty,' Chaim said. 'What's to stop her double-crossing us?'

'Nothing,' Paul admitted, 'but I think I know her well enough by now.'

Chaim snorted in derision but Paul continued. 'She's told me things,' he said. 'Her hatred for Samuel is real.'

'You'd better be certain of that,' Chaim said.

'It's a gamble,' Paul said. 'But I don't see any other way of defeating Samuel. We need allies. She's going to organize a meeting of the other gang leaders.'

Chaim stared in disbelief. 'That's your plan? We're going to put your trust in the worst bunch of cutthroats in the whole of London!'

'Samuel has an army,' Paul said evenly. 'That means we need soldiers too.'

'So who's coming?' Chaim asked.

Paul ran through the gang leaders' names. 'There's a man called Barton . . .'

'You can stop there,' Chaim said. 'You've just confirmed my worst fears. If Razor Barton's involved, then you're in hock to the worst there is.'

'I thought Samuel was the worst there is,' Paul snapped.

'Do you have any idea who you're dealing with?' Chaim cried, ignoring him. 'You're selling your soul to the Devil.'

Forty-six

Knuckles rapped on the hotel bedroom door. Paul swung his legs off the bed and answered the knock.

'I'm sorry to disturb you, sir,' said the concierge, 'but there is a gentleman in the foyer.'

Paul noticed a slight hesitation over the word gentleman and smiled to himself. He tipped the concierge.

'I'll be down presently,' he said, copying the rhythms of speech he had been hearing around him.

He squirmed into his clothes and pulled on his boots. He slipped on a thick jacket and examined his reflection. Was this it? He looked out at Covent Garden then made his way downstairs. O'Shaughnessy was waiting for him. His face was lined with a thick layer of stubble and his eyes were bloodshot.

'You've been drinking,' Paul observed. O'Shaughnessy sniffed but he didn't answer. 'Do you have some news for me?'

'Everything's arranged,' O'Shaughnessy replied. 'I'm to take you to the meeting. You're to come right away.'

'Why the rush?'

'Why do you think?' O'Shaughnessy said. 'The gangs don't trust you. They want the meeting at a time and place of their own choosing. That way you can't pull any funny tricks.'

'Where?'

'A warehouse near St Katherine's Dock,' O'Shaughnessy said. 'Kit says Samuel's less likely to find out that way.'

'Wait there a moment,' Paul said. He scribbled a couple of notes and instructed the concierge to see they were delivered as a matter of urgency. Another tip followed. 'Let's go.'

He hailed a hansom. He didn't exchange a word with O'Shaughnessy all the way there. Soon, the masts and sails of the moored vessels came into view. The myriad smells of the port muddied the air. The cab rattled away in the direction of Commercial Road.

Paul shot a glance at the monumental, smoke-blackened building. 'How am I to know you're not leading me into an ambush?'

'There's no guarantees,' O'Shaughnessy answered. 'There's no need to worry though. I don't give a fig for you, mister. I'd sell your hide to Samuel tomorrow. But I'd do anything for Kit.'

Paul considered his words for a moment. 'You first.'

O'Shaughnessy shook his head and led the way inside. As Paul followed, he allowed his newly acute senses to probe the warehouse's interior. He made out shifting feet. There had to be at least a dozen people, maybe twenty. He breathed in the acrid reek of tobacco and a faint trace of alcohol. Then a welcome scent reached him. It was Kitty Flaherty's perfume.

'In here,' O'Shaughnessy said.

Paul shoved him forward, roughly enough to make him lose his balance. 'After you.'

O'Shaughnessy stumbled inside. Immediately, Paul glimpsed a shadowy figure moving towards him. He flashed out a hand. Searing heat met his attacker and a scream cut through the gloom. Noticing a broken barrel over to his right, Paul kindled it with a jet of flame, illuminating the gathering. He took advantage of the garish light to survey his surroundings. His victim was bent double, nursing a blistered arm. Mrs Flaherty was sitting on a crate, the trademark smile playing on her lips. Up to two dozen men were standing or sitting around her.

'What was the meaning of that?' Paul demanded, indicating the wounded man. 'I came here in good faith.'

'These gentlemen insisted on putting you to the test,' Mrs Flaherty explained. 'Their trust isn't easily won.'

'I assume I've passed,' Paul said.

Mrs Flaherty introduced those present. She lingered over the names Razor Jim Barton and Ger Willis, alerting Paul to their importance as movers and shakers in the East End underworld.

'How many gangs are represented here?' Paul asked.

'Four,' Mrs Flaherty informed him.

'And what unites you all?' Paul asked. He let the question hang then answered it himself. 'It's Samuel Rector, isn't it? Now here's another question for you:

288

why haven't you moved against your common enemy? Answer: he's too strong.'

Barton gave an almost imperceptible nod, as if he resented admitting it. 'I'll give you that. It don't mean we should join you though, do it?'

Paul heard footsteps behind him. It was Bill and Jim. They stood to either side of him.

'I know more about Samuel than any of you,' Paul said. 'I know his strengths and his weaknesses.'

'How can you?' Barton demanded. 'None of us have ever seen you before.'

'I don't think you appreciate what I'm telling you,' Paul said. 'Samuel and me, we're family.'

A murmur ran round the room.

'That's right. Only he's the black sheep,' Paul said. 'He dies, or I do.' There was more movement behind him. It was Chaim. 'Accept my leadership and I will take you to victory. No more Samuel Rector. You will have free rein to run the East End as you like.'

'Are we supposed to take your word for all this?' Willis demanded. 'I mean, look at you. You don't even look like you're ready to shave yet, never mind take on the Satan of Spitalfields.'

'Haven't you had enough demonstrations yet?' Paul asked. He sighed. 'Go on. Pick your man.'

Willis waved one of his men forward.

'Take him, Slugger.'

The man was lean and shaven-headed. Slugger drew a cudgel and strode towards Paul. He took a swing but missed. Paul crouched low, facing him. He couldn't help marvelling at his own prowess.

It's true. I'm changing. I can anticipate his every move.

'You'll have to do better than that,' he told Slugger,

waving him forward. He was enjoying his new strength and agility. Slugger swung again. As he did, Paul shot out a leg and upended him. Paul leapt on top of his opponent and fixed him with a stare.

'What's he doing?' Barton demanded.

'Watch,' Mrs Flaherty told him.

Paul held Slugger's startled look and opened the gates of Hell. The man started to rock his head back and forth.

'No,' he cried. 'No!'

'It's true,' Willis gasped, 'he is related to the guv'nor. That's the trademark of the Satan of Spitalfields. We've all seen Samuel do this to his enemies.'

Paul sensed the gathering leaning forward. Oh yes, he thought, you all recognize the death stare. He continued the demonstration. Slugger's boots were kicking on the wooden floor. His breath was coming in hoarse whimpers.

'Do I need to continue?' Paul demanded.

Spittle was bubbling on the terrified man's lips. A gurgle of horror rose in his throat. 'Please,' Slugger begged.

'Enough,' Willis yelled.

'But I'm just starting to enjoy myself,' Paul taunted.

'Enough, I say,' Willis repeated. 'Let him up.'

Paul relented and walked to the middle of the warehouse floor.

'Now listen to me, *gentlemen*,' he said, heavy on the sarcasm, 'I'm just overwhelmed that you've accepted my leadership. But you must understand what it means.' He waited a beat. 'You're all answerable to me now.' He met the gang leaders' eyes. 'Pass this on to your foot soldiers, if I give an order they don't hesitate, they don't look to you for confirmation, they obey without question. Is that understood?'

There were a few grudging nods. Dissatisfied, Paul unleashed a stream of flame. He watched the effect on his audience. After a few moments, he roared the question a second time. 'I said, is that understood?'

His audience chorused their answer. 'Yes.'

'Good,' Paul said. 'The moment it goes dark, there are preparations to be made. I'll need twenty strong men. Arrange it for me.'

He whispered in O'Shaughnessy's ear. 'Get in touch with Kidd. Tell him it's time to move the barrels.'

O'Shaughnessy did as he was told, though with obvious reluctance. As Paul strode from the warehouse, flanked by Bill and Jim and followed by Chaim, he caught Mrs Flaherty's eye.

'How did I do?' he asked.

'Just fine,' she replied. 'Now you've got to put those fine words into action. Sammy ain't no ordinary street villain.'

Paul nodded. 'I know.'

He continued out into the murky, winter light. For all his confident appearance, his heart was thudding so hard he could barely breathe.

Forty-seven

It was just before midnight when Paul heard it.

'What's wrong?' Chaim asked, scrambling up from the trench where he'd been sheltering from the biting wind.

Chaim wasn't the only one who had seen Paul stiffen and peer into the darkness towards Whitechapel. Mrs Flaherty appeared. Barton and Willis signalled to their men to stop talking. 'Listen.'

There were shaken heads all round. Paul ran his gaze over the motley force he'd managed to assemble. It was one hundred strong, mostly made up of the most desperate ruffians and thugs armed with knives, cudgels and cleavers. There were rumoured to be one or two concealed pistols. They were using the construction site for the new railway terminus as a series of ramparts against Samuel's army of the night.

Bill was next to notice it. A veteran of many military campaigns, he recognized the tramp of feet. But this was different. There was no jingle of harness, no slap

292

of sword against thigh, no orderly march. The throng that was closing on Aldgate from the graveyards of Whitechapel and Mile End, Bethnal Green and Hackney, Shoreditch, St George's and Spitalfields, was chaotic and unnatural. Some of the unseen feet tramped, others dragged, still others scampered ahead.

'He's right,' Bill said, 'they're coming.'

'Pistols,' Paul shouted across the site, 'show me who's armed.'

Bill produced his weapon. The moonlight caught one or two ancient muskets and half a dozen more pistols.

'And the rest,' Paul commanded. 'If you want to live, you won't hold anything back to settle scores later. I want to see those guns.' He counted. 'A dozen, is that all?' Barton and Willis produced their own weapons. 'Fourteen,' Paul amended. 'It will have to do.' He glanced at Chaim and Jim. 'Is everything in position?' Chaim nodded.

Paul called every armed man into the trench facing east and gave them their instructions.

Soon, dark figures started to loom in the distance. Half a dozen were closing fast, dropping occasionally onto all fours. These were the transformed Rat Boys. Behind them lumbered the ranks of the undead.

'What if we hit Betsy or Izzy?' Chaim hissed.

'I don't see them,' Paul replied, 'but it's a chance we've got to take.' He crouched forward. 'Each man pick a target. Wait until they're in range.' Finally, the Rat Boys were close enough so that he could see their features. He flung out an arm and a fireball engulfed Ezra who tumbled, twisting and writhing to the earth. A musket ball smashed Enoch's skull. Ethan was faster, leaping into the trench with an inhuman scream. He tore open the throat of the man next to Bill. Swinging round, Bill hacked the boy down.

'Chaim, Jim,' Paul cried, 'pick up those guns.'

Bill picked one up and presented it to Chaim. 'I don't know how to fire it,' Chaim protested.

'I'll show you, lad,' Bill told him, reloading it.

But when Jim reached for the second pistol, the strangest thing happened. It started to slide out of his reach. 'I've seen this before,' he cried. 'It's one of them boys. He can move things with his mind.'

Paul leapt forward, crashing his elbow into Jasper's face. He wrestled the boy to the ground and seized him by the throat. The will to destroy welled up inside him and Jasper was consumed by fire. Paul watched the boy die then he felt Jasper's power flow through him. He patted James's shoulder. 'Take the gun, James. Use it.'

'Here they come,' Mrs Flaherty shouted, pointing at a packed mass of shuffling creatures.

'Take cover!' Paul yelled.

As the defenders around Aldgate ducked down behind whatever cover they could find, Paul hurled jets of flame at a dozen concealed dumps of explosive. One after another, they detonated, sending the bodies of the undead hurtling into the night. Already, police whistles could be heard piercing the air in the distance.

'The Peelers are on their way,' Willis said.

'Does it matter?' Paul demanded. 'Their presence won't affect the outcome of the battle.'

The explosives barely thinned the mob of risen dead. On they came, a tramping silent horde.

'Get at them!' Paul yelled.

Soon, the scene was an horrific mêlée as the defenders slashed and bludgeoned their way into the mass of walking cadavers. Half a dozen gang members were dead, overwhelmed by the creatures Israel had raised from the grave.

'Where's Samuel?' Paul cried, scanning the crowd. He laid his hands on the nearest of the undead, encasing the ghoul in flame. But when he tried the trick a second time, his hands barely glowed.

'What is it?' Chaim asked.

Paul wiped the sweat from his forehead. 'I don't know.' His head was swarming with nightmarish visions. His demon side was growing stronger, poisoning his thoughts. He sank to his knees, clutching his head. Lud's scarlet eyes blazed in his mind.

'Paul!' Chaim cried. 'We need you.'

The undead were making inroads. More men were dying. Pistols and muskets crackled briefly then fell silent. They were out of ammunition. But still the night creatures came. The undead were on the march.

'Try to hold them off,' Paul panted, clawing at his temples. He fell back and knelt, gulping in the winter air, trying to clear the demon contagion from his thoughts.

We're on the brink of defeat. That's when he heard Barton's voice.

'Clear out, boys,' he bawled. 'It ain't worth it. They're slaughtering us.'

'You can't go,' Paul cried.

'Don't tell me what I can or can't do,' Barton retorted. 'You said we was going to remove Samuel. Well, I don't see us winning now, do you? You can't even stand. This is a bleedin' massacre, this is.'

Willis and the other gang leaders had come to the same conclusion. Men were streaming from the field of battle.

'Come back!' Paul roared.

But the fleeing men took no notice. Paul counted the remnants of his force. Bill and Jim were still standing. So was Chaim.

'Where's Kit?' he asked.

'Where do you think?' Bill snorted. 'Gone, just like the rest of the sewer rats.'

'I tried to tell you,' Chaim said. 'Her and that O'Shaughnessy were the first to bail.'

Paul turned and counted the ranks of the undead. There were still twenty of the things standing. At their head stood Jacob and Ethan.

'You and me, renegade,' Jacob shouted, by way of a challenge.

Paul scrambled over the workings towards him. 'It suits me. Just us two.'

Chaim grabbed his sleeve. 'What are you doing? You don't even know if you've recovered your powers yet.'

Paul brushed him away. 'I've got to buy time,' he said. 'We're in danger of being swept away.'

He took several steps forward. Jacob grinned and raced into the attack. Such was the speed of the assault, Paul saw him only as a blur. Then the boy's yellowish teeth were snapping at his throat. Paul clung to Jacob's shoulders, trying to hold him off. He could feel hot spittle on his face.

'I'm going to rip your throat out,' Jacob shrieked. 'You've butchered four of our boys.'

Paul focused on Jacob's face. Dark shapes still fluttered at the edge of his vision. But he was beginning to focus them. His power was returning. Concentrating everything he had on his hands, Paul summoned all his strength. Jacob started to howl. Paul rolled him over. Flames started to lick Jacob's flesh. His skin was crisping and blackening. As the Rat Boy threshed beneath him, Paul clung on. It was over within seconds. But even as he was about to rise, Paul felt a searing pain. Razor sharp claws were digging into his back. It was Ethan. The assault lasted just a few seconds. There was a loud report and the boy fell to the earth, quite dead. Paul spun round. Bill's pistol was smoking.

'I saved a single shot,' he said. 'It was for myself, see. Well, I didn't want those things cannibalising me.'

Paul turned to look at the undead. To his surprise, they were as still as statues. Then, one by one, they crumpled to the ground. Everybody stared at Paul, wanting an explanation.

'I don't know why've they stopped,' he said.

He searched the gloom for Samuel. Three or four policeman were hurrying towards them when a huge explosion stopped the police in their tracks. The four remaining defenders spun round and gazed in the direction of the City.

'What in God's name was that?' James asked.

A sickening wave of foreboding swept through Paul. *It can't be.* 'Follow me,' he said, running towards Mitre Square.

'What about Aldgate?' Chaim said. 'We can't abandon it?'

'Don't you understand?' Paul cried. 'This battle wasn't for real.'

'Say that again!' Chaim panted.

'The whole thing was a diversion,' Paul told him.

'Why didn't I see what he was doing? *This* is the reason Samuel isn't here. Lud has been fooling us all along. We put all our efforts into defending Aldgate, the East Gate. But there are four gates, Chaim. *Four!'*

They were running up Mitre Street when they saw the crowds.

'What's going on?' Paul asked the first man he saw.

'There's been an explosion,' the man told him. 'Camomile Street's in flames.'

Paul hung his head.

'I still don't understand,' Chaim said.

'It's simple,' Paul said. 'We've lost.'

'How?' Bill protested. 'How have we lost? We repelled those things, didn't we?'

'Oh, we fought them off all right, and all the while we were cutting them down, Samuel was here. Lud's been controlling those things from his crypt while Samuel got on with the real business.'

Three pairs of questioning eyes fixed him.

'While we've been occupied at Aldgate, Samuel's broken the second seal. He's breeched Bishopsgate.' He pointed. 'This was the southern gate of the Roman city, one chamber of London's dark heart.' He screwed his fists into his face. 'Lud's played me for a fool all along.'

The words had no sooner left his lips than a familiar figure appeared at the top of the street. The boy dodged and weaved his way through the pressing crowd.

'Now what?' Bill asked.

Malachy emerged from the confusion. 'You finally got here then?' There was a gleam of triumph in his eyes.

'What do you want?' Paul asked, his skin burning with humiliation.

Malachy grinned. 'I've got a message from the guv'nor. He's waiting for you at the Rats' Nest. If you want Bets and Izzy back, you'll have to come and get them.' Without another word, he scampered away into the throng.

'What do we do?' James wondered out loud.

'What *can* we do?' Chaim said. 'That monster will kill them for sure. We've got to go.'

'You know it's a trap, don't you?' James said.

'Of course it's a trap,' Bill snapped. 'But what choice do we have? When I think about that poor girl . . .' He clenched his fists. 'We've nothing left to lose.'

'Bill's right,' Paul said. 'We've got to face Samuel. Somehow, we have to defeat him. Thanks to my stupidity, he's already taken Bishopsgate. If we fall, nothing can prevent him taking Aldgate too. Half the crypt's seals will have been broken. He'll be unstoppable. Then he will be able to break through the Bridge Gate and Ludgate too. He is on the brink of changing history for ever. We will have handed him his final triumph.' Horror was written on his features. 'Lud could be free in days.'

'What do you want?' Paul asked. He..

forty-eight

'So we're back where it began,' Chaim said.

Paul could hear the weight of disappointment in his voice. A pall of smoke hung over the Flowery. Smoke and soot from the explosion at Camomile Street was settling on the roofs. Wreaths of mist were curling around the neighbourhood. There was the odd drunken shout, the occasional raucous yell, but quiet was coming to Spitalfields.

'How do we do this?' Bill murmured, his gaze climbing the floors of the Rats' Nest.

'There's one way in,' Paul said. 'We go through the front door.'

'That's it?' James asked. 'We just present ourselves to him?'

Paul was numb. Nothing had turned out as he hoped. Lud had outwitted him. Kit had betrayed his trust and fled the field of battle.

'Unless you know how to sprout wings,' Paul answered, 'it's the only way in.'

Bill shoved at the door. 'It's locked.'

'Can't you open it, Paul?' James said.

'Maybe I can,' Paul said.

He focused on the door. The familiar black shapes spiralled, creating a tunnel whose end point was the lock. For a moment nothing happened. Paul steeled himself once more, driving everything else from his mind. There was the rasp of bolts, the click of the lock and it creaked open.

I did it. It's still there. I've got Jasper's power. He felt a surge of optimism. He squinted into the shadowy interior. A shaft of moonlight lanced across the staircase. The only other light came from the top floor, a candle or an oil lamp.

'How many of them are in there?' Bill asked.

It was Chaim who answered. 'There's Samuel, of course, and two Rat Boys, Noah and Malachy.'

'What about them walking stiffs?' James asked.

Paul shook his head. 'I don't think we've got anything to worry about there. Samuel doesn't need them any more.'

James brightened. 'So we outnumber them?'

'Don't get your hopes up,' Chaim said. 'I've seen him at close range. With his monstrous strength, Samuel is worth any three men.'

'That ain't all,' Bill said. 'He's got Bets as a hostage.'

'And Israel,' Chaim reminded him.

Paul gestured for them to be quiet, and led the way up the first flight of stairs, stopping on the landing. He glanced back. Bill was immediately behind him, armoured with a cleaver. James and Chaim were following, each brandishing a cudgel. Paul was about to start up the second flight when he heard somebody shifting their weight. He spun round just in time to see Malachy and Noah coming at him, slashing with their claws.

'Look out!'

Malachy crashed into him, slamming him against the wall, while Noah threw himself at Bill. In the cramped stairwell, James and Chaim could only look on helplessly while a desperate struggle followed. Malachy was in a frenzy, tearing and slashing at Paul. For a few moments Paul could only fend off the blows. Then he remembered the power he had taken from Jasper. He fixed Malachy's belcher with a stare and the neckerchief tightened around the boy's throat. The moment Malachy started to choke, Paul laid flaming hands on him. He was dead in seconds. Noah saw what had happened and fled upstairs.

'Are you all right, Bill?' Paul asked.

'A few scratches, that's all,' Bill told him. 'What about you?' He stared. 'What in God's name are you doing there?'

Paul's hands were still planted on Malachy's blackened chest. He could feel the boy's life force pulsing inside him. 'Look away if you like, Bill. I have to drain him of every ounce of his life force. If I'm right, his strength is my strength.'

There had been times he had denied his true nature, but here he was, stripping his supernatural foes of their abilities, growing in power as his victims perished. Until this day he'd thought himself too young, too weak, too inexperienced. Hadn't he reached this point more by luck than by choice? He'd been out of his depth. No more. He could see the way ahead. He would break his enemies and make their powers his own. One day his powers would eclipse Lud's. When that time came he would release the demon and crush him. For the first time, all this talk of destiny had the ring of truth.

I am one demon who can be all demons.

He hurried up to the Rats' Nest. Through the open door he could see Betsy and Israel. Each of them was bound to one of the timbers that supported the roof. They were both gagged. Wide eyes stared at him. What were they trying to tell him?

'Where's Samuel?' Paul asked, stepping into the room.

His answer came in a sudden explosion of sound and movement. First, a huge fist crashed into his head, sending him sprawling on the bare floor. In the same split second, the door slammed. Outside on the landing, Noah was barring entry to Bill, James and Chaim. Through a grey, numb mist, Paul could hear the ferocious struggle. He rolled onto his back and groaned. Immediately, Samuel hove into view above him. His black eyes were aflame with hatred.

'Well, if it ain't the renegade,' he snarled, simultaneously driving his right boot into Paul's ribs. He screwed the boot in hard. Paul felt at least one snap and screamed. The boot slammed into him a second time and the white heat of pure agony ripped through him.

'Do you still think you can defeat me?' Samuel bellowed.

Paul tried to hug himself in a vain attempt at self protection but Samuel pounded him with three more savage punches. Paul's face was already a mask of blood. There was only one thought in his head.

He's going to kill me.

Samuel's elbow crashed into the centre of his chest and the breath went out of him. Paul writhed and twisted on the floor, desperate to wriggle away from the bone-crushing impact of Samuel's boots and fists. He couldn't breathe, let alone resist.

'Is this it?' Samuel taunted. 'Is this the retribution you promised to hand out?' He dragged Paul to his feet. 'Can you really be the appointed champion of the priests of Beltane?' He spat. 'Why, I've fought tougher men in the ring. Kit Flaherty's old fellow put up more of a fight than you.'

A voice interrupted him. 'Yes, and you slaughtered poor Danny.'

Samuel's head snapped round. 'Kitty! Now ain't that a coincidence.'

Mrs Flaherty was standing by the window. 'It ain't no coincidence, Samuel. I've been biding my time. You're going to pay for what you did to me, to Danny, to everybody you ever hurt.'

'Fighting talk,' Samuel said. 'Tell me, how did you get up here?'

Mrs Flaherty wasn't alone. O'Shaughnessy had a pistol pointed at Samuel's head. 'You showed me how, Samuel,' she said. 'I lived with you once, remember. You was a good teacher in the thief's arts, I'll give you that. We used your secret route. We came over the rooftops.'

'Clever girl,' Samuel said. He stood facing her, hugging Paul's bleeding body to him. 'I like you, Kitty, I really do. Hard as hobnails, ain't you? It seems you're more of a man than this ancestor of mine.' He tightened his grip on Paul's limp form then shifted his stare to O'Shaughnessy. 'You've got one shot, mister. You'd better kill me stone dead or, so help me, I'll crush you with my bare hands. Do you think you can do it?' He laughed then bellowed the question again. '*Well, do you?*'

O'Shaughnessy's finger was on the trigger.

'What's the matter?' Samuel asked. 'Is your hand trembling? Come on, I'm a big enough target.' He cast Paul aside and threw out his arms. 'Go on, do your worst.'

'Aim for the head!' Mrs Flaherty screamed, sensing the paralysis that was numbing O'Shaughnessy's muscles.

Samuel sprang forward. There was an ear-splitting explosion as the pistol went off. Through a booming tunnel of pain, Paul could feel the spatter of hot blood. It belonged to the Satan of Spitalfields. Samuel was reeling slightly but still standing. O'Shaughnessy had lost his nerve. That precious single shot had failed to kill Samuel outright. To Paul's horror, Samuel clamped a huge hand to his own shoulder. He turned his palm over and showed the blood to O'Shaughnessy.

'It's a flesh wound,' he chuckled.

'Sweet Lord,' O'Shaughnessy croaked, the blood draining from his face.

'Kit told you to aim for my head,' Samuel said. He tapped a thick finger against his brow. 'Are you hard of hearing, or just plain stupid?'

Paul was starting to recover from Samuel's assault. He could hear Betsy murmuring something against the gag. *Untie me.* Taking advantage of the fact that Samuel was preoccupied, he rolled over and winced as fresh stabbing pains gouged through his side. He fastened on one thought.

I am one demon who can be all demons.

He had to use Jasper's mind trick while Samuel had his back turned. He willed Betsy's ropes to loosen. As he looked on, they gradually uncurled. Given the chance to squirm free, Betsy ripped away her bonds. Paul saw her fumble in the folds of her dress. She had a knife. Betsy started sawing at Israel's bonds for a moment then he was free. She pressed a finger to her lips. Paul nodded. But no sooner had hope been lit than it was extinguished. Samuel snapped O'Shaughnessy's neck with one sudden squeeze then clubbed Mrs Flaherty to the floor with the back of his hand.

'Think you're going to stop me, do you?' he bawled.

Untying his belcher, he staunched the flow of blood, lodging the neckerchief under his shirt to cover the wound. He turned. Betsy concealed her knife before he could see.

'What's this?' Samuel said. 'Get yourself free, did you?' His eyes rested on Betsy for a moment. 'Maybe you're not quite the miserable little mouse I always thought.' He looked down at Paul next, then at Israel. 'It won't do any of you much good, mind. It's over.'

Even as he spoke, a rush of hot air filled the room. Dust whipped and spiralled. Thick braids of cobwebs danced in the updraught. It was Lud.

'No mistakes, Samuel,' the demon instructed. 'You must control your natural instincts. Revenge comes second. Put the girl to the back of your mind.' Seeing Betsy's expression, he laughed scornfully. 'Concentrate, Samuel. You can have your fun when you have destroyed the renegade. With him out of the way,

306

our victory is certain. The first seal is already broken. The second has been weakened. Once this boy is dead, my rise will be inevitable, and you will sit at my right hand.'

Samuel raised his boot and drove it into Paul's face. He was out to crush his descendant's skull. A hurricane of agony howled through him. One more and it would be over. Paul's thoughts raced.

One demon who can be all demons.

His strength is my strength.

Betsy threw herself at Samuel. 'No. Please no.'

But Israel knew it was too late. He could only look on in horror as he saw the tell-tale signs of death. 'It's no use, Bets,' he said. 'Paul's already dead.'

Paul's eyes rolled back in the sockets. A deathly pallor came into his face. He shuddered for a moment then fell still.

'You must make sure,' Lud commanded. 'Destroy him, Samuel. Smash his skull in. Do it!'

Betsy was on her knees, sobbing. Her fingers were on Paul's throat. 'There's no pulse. He's gone.'

Israel reached for Paul but Samuel flung him across the room. 'No you don't, Izzy. There'll be no resurrection this time.'

Still Lud wasn't satisfied. 'Don't let yourself be distracted, Samuel. Forget the others. It's the renegade that matters. Pound him into dust!'

Samuel frowned. 'But I killed him. Nobody could survive that. See, he's going cold already.'

'Don't let outward appearances fool you,' Lud was roaring. Then he saw something. He screamed a warning. 'Don't you see? It's a trick. The renegade isn't dead. He's taken Malachy's powers.'

Samuel half turned. Malachy's nickname came to his lips. In the same moment, a look of horror and understanding crossed his face. He gasped in realization. 'Play Dead.'

Weakened though he was, Paul shook off the half-death that was Malachy's power and clutched Samuel's ankle. Flames licked at the monster's flesh rather than consumed it but Samuel roared in pain nonetheless. Betsy took advantage of the moment and plunged her knife into his chest, striking for the heart.

'That's for Molly, that is,' she shrieked.

Samuel tried to shake her off but she clung on, driving the blade deeper. The slabs of muscle that covered Samuel's chest prevented Betsy delivering the killer blow but it made him stagger. Encouraged, Israel struggled to his feet, snatching up a pewter jug and pounded it into Samuel's face – once, twice, three times, as hard as he could. Burned, cut and half-blinded, Samuel was swinging his huge fists, trying to land a punch on his tormentors. He was like a bear set upon by hounds. Still, he didn't fall. Then another voice crackled behind him.

'What did your Master say, Sammy?' Mrs Flaherty shrieked. 'Females are worthless? Maybe demon kind aren't as superior as they think. It's a pair of these worthless females who are going to finish you.' She was pointing O'Shaughnessy's pistol at his head. 'And I ain't going to make no mistake.'

At that moment, the door burst open. Paul could see Noah unconscious on the landing. Though bruised and cut, Chaim, Bill and James had triumphed. But they weren't alone. Beside them stood two officers of the Metropolitan Police.

'Put the gun down, Mrs Flaherty,' one of them said.

The second – a sergeant – seemed to know her. 'If you shoot Rector, Kitty girl, you'll hang on the same gallows as your former lover.' He saw her finger tighten round the trigger. 'Don't do it Kit. I wouldn't want to see that lovely neck all twisted out of shape on account of this abomination.'

Paul looked around the room for some sign of Lud, but the demon master had vanished. He managed to drag himself to his knees. Of course, if history was to stay true to its original path, Samuel must live to face justice.

'Do what the officer says, Kit,' he said. 'The best revenge you can have is to see Samuel dance at the end of a rope.'

Mrs Flaherty hesitated, the barrel of the pistol still pressed to Samuel's head.

'Please Kitty,' Paul pleaded. 'He isn't worth it.'

More police were pounding up the stairs.

'Listen to the lad,' the officer said. 'He won't wriggle out of it this time. We've got all the witnesses we need and not even Samuel Rector will break free of the cell we've got prepared for him. We've been waiting for this moment for years. What's it to be, Kit? Are you going to throw it all away or are you going to show a bit of the cunning that made your reputation.'

Kit met the policeman's eye. 'Well, ain't this ironic, Sergeant Hale?' she said. 'All the times you've tried to put me away and now here we are on the same side.'

Sergeant Hale nodded. 'That's the way things turn out sometimes.'

Mrs Flaherty disarmed the pistol then whipped it across the back of Samuel's skull. He sank to his knees.

'You can do it again if you like, Kitty,' Sergeant Hale said with a wink, 'I ain't going to stop you.'

Mrs Flaherty had tears in her eyes. She continued clubbing Samuel until he was barely conscious. Then the police handcuffed him and bound him in chains. An entire crowd of armed officers flanked him as he was removed from the Rats' Nest.

'Are we all free to go?' Mrs Flaherty asked Sergeant Hale.

'Perfectly free,' Sergeant Hale confirmed. 'There's nothing I can hold you on. Just give your names and addresses to the constable on your way out. You'll be needed as witnesses.'

'You're coming with me,' Mrs Flaherty said to Paul. 'I've got a soothing touch for those wounds.'

Paul put up no resistance. 'O'Shaughnessy?' he asked.

Mrs Flaherty shook her head. 'He's gone.'

As the six allies against Lud trudged out into the darkness and the cold, Betsy took Israel's hand.

'See,' she said, gazing up at the stars, 'we did it Moll. We finally found the courage to stand up to him.'

forty-nine

Samuel Rector stirs in his dark, airless cell. The stench of brimstone is in his nostrils.

'Master.'

He eases himself up on the stone bed where he has been lying. The familiar black vortex swirls before him.

'You failed me, Samuel.'

Samuel drops to his knees. 'Master.' He averts his eyes from the demon master's stare. 'You've got to forgive me.'

'Do I?' Lud demands. 'And why is that?'

Samuel keeps his head bowed. He fails to offer a reason.

'You underestimated the renegade,' Lud says. 'Even when I commanded you to complete the kill, you failed to make the right choice.'

'How was I to know he could take the boys' powers?' Samuel whimpers. 'He weren't nuffin'. I thrashed him to within an inch of his life.'

'Miserable fool,' Lud growls. 'Brawn isn't his strength. Didn't you hear what he said: a demon who can be all demons. He is beginning to understand his nature. If he slays a demon brother, he can assume his powers.'

'But that don't make him more than a scavenger,' Samuel protests, 'stealing off others.'

'Does it matter how the renegade did it?' Lud says. 'The point is, he won.'

'Why couldn't he fight me . . . ?'

Lud's features light with intense black flames. 'Fight you fair, is that what you were going to say? You're a damned fool.' His presence dims. 'The struggle goes on, Samuel, but you won't be a part of it. Already, one of my disciples is moving against the renegade. I am about to strike at him where he is most vulnerable. I plan to tear open his soft, sentimental heart.'

'Don't leave me, Master,' Samuel pleads.

Lud's eyes flicker one last time.

'I wash my hands of you,' he says.

'No!'

'You are no use to the demon cause.'

'I am your loyal servant.'

'You are nothing,' Lud snarls. 'Kill yourself, Samuel. Do it now.'

Moments later the turnkey is alerted to an incident by the shouts of the other prisoners. He peers into the cell to see Samuel hurling himself head first against the stone walls. Again and again Samuel crashes his skull into the wall. It takes a dozen warders to restrain him.

By the time they carry him to the infirmary, he is barely breathing but he will live to kick at the end of the hangman's noose.

Fifty

*F*ar in the future, on another February day, a ghost train arrives silently at Whitechapel Underground station. Out steps a tall, lean man with lank, black hair. He steps onto the empty platform and breathes in the night air.

'You did it, Master,' he says, deep satisfaction in his voice. 'Guide my footsteps to the girl. I will not fail you.'

He closes his eyes and takes his instructions from Lud. Then, jogging past a startled night cleaner, he vaults over the ticket barrier and strides along Whitechapel High Street. It will take him three quarters of an hour to make his way along the largely deserted streets to the estate where the girl lives. He is in no hurry. He may take her today. He may enjoy himself first in the fleshpots of London and make his move later. Either way, he will complete his mission.

Soon, he is making his way into the Close where Netty

313

Carney lives with her mother. He watches the lighted window and smiles.

'You can't imagine the adventure that awaits you,' he murmurs. 'Get ready for the trip of a lifetime.'

cut arms. She squeezed his arm. 'So what are you

Fifty-one

It was weeks before Paul recovered fully from his
injuries, but he was in time to watch Samuel hang.
He stood beside Kitty Flaherty in the Old Bailey,
staring up at the scaffold. Enormous crowds packed
Newgate Street for the occasion. Every window overlooking the scene was thronged with people trying to
get the best view of the spectacle. Most had paid a
substantial sum for the privilege.

'Your friends didn't come then?' Mrs Flaherty said
as they walked away.

'No,' Paul told her. 'I think they've seen enough
death and suffering. They're waiting at a coffee shop
down Fleet Street. We will join them after we see
Samuel hung.'

Mrs Flaherty slipped her arm round his. 'You should
stay. I need a new lieutenant.'

Paul shook his head. 'Thanks for the offer, Kit, but
no thanks.'

Mrs Flaherty watched him for a moment then gave a

315

sad smile. She squeezed his arm. 'So what are you after, Paul Rector?'

'I want the horror to end,' he said simply.

'But it has,' Mrs Flaherty said. 'The East End ain't going to see the likes of old Sammy in a while.'

'Samuel was just one of the boils,' Paul said, 'a symptom of the contagion. He wasn't the plague itself. I've got to destroy Lud.'

'Don't you think that's a bit of a tall order?' Mrs Flaherty asked. 'Samuel damned near killed you. Why risk worse? You and I could have a fine old life here.'

'I'd love to stay,' Paul said. 'But I can't. While Lud exists, the threat to this city remains. I've got to go on.'

'You're throwing your life away,' Mrs Flaherty protested. 'If you'd fought Samuel on your own, you'd be six feet under by now.'

'I know,' Paul said, 'and don't think I'm not grateful.'

'I don't want your damned gratitude!' Mrs Flaherty retorted fiercely. 'I want you to stay alive, you young fool. If Samuel very nearly killed you, imagine what horrors still lie in store. There might be worse than the Satan of Spitalfields. What makes you think you can defeat Lud?'

'I've learned something about myself,' Paul said. 'I know why I'm different to all the rest of demon kind.'

'You knew that already,' Mrs Flaherty objected. 'It's the fact that Lud can't control you.'

'There's something else,' Paul said. 'I am the demon who can be all demons.'

'What's that supposed to mean?'

'I didn't understand until that last battle,' Paul said. 'I took Jasper's powers, and Malachy's. That's what I have to do. If I consciously kill another demon, I can absorb his strength, his abilities.'

'So you've got to become a murderer?'

'If you want to think about it like that, then yes.'

'Take it from one who knows,' Mrs Flaherty said. 'You can't make good out of evil. There's always a price to be paid. I've been up to my arms in the dirt of the East End for years. You know what that's got me? Dirty hands! All the time you're fighting them monsters, Paul, you'll be turning into one yourself.'

Paul smiled thinly. 'I've heard that said before, Kit.'

Mrs Flaherty tossed her hair in frustration. 'You hear it but you don't take no notice, do you? It'll turn you bad, Paul.' She clamped her hands to his face. 'It'll make you like Samuel. I don't want that to happen.'

Paul peeled her hands from his cheeks. 'Maybe it doesn't have to.'

Her face fell. 'So your mind's made up?'

'It is.'

They continued in silence to the coffee shop where his allies in the fight against Samuel were waiting.

'Here he is!' Bill beamed. 'And don't he look a hundred times better than the last time we saw him?'

Mrs Mayhew smiled. 'Are you recovered, Mr . . . Rector?'

'Yes,' Paul said, 'I'm much better. Kitty would make a good nurse.'

'She would not!' Mrs Flaherty objected. 'I couldn't live on a nurse's pay, no way. I like my little luxuries too much. If the choice is a life that's long and honest, but poor, or one that's short, dangerous and rich, I'll take the second one any time.'

Mrs Mayhew obviously disapproved of Mrs

317

Flaherty. 'Not all of us agree with you, Mrs Flaherty.' She glanced at Betsy. 'Do you have something to say, my dear?'

Betsy walked across to Paul and planted a kiss on his cheek. 'I'm to work with Mrs Mayhew rescuing girls who are in the same straits as I was, Paul. What do you think of that? I've got my own room and I have a few shillings to spend on myself. I'm going to get myself a little dog, like poor Molly always wanted.' She glanced at Mrs Mayhew who nodded. Betsy's eyes lit with excitement. 'I've another bit of news. Mrs Mayhew wrote a letter to the authorities in Australia. It's my father, Paul. He's alive.'

Paul took a moment to digest the news. 'You deserve to be reunited with your family.'

'It ain't that easy,' Betsy said sadly. 'He's all but penniless and I've no money to pay his passage home.'

'You do now,' Paul said, 'I have set up a trust for just such an eventuality. I was wondering who the money should go to. I can't think of a better cause than your happiness.' He handed her a card. 'This is the name of my solicitor.' He then produced a letter and proceeded to fill in some details. 'This will authorize you to draw the funds you need to bring your father home.'

Betsy's eyes widened. 'You'd do this for me?'

Paul embraced her. 'You deserve it, Bets.' He whispered in her ear. 'I owe you my life.' He then turned and said his farewells to Chaim and Israel.

'Izzy's mastering those dark thoughts of his,' Chaim said.

'That's right,' Israel said, 'I'm back in school. Now that the Rat Boys' power is broken, I think I'm going to be all right.'

'I'm pleased,' Paul said. 'Excuse me a moment.' He paused watching the group exchanging their stories then made for the door. By the time Chaim went to look for him, he was long gone, making his way to Aldgate. His friends would go to his rooms at Hummums but they would discover that he had paid his bill and checked out. None of them would ever see him again.

As Paul crossed the road, he wasn't aware of four spectral figures watching from a rooftop.

'He did well,' Cormac said. 'There was a moment when he overused his powers. I thought he had opened the door too wide. Lud could have overwhelmed him then.'

'The boy must learn to use his powers sparingly,' one of the fire priests observed. 'The demon lord is waiting for the slightest misjudgement.'

'Will you tell him what the Courts of Destiny have decreed?' another asked Cormac.

'That he will never see his mother,' Cormac sighed, 'that he will never live in the home where he grew up, that he will never know the joy of family and friends? How can I? If he fulfils his destiny, he will know soon enough.'

The hooded men watched Paul step further back into London's past, into Hell's Underground. Without another word, they faded from view.

Fifty-two

$\mathbb{R}$obert Stephenson is completing the tour of the new Minories station.

'Do you really think traction is the best way to bring the trains into the platform?' asks Arthur Winchcombe, one of the investors.

'Given the gradient, it is the best solution for the present,' Stephenson says. 'We will look at it again in a few months time.'

Winchcombe's wife, a portly lady in her late fifties, isn't interested in railways. She does have a question, however. 'Wasn't it terrible about poor Mr Strachan?'

Stephenson clears his throat to give himself time to frame an answer. 'It was most regrettable, Mrs Winchcombe.'

'Slain by his own child in a fit of madness,' Arthur Winchcombe says. 'A bad business, Robert. Where is the child now?'

With great reluctance, Stephenson fills in the details. 'She is a patient at the Bethlem Royal Hospital.'

'And is there any change in her condition?' Mrs Winchcombe asks.

'Sadly,' Stephenson replies, 'there is none. She repeats the same few words over and over again. "The Demon Seed".'

'Dear me.' Mrs Winchcombe is about to ask another question when she sees a slight figure making his way across the railway line. 'I thought the public were being kept away until the opening.'

'They are,' Stephenson says. He walks towards the trespasser. 'You, what's your name?'

The answer surprised the engineer. 'I'm Paul Rector.'

Stephenson is tongue-tied for a moment.

'Rector?' Mrs Winchcombe says. 'Wasn't that the name of that dreadful murderer? I believe they're hanging him this very day.'

Stephenson glances at her. 'It must be a coincidence, madam.' When he turns back, the boy has vanished. 'Where did he go?'

Even as he asks the question, there is a deep rumbling in the earth below their feet.

'What's that?' Arthur Winchcombe asks. 'There are no trains running yet, are there Stephenson?'

'Of course not,' Stephenson replies.

'So what's that noise?' Mrs Winchcombe asks.

Stephenson cannot think of an answer but, just for a moment, he fancies he glimpses a train on the platform. It has a single passenger, a boy called Paul Rector.

Then it is gone.

EXCLUSIVE EXTRAS

Behind the scenes with Alan Gibbons . . .

Meet the Bodysnatchers

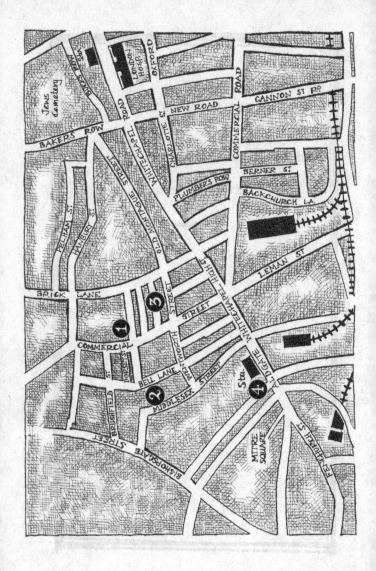

Fact Zone:

Setting the Scene for *Renegade*

1. Christ Church, Spitalfields

2. Bell Lane, location of the Jews' Free School, established in 1822

3. Flower and Dean Street

4. St Botolph's Church

About the Author

Name: Alan Gibbons
Place of Birth: Warrington, Cheshire
Lives in: Liverpool
Occupation: Author and educational consultant

1. Why do you think people like horror stories?

The world is a scary place. All kinds of terrible things happen and we have no control over them. When you write a horror story it is a way of bringing some of those demons out from under the bed and giving them a name. Sometimes you can even conquer them. Plus we all love scaring the living daylights out of ourselves for no better reason than that it's fun!

2. Who's your favourite villain?

Honestly, there are so many. Here are some of the amazing characters that have done it for me. In no particular order they are: Bill Sykes from *Oliver Twist*, Bram Stoker's *Dracula*, Venom and Dr Doom from Marvel Comics, Jack Nicholson in *The Shining*, Freddy Kruger, Davros from *Dr Who*, Darth Vader, Sauron from *Lord of the Rings* and the Mekon from *Dan Dare*. Oddly, even though I am not a fan of DC Comics, they give me my favourite screen villain, Heath Ledger's The Joker. He is amoral, violent, dark and unpredictable, pretty much like Lud.

3. Do you believe in good and evil, or is there a 'demon seed' in everyone?

No, I don't believe pure good or pure evil exists, though a figure like Hitler makes you wonder.

Everyone has the capacity for great good or great wickedness. It depends on the conditions in which you live. Sometimes it is enough to stand back to allow evil to conquer. The way I see it, a small minority of people always seems to try to do the right thing. Another small minority tends to be selfish and destructive. These two minorities fight for the soul of the vast majority of us, the ditherers.

4. Have you ever had a supernatural experience?
Never, but I have had a few moments of out of body delirium. One was when England won the World Cup in 1966. Another was when Crewe Alex were promoted to Division Three in 1968. Then there were Man United's European triumphs in 1968, 1999 and 2008. Another one will be when the telly dumps that stupid Big Brother.

5. If you were a Rat Boy, what would your special power be?
Occasionally, my wife thinks I am one. This might sound spooky but I'd quite like the power of the dream-walker to come in Book Five, *Blood Lust*. He can enter people's dreams and fight their nightmares. This character was inspired by Dr Strange, again from Marvel Comics.

6. What's the strangest thing you've ever eaten? Don't say a rat!
I've eaten crocodile, kangaroo, ostrich, frog's legs, snails, raw beef in Brazil, raw fish in Norway. Grossest of all is something we ate when I was a boy in the Cheshire countryside. They are called sweetbreads and they are . . . well . . . pig's pancreas glands. Yummy!

Bodysnatching in the 1800s

A fate worse than death: Until the 1830s, dissection was inflicted on the worst of murderers. Only beheading, hanging, drawing and quartering, or burning alive exceeded it in severity.

Supply and demand: With the expansion of medical schools, demand for fresh corpses to study far outweighed supply – and so the practice of bodysnatching was born . . .

The fresher, the better: Some Edinburgh bodysnatchers even resorted to murder, as they were paid more for very fresh corpses.

By the late 1820s, bodysnatching was so prevalent that friends and relatives would watch over the body both before and after burial to stop it being stolen.

Weeping women: Bodysnatchers sometimes hired women to attend funerals as grieving mourners and scope out any potential problems before they made their move.

End of an era: The Anatomy Act of 1832 effectively ended the bodysnatching trade by allowing unclaimed bodies and those donated by relatives to be used for the study of anatomy.

The Police in 1830s London

Renegade takes place at a time of change. London's first professional police force was the Bow Street Runners. This unit was set up by Henry Fielding in 1749, five years before his death. Fielding was a magistrate and a novelist. He wrote the novel *Tom Jones*. At first there were only eight Runners to police the whole of London. The Bow Street Runners wore blue uniforms and top hats!

In the early nineteenth century, people had decided that a new police force was needed. In 1829, Parliament passed the Metropolitan Police Act to set up a new force. The Home Secretary in charge of this change was Sir Robert Peel. The two parts of his name gave rise to two nicknames for the police, 'Bobbies' and 'Peelers'.

The Jews in London

Jewish people have lived in Britain at least since the time of William the Conqueror and probably as far back as the Romans. In the twelfth century there were massacres of Jews in London and York, but events like this and prejudice against Jews, called anti-Semitism, didn't stop the development of a Jewish community.

By the nineteenth century some British Jews were being honoured for their contribution to the country. In 1837 Queen Victoria knighted Moses Montefiore, and in 1855 the city had its first Jewish mayor. Nevertheless, in spite of this recognition, in Victorian times many London Jews were poor and often crowded into the East End.

Lots of Jews spoke Yiddish. Mum is *Mamme*; Dad is *Tatte*; Grandad is *Zaydeh*. I like words like *meghuggeneh* for fool and *shlep* for go or travel. You can still walk round East London and see buildings that started out as Protestant Hugenot churches, then became Jewish synagogues and have now become mosques where Muslims worship. This is the living history of the East End.

The Jews' Free School was established in 1822 in Bell Lane in the heart of the East End and remained there until the Second World War. The school is now in Kenton, Middlesex. It was on a visit to JFS that I first got the idea for basing some of my characters like Chaim in the original school in Bell Lane.

History of the London Underground

The London Underground is more than 140 years old, 253 miles long, and weaves its way beneath London's most historic sites, disturbing what was laid to rest centuries before. Although the fictional events of *Renegade* take place several decades before construction began, this deep network of tunnels beneath the city has long been associated with strange tales and ghostly sightings.

At Elephant & Castle station, staff have reported hearing the steps of an invisible runner along the platform, strange tapping noises and doors being thrown open with no apparent cause.

On the Bakerloo Line, northbound, some passengers have reported seeing the reflection of someone sitting next to them, even though there is no one in the seat.

Covent Garden station is said to be haunted by the ghost of an actor who was fatally stabbed on the Strand in 1897.

At Farringdon station, the screams of thirteen-year-old trainee hat maker, Anne Naylor, murdered by her employer in 1758, can sometimes be heard echoing across the platforms late at night.

The British Museum station (closed in 1933) has been linked to the 'curse' of Amen-Ra's tomb. Reports say that this Egyptian princess returns from the grave at night to wail and scream in the tunnels, and she has been heard more recently further down the track, at Holborn station.

Local legend has it that under Crystal Palace Park there is a train bricked up, complete with dead passengers and crew – and sometimes the hands of the dead reach up from the ground to try and grab the living . . .

Most people never realise that the trains they use every day run deep underground, passing by London's countless plague pits, dug during the outbreak of Bubonic Plague in the seventeenth century. In fact, just behind a wall near Elephant & Castle there is one such pit. Although no ghostly activity has been reported, few staff are willing to go down there, particularly at night.

If you want to retrace Paul's journey through the East End, why not follow it with a visit to the London Transport Museum in Covent Garden. And next time you're travelling on the London Underground, whether you're looking at the destination board for the next train, or just reading a book, remember you can never be sure exactly who, or what is behind you . . .